INTRICATE LIAISONS

Recent Titles by Pamela Oldfield from Severn House

The Heron Saga
BETROTHED
THE GILDED LAND
LOWERING SKIES
THE BRIGHT DAWNING

ALL OUR TOMORROWS
EARLY ONE MORNING
RIDING THE STORM

CHANGING FORTUNES
NEW BEGINNINGS
MATTERS OF TRUST

DANGEROUS SECRETS
INTRICATE LIAISONS

INTRICATE LIAISONS

Pamela Oldfield

This first world edition published in Great Britain 2004 by
SEVERN HOUSE PUBLISHERS LTD of
9–15 High Street, Sutton, Surrey SM1 1DF.
This first world edition published in the USA 2004 by
SEVERN HOUSE PUBLISHERS INC of
595 Madison Avenue, New York, N.Y. 10022.

British Library Cataloguing in Publication Data

Oldfield, Pamela
    Intricate liaisons
    1. Young women - England - History - 19th century - Fiction
    2. Love stories
    I. Title
    823.9'14 [F]

    ISBN 0-7278-6091-7

Typeset by Palimpsest Book Production Ltd.,
Polmont, Stirlingshire, Scotland.
Printed and bound in Great Britain by
MPG Books Ltd., Bodmin, Cornwall.

One

H arriet Lester tiptoed into her mother's room to collect her breakfast tray. Most of the toast remained untouched, she noticed, but at least the lightly coddled egg had been eaten.

'Hardly enough to keep a flea alive!' she whispered. Her mother had fallen asleep again and Harriet paused for a moment to consider Agnes's sleeping form. As she looked at the small figure lying alone in the double bed, Harriet felt a rush of tenderness laced with fear. Before Agnes had been widowed she had led a full life, raising a family and working for charity but after an emotional collapse she was still frail and the doctor had been forced to admit that any further improvement now seemed unlikely. Harriet glanced round the familiar room – curtains pulled to keep out the sunlight, windows closed against draughts, three boxes of pills on the bedside table next to the small handbell. There was a faint smell of lavender from the clothes in the chest and the brass-framed clock on the mantelpiece ticked steadily.

With a sigh, Harriet carried the tray from the room, leaving the door ajar so that when Agnes rang her bell she would hear it. She went down the wide oak staircase and into the kitchen, where she found the gardener emptying vegetables from a trug on to the large scrubbed table.

''Ere you are, Mrs Lester.'

'Good morning, Alfred. Those carrots look nice.'

'Aye. They done well this year.' He rubbed one with his thumb. 'Four decent leeks there, too, and some early beetroots

1

but they're hardly more than thinnings. Still, what can you expect at the end of April? We could do with a bit more rain.' Alfred Cummings sighed and shook his head. 'The slugs have been at work again and as for the field mice . . . Dratted varmints! They've played merry hell with the peas I planted.'

'Don't worry, Mr Cummings.' Harriet was used to his grumbles. 'We'll manage with these. I've still got some cold potatoes from yesterday.'

They would *have* to manage, she told herself ruefully. On the surface, the family lived in some style but in fact they had very little income. Her father's death had left the family almost destitute and they now lived on the outskirts of town, where they shared Havely House with Agnes's uncle Robert.

Agnes Burnett was a semi-invalid and 25-year-old Harriet now ran the household as well as devoting a considerable amount of time to her charity work as member of the Board of Guardians at the local workhouse. Her husband, Godfrey Lester, earned what little income they had by translating for two of the London publishers. Italian was his forte and he was kept busy upstairs in the library-cum-study – a large room which he shared with elderly Robert Burnett.

As Harriet washed the vegetables under the tap to remove the soil, she thought about her husband and as usual she smiled. She still loved him with a passion that sometimes frightened her. Her only regret was that they had no children but she tried to persuade herself that this was fortunate as they had so little money and that a child would come along when their circumstances had improved and the time was right.

''Scuse me, Mrs Lester.'

Cummings was back, his cap in his hands. 'I forgot to ask if I could have that Italian stamp that came yesterday. The postie mentioned it and my little nephew – he's getting really interested and—'

'Italian stamp?' Harriet shook her head. 'I think you're mistaken. We don't know anybody in Italy.'

'That's odd. I'm sure he said Italian.' He frowned, then brightened. 'He's got more than twenty now, has Timmy.

Stamps, that is. Very bright he is, for a cripple. He can even read!' He grinned. 'He spends hours with his stamp book and the old atlas you sent over. My sister's employer has given him a little magnifying glass for his birthday so he can study them proper like.'

Harriet nodded distractedly and the gardener withdrew, closing the back door gently behind him. Puzzled, Harriet concluded that the stamp referred to was probably on a letter from an Italian publisher. She would ask Godfrey later.

Half an hour later she had just pulled a tray of jam tarts from the oven when the front door bell jangled and she hurried along the long passage to answer it. Gone were the days when Izzie the maid did all the running to and fro and Cook reigned in the kitchen.

Eveline Boothby waited on the step and Harriet welcomed her friend warmly and invited her inside.

'You must have smelled the jam tarts,' she told her. 'Come along to the kitchen. I'm in the middle of baking.'

Eveline followed her into the spacious kitchen and settled herself comfortably on a chair by the table. She was a wealthy middle-aged spinster with a thin face and iron-grey hair. Small dark eyes and a firm chin added to the stern impression but Harriet knew she had a kind heart as well as a strong will and greatly admired her. Eveline was also a member of the Board of Guardians at the Maybourne Workhouse and one glance at her face told Harriet that she had brought a problem with her.

'I saw Daisy Pritty today,' Eveline began without preamble. 'She was—'

Harriet, sliding a second batch of tarts into the oven, turned eagerly, her heart leaping. 'Daisy is out of prison? That's wonderful news!' She uttered a silent prayer of thanks. Now perhaps Daisy could make a fresh start.

Eveline smiled. 'I knew you'd be pleased. She was towing her daughter, Molly. The poor little mite looked totally bewildered. Having been brought up in the workhouse it was probably the first time she's been out in the town.'

Harriet had grown fond of the wayward Daisy although

the rest of the Guardians considered her a failure. A work-house child, now a young woman, Daisy had resisted every effort to help her and had eventually been arrested and sent to prison for fighting in the street.

Harriet closed the oven door and straightened up. 'How long has poor Daisy been in prison? I lose track of time.'

'*Poor* Daisy? I'd hardly call her that. I know you see her as misunderstood but in reality she is simply a rebel. How long has she been in prison?' She shrugged. 'I don't know. Four years – maybe five! They kept extending her sentence because her behaviour was so bad. She's a fool to herself, that girl.' Eveline shook her head and accepted a cup of tea and a still warm jam tart. 'Mm! Delicious!'

Aware of a frisson of excitement, Harriet settled opposite her at the table. 'So she must have collected Molly from the workhouse – but what next? Does she have a job?'

Eveline shrugged. 'You know Daisy! I wanted to speak with her and waved but when she saw me coming . . .'

'Let me guess! She crossed the road to avoid you!' Harriet's laughter was tempered with regret. 'She's incorrigible!'

'Exactly!' Eveline rolled her eyes. 'Dragging Molly after her. That poor little tot!'

They exchanged exasperated looks and Harriet bit back the urge to apologize for Daisy's behaviour. She was not responsible for the young woman, and her mother had warned her against becoming too closely involved.

Harriet broke the silence. 'Do you think Daisy will seek out that awful Digby Wise? She wouldn't be that foolish again, would she?'

'I don't see why she would. Molly's not his child.'

Digby Wise, commonly known as Digger, had once been Daisy's partner in crime but he had also been the reason for her imprisonment.

Harriet sighed. 'But if she loves him . . .'

'She only thinks she does. I doubt she knows the meaning of the word.'

'Oh, that's too harsh!' Harriet protested. 'We can all love,

surely. We may not love wisely but if she loves the awful
Digger . . .'

'Let's hope she doesn't! For the man's a rogue and will
bring her down to his level.'

Harriet sighed, aware of the truth of Eveline's prediction.
'If only Daisy could find a nice husband and settle down,'
she said. Since her own marriage, she was inclined to think
that a good husband was all a woman needed.

Eveline laughed. 'Where would a woman like Daisy find
a *nice* husband?'

'Goodness knows – but it's her only chance, poor girl. If
she was happy maybe she wouldn't feel the need to behave
so badly. Another baby would keep her busy and out of
mischief.' She had a brief but delightful vision of a contented
Daisy rocking the cradle while Molly, prim and clean, sat
beside her with a doll. A devoted husband hovering nearby
completed the tableau.

Eveline patted Harriet's hand. 'Not every marriage is as
happy as yours, my dear. She might choose a lazy, foul-mouthed
bully and be utterly miserable! It happens all the time.'

'But a *nice* man . . . Someone like Godfrey – gentle, consid-
erate, loving . . .' With a laugh she held up both hands before
her friend could protest. 'Sorry! I know I'm biased. You've
told me before!'

Footsteps sounded in the passage and Godfrey put his head
round the door.

'Do I smell cakes?'

Eveline said, 'Speak of the Devil!'

Godfrey was smiling and Harriet's heart skipped its familiar
beat as she looked at him. He was tall, with fine auburn hair
and pale-grey eyes. She jumped to her feet. 'You smell jam
tarts! I'll give you some to take upstairs with you – and tell
Robert that we won't be eating until quarter past one as I
was a bit late getting started. I had to finish my letter to young
Sam.' She turned to Eveline. 'My brother insists that he hates
boarding school but I know that's just affection. He's doing
very well there and has plenty of friends. Which reminds

me . . .' She turned back to her husband. 'Cummings asked me for an Italian stamp. I told him we didn't have anything from Italy yesterday but then I thought—'

'From Italy? No! *No!*' He accepted the plate of tarts. 'Who told him that?'

'The postman apparently.'

'He had no right to discuss our post with someone else.' He looked flustered. 'Anyway he was wrong. There was no letter from Italy.'

Surprised by Godfrey's attitude, Harriet changed the subject. 'Apparently the lad has more than twenty stamps and is devoted to his collection. Poor child. Those poor useless legs – but at least he has wits and can amuse himself.' She watched Godfrey retreat with four jam tarts on a plate and smiled at Eveline. 'My great-uncle is putting on weight but he was very thin when we first moved in, so it won't do him any harm.'

'What happened to the boy's legs?'

'He was born that way. The midwife thinks the bones didn't grow properly before he was born.'

Eveline leaned forward eagerly. 'But there may be something the doctors can do. A London doctor, perhaps, who specializes.'

'They couldn't afford it, Eveline. Cummings's brother-in-law is a farm labourer but he's not very strong, something to do with his chest, and is in and out of work. They went into the workhouse once when he lost the farm cottage but they were out again a fortnight later and swore they'd die rather than go back.' Harriet bit into a second tart, scattering crumbs in all directions. At this rate, she thought, there would be no tarts left for teatime.

Eveline sighed. 'I hate to think how badly people regard the workhouse. It's there to *help* people. That's why they were built – to avoid desperate people dying on our streets. Why does nobody see it like that? It's not a *prison!*'

'It's the slur on a man's reputation,' Harriet suggested. 'Going into the workhouse for any length of time is like admitting that you have nothing. It's an admission of total failure. Rather like confessing that you can't support your family or yourself.'

'But plenty of people survive the experience and make a better life for themselves. Think of Mrs Bly – do you remember her?'

'Most certainly I do. We gave her a mangle and she set up as a washerwoman. I met her one day last week and she was cheerful and doing well enough. She has remarried – a coalman – and is expecting another child.'

Eveline smiled. 'So she has a *nice* husband!'

'If only Daisy could be that fortunate!' She regarded Eveline with a determined glint in her eye. 'I shall find a way to save that young woman if it's the last thing I do!'

That night Harriet lay in bed beside Godfrey. He slept but she was wide awake and all her thoughts were about Daisy Pritty and Molly. There must be a way that they could be saved from disaster, she reflected, thinking of the first time she had seen Daisy – a wild young woman with her bonnet askew and blonde curls flying, brawling in the street until a stab wound had laid her low. Sedate Harriet had been fascinated by her defiant, outrageous behaviour.

'I envied you, Daisy,' she whispered. 'You had courage when I had none. Your life was exciting and mine was dull.'

But admiration was not the only reason for Harriet's devotion. She also knew that Daisy Pritty was the unfortunate woman *she* might have become. Only Agnes and Godfrey knew that Harriet had been born in the Maybourne Workhouse years earlier when circumstances had conspired to allow childless Agnes to pass off the orphaned baby as her own daughter.

'Poor Mama!' murmured Harriet.

When Harriet first learned the truth about her birth she had been devastated, but eventually she realized the true extent of her good fortune. Without Agnes's sacrifice, her own life might have mirrored Daisy's. For the best part of five years Harriet had fought unsuccessfully to have Daisy released from prison but now she was free.

'And you must never go back!' Harriet told the absent Daisy.

Restlessly she turned over in bed and tried to make her mind a blank but instead she thought about young Molly and pondered *her* future. What chance was there for a child born in prison and then sent to the workhouse while her mother finished her sentence? Would Molly grow up like her mother on the shady side of the law? Harriet found this prospect unbearable.

Beside Harriet, Godfrey turned over and reached for his half-hunter watch on the table beside his bed.

'Half past one?' he grumbled.

'What woke you?' Harriet asked, sliding an arm around him. 'A bad conscience?' It was a joke her father had sometimes used when either Sam or Harriet had been restless in the night.

'A bad conscience? Why do you say that?'

To Harriet's surprise he spoke sharply. 'It's a joke,' she told him. 'Papa always—'

'What makes you think there's something wrong with my conscience!' He propped himself on one elbow and she fancied that he was glaring at her.

'Nothing, Godfrey . . . I've been awake for hours,' she said hastily. Godfrey was never at his best when he first awoke from sleep. 'I keep thinking about Daisy and—'

'Don't!' he advised. 'You'll have nightmares!' He gave her a quick kiss and turned away from her. 'I might go up to London tomorrow. My copy-editor has some queries. It should only take a few hours.'

'He usually sends his queries by post.'

He gave an exaggerated sigh. 'Well, this time he wants to talk face to face. There's a chance, too, that the author will be in London. They might think we should meet.'

'At least you'll get a decent meal. They always treat you well.' She thought about it, trying to overcome the familiar sense of loss. Because her husband worked at home she took his presence for granted and on the rare occasions when they were apart the hours dragged. 'Shall I come up to town with you?' she suggested suddenly. 'At least we'd be together on the train going up and coming back and I could go window-shopping and—'

'No, dearest,' he said firmly. 'It's a waste of a fare. It's not as though we can even eat together, for I shall be tied up with business.'

'And your visiting author. Is it a man or a woman?'

Abruptly he turned back to face her. 'What does it matter?'

'I was curious, that's all. Do take me with you, Godfrey.' Irrationally, the more he tried to dissuade her, the more she fancied the idea of a few hours in London.

'It's just not sensible, Harriet. And your mother will hate being alone.'

'She won't be alone. Great-Uncle Robert will take up her meal if I prepare something simple and leave it ready. Soup and bread and rice pudding. He likes to feel useful. Sometimes he reads to her. Do say yes, Godfrey.' She waited for his answer.

'I've already said no. It's better if I go alone. Anyway, it's Thursday tomorrow and you have a meeting at the workhouse.'

'So it is! Botheration!' Harriet had forgotten that fact. She tried never to miss one. It was something her mother had instilled into her. 'If you join the Board of Guardians you should consider it a duty, not a chore,' she had told Harriet. 'You do it wholeheartedly or not at all.' Harriet sighed, trying not to feel hurt. She knew that Godfrey was being entirely reasonable but she wished he had sounded a little more regretful. She snuggled closer. 'You'll miss me!' she joked.

'I'll only be gone a few hours. Go to sleep, Harriet.'

Slowly Harriet withdrew, then turned over so that she faced the large window, through which a bright moon was shining. Somewhere in the darkness a fox barked and she hoped Jasper, the cat, was safe. She told herself that she was being foolish to make such a fuss. Most women were alone all day while their menfolk toiled in the fields or on the dockside. Her father, George, had often been at sea for weeks at a time, sometimes months, but Godfrey was always with her. Perhaps he found it restricting, being at Havely House day in, day out. When they had first met he had just returned from travelling in Italy. Perhaps, she thought, her husband found it stimulating to have a few hours in London away from the family. It was nothing to do with missing or not missing her – it was simply a welcome change from his usual routine. Something to look forward to. She had her own break from the daily round of housekeeping by attending her meetings at Maybourne Workhouse.

Yes! she told herself firmly. He's entitled to a break. She could perfectly understand how Godfrey felt and there was no reason at all why she should fret about it. Go to sleep, Harriet! she told herself.

When the church clock struck two, however, she was still wide awake and at that time of the night each and every fear she had ever had resurfaced to torment her. Would her mother ever recover fully? Would she, Harriet, ever bear her husband a child? Had the people of Maybourne ever forgotten the scandal of her father's suicide? Would Daisy ever give up her wild ways? Did Godfrey love her as much as he did on their wedding day . . . ?

Ten minutes later, still worrying, Harriet slipped into an uneasy sleep.

The following morning, the meeting of the Board of Guardians began promptly. The room was large with a high ceiling and, consequently, chilly. Economies meant that the fire was no longer lit and the air smelled raw and unwelcoming. The fireplace contained cold ashes covered by a fall of fresh soot. Harriet, prewarned, had dressed warmly and had thrown a heavy shawl around her shoulders. Waiting for the others, she gazed round idly at the large cupboards, the jute carpet frayed along one edge, the few oil paintings on the wall. The high windows revealed nothing but sky and the branches of a nearby sycamore. Today she found the familiar room comfortable enough as they settled round the large table but she could still recall her first visit when she accompanied her mother as an interested onlooker. Then she had found it austere and unwelcoming.

Now she had replaced Agnes on the board and took it all for granted. As chairs were pulled into place and note-books opened, Harriet made an effort to concentrate on the proceedings. Those present were the usual – Charles Swift who was the Workhouse Master, his assistant Mrs Fenner, Eveline Boothby, Edgar Laycock and Harriet. Five years earlier, when Harriet had first joined, James Wellbury had also been a member of the board and Harriet had expected him to become her father-in-law. Her father's suicide, however, had put an end to her relationship with his son, Marcus. James Wellbury had felt it necessary to resign from the board, presumably to avoid confronting her at every meeting.

' "Item One – Two inmates suffering with suspected influenza . . ." ' Mrs Fenner glanced up. 'Doctor Fletcher is almost certain. There seems to be a small, localized outbreak in the South-East. Seven cases in Margate and a few in Dover so far. "Item Two – Molly Pritty was removed by her mother, who spoke about taking her to London." Lord help the child if that happens!' Mrs Fenner shook her head. ' "One blanket stolen, one rug to be replaced, the cook off sick . . ." ' She glanced up again. 'Now some good news! "Item Six – Jim Wheeler moved on towards Canterbury and Meg Linnet found employment at Hanks Farm north of Maybourne. To live in." '

She sat down and Charles Swift leaned forward, dipped a pen into the inkwell and signed the book with his usual flourish.

Harriet said, 'Any sign of Daniel Stick or have we seen the last of him? Nasty little troublemaker!'

Swift said, 'We can only hope he's left the town for good. No one's set eyes on him for a week.'

Eveline asked if the influenza was likely to spread within the workhouse.

Swift steepled his fingers. 'We've washed down the walls of the infirmary as the doctor recommended and will do it on a daily basis if necessary. The two inmates are old Mr

11

Budgen and Lois Carter, who we think brought it in with her last week when she was admitted. She's in a very bad way, seemingly, and Doctor Fletcher fears we could lose them both.'

Eveline tutted. 'Are they on a special diet?'

He shrugged. 'The old man can't keep anything down but the woman had an egg yesterday and milk this morning.'

Eveline nodded approval but added, 'I'll send in some calves-foot jelly later this afternoon. Enough for two.Very restorative, calves-foot jelly. My aunt swore by it. Give it to them immediately, because it doesn't keep well.'

'You're most kind.' Swift inclined his head graciously and Harriet's mouth tightened. She sometimes felt that Charles Swift was an actor playing the role of a workhouse master.

Mrs Fenner noted the offer in the book.

Harriet said, 'I suppose there is no work we can offer Daisy Pritty.'

Edgar Laycock snorted. 'With a prison record? I hardly think we could recommend her to anyone. We know she's a thief as well as everything else.'

'That was nearly five years ago!' cried Eveline. 'She's paid her debt. She should start with a clean slate.'

Mrs Fenner shrugged. 'We all know that's almost impossible. Everybody knows Daisy Pritty's no angel.'

Harriet ignored her. 'I could speak to Albert Hawke, the undertaker. She once worked a few hours for him.'

Edgar Laycock snorted. 'God help her employer, that's all I can say!'

Harriet hid her annoyance. Edgar Laycock had a rough edge to his tongue and did not suffer fools gladly but he was wealthy and generous – and the workhouse was often the beneficiary. Mrs Fenner wrote again.

'*If* she wants a job.' Swift looked at Harriet. 'Try by all means, but if she has made up her mind to go to London . . . I, for one, see no reason to prevent her. Maybourne would be well rid of her.'

Mrs Fenner nodded. 'Word is that's where Digby Wise has gone. She'll be looking for him, no doubt.'

Time passed, the meeting continued and 'matters arising' were laboriously dealt with. Harriet often wished she could turn a handle and speed up the process which was punctuated repeatedly by countless small irrelevancies and petty disagreements. Today's business was much like any other week's. One woman was applying for relief – a bold, dark-skinned woman who looked like a gypsy and who claimed she had been robbed of a shilling while sleeping rough the previous night. Her voice was husky and her accent foreign. She offered to read their palms for a penny each but there were no takers. Harriet avoided the woman's eyes, wishing she dared offer her palm. She wanted to know if she would ever have a child, but nothing would induce her to share this desire with anyone else. Thinking about a baby reminded her that Godfrey was in London and she wondered how he was getting on. A glance at the clock told her that he would be home in three hours' time and she felt a surge of joy at the prospect of his return. How on earth would she have borne it if Godfrey had been a military man away at the wars? How she pitied soldiers' wives their lonely days and loveless nights. And poor Eveline. How did she bear her solitude?

Swift regarded the gypsy woman uneasily. 'Indoor relief only. Three nights' stay,' he said at last, 'but then you must move on. Wait outside the door now until we have finished the meeting.'

She left the room but was passed by the nurse, who came in and then whispered something in the Workhouse Master's ear. He rolled his eyes, nodded and muttered, 'Thank you.' When she had gone he said, 'Lois Carter has passed away. Not unexpected, I'm afraid. Let's hope she isn't the first of many!'

Harriet said, 'I have to see the undertaker when I leave here. Shall I notify him for you?'

'Please, Mrs Lester. That will save Mrs Fenner a walk. She will be busy helping the nurse with the body.'

Harriet found Albert Hawke, the undertaker, enjoying a pipe in his yard while Snapper, his dog, dozed nearby.

She smiled. 'What's the matter with Snapper? I thought I'd get the usual frenzied welcome.'

'Afraid not. Not any more. He's going deaf, poor old thing.'

Albert Hawke eyed Harriet with obvious admiration and she hoped she wasn't blushing. She told him about the death at the workhouse and he promised to attend the following day to measure the deceased for a coffin. When the preliminary details had been written down, Harriet turned her attention to the real purpose of her visit.

'Did you know that Daisy Pritty was out of prison?' she asked casually. 'She's collected her daughter from the workhouse and we're worried about what will happen to her.'

She saw with relief that Albert Hawke was immediately concerned. 'She could make something of her life, that one,' he said. 'A bonny lass. And with a kiddie now.' He squinted up at her, a half smile on his face. 'I daresay you're going to ask me if I can give her some more work.'

'Yes, I am.' Harriet regarded him hopefully. 'We're afraid she'll run off to London. That's her plan – and you know what happens to young women in that fair city!'

He shook his head. 'Nothing good, I reckon. Too much temptation. Too many ways to go wrong again. Land herself back behind bars. Yes, I could give her a few hours work, but will she take it?'

'I don't know, Mr Hawke, but we have to try. She'll need a proper job if she's going to find a room and look after Molly, but that won't be easy to find. People won't trust her but you can't blame them, and a prison record doesn't help. But I'll make some enquiries. If I find her, I'll send her round to you, shall I?'

'By all means, Mrs Lester. It's worth a try. What's it say in the Bible? "If one sinner repenteth . . . ?" Summat like that.'

As soon as that was settled Harriet was prepared to go, but courtesy demanded that she first enquire after the undertaking business. By this time Snapper had woken and he rushed to greet her, wagging his tail enthusiastically as she bent to pat his head.

'How's business?' Albert echoed. 'If I say it's booming, folks give me a funny look, but there you are. It *is* booming. Not so much because too many folk are pegging out but because the work's changing. I can do a better class of funeral now – better coffin, better cortège and I can supplement some of the more important funerals that are handled by others – supplying drapes, candlesticks, feathers for the horses and suchlike. Not to mention my own funeral carriage.' He smiled with satisfaction. 'You could say business is good, Mrs Lester, and thanks for asking.'

She hesitated. 'Are there many deaths from the influenza? Is it spreading, would you say?'

He nodded. 'From what I'm hearing in the trade, it seems likely. So you take care. If you think you might have it, make yourself an infusion – vinegar, honey and onions boiled together. My old ma used to swear by it. Makes you sweat, mind you, but it does the trick.'

Thanking him for his help, Harriet set off again in the direction of home.

She had walked for less than five minutes when she spotted Daisy Pritty talking earnestly to a young man. Prison had not changed her much, thought Harriet, with the familiar surge of admiration. She was as pert and pretty as ever, the blonde curls escaping from her bonnet still framing her face, but she was thinner. A small girl was holding on to her skirt. Molly was the image of her mother, with a mop of fair curls and a round face which was only spoiled by a miserable expression. Deciding not to alert Daisy to her presence, Harriet approached warily. Daisy, busy with her conversation, failed to see Harriet until the latter touched her arm.

'Daisy! How good to see you again – and this must be Molly.' She smiled cheerfully as Daisy glanced around for a way of escape. Harriet saw with a shock that the young man was one of Daisy's earlier associates – a villain known as Squinty for obvious reasons.

Daisy said, 'Oh! Hello. Yes, this is Molly.' She tapped the girl on the head and said, 'Say hello to the lady!'

The girl hid her face in her mother's skirt and said nothing. Squinty, sensing impending interference, mumbled something and hurried away.

Daisy scowled. 'Now look what you've gone and done! You've scared him off! Gawd knows when I'll find him again.' She leaned down to free her skirt from Molly's clutches. 'Get off me skirt, will you! You're a big girl now.'

The child began to cry but Daisy ignored her. Harriet bit back words of censure, reminding herself that Daisy hardly knew the child and was not yet used to being a mother. She said quickly, 'Mr Hawke, the undertaker, is eager for you to work for him again. Would you be willing? You'll be needing a job and he's a—'

'The undertaker? I remember him. Decent sort of chap . . .' She watched Squinty disappear round the corner and tutted to herself. 'I need Squinty to tell me where Digger is. He doesn't know I'm out yet and I want to surprise him. He'll be that thrilled!'

She beamed in hopeful anticipation and Harriet's heart ached for her. If she was any judge of character, the wily Digger would be hiding out in London, trying not to be found by his erstwhile companion.

Daisy was warming to her story. 'He's also got a bit of money of mine. He's minding it for me . . . sort of. Squinty knows where he is, I'm sure he does, but he makes out he doesn't. Lying little toad! He hasn't changed much in the last few years – leastways, not for the better.'

Harriet tried again. 'I can ask around for you for a job but in the meantime a few hours a week at Mr Hawke's yard would be a start. If you pop in to speak with him . . .'

Daisy, unimpressed, glanced down at her daughter and gave her a slap. 'Stop sucking your thumb! I've told you. Only babies suck their thumbs.' She looked up at Harriet. 'That blooming workhouse. They've let her get away with murder. She wet the bed last night! Gawd! I don't know what I'm going to do with her.'

'I don't think you'll find Digby Wise,' Harriet told her.

'Rumour has it he's in London and it's a big city. You'd be better off staying in Maybourne, where you have friends and can make a home for your daughter. She's a sweet child.'

As though to disprove this fact Molly took her thumb out of her mouth long enough to pull a face at Harriet.

Hastily Harriet looked away but Daisy said, 'Sweet child? Who're you kidding? She's 'orrible – just like I was at her age!'

Harriet searched her mind for a conciliatory reply but before she found one Daisy had spotted another acquaintance and was waving frantically to her. Without another word to Harriet she dashed across the road, dragging a protesting Molly with her, and within seconds she and the young woman friend were deep in conversation. As Harriet watched, a black cat appeared in a nearby doorway and Molly moved cautiously towards it. When allowed to stroke it, the little girl's expression changed. A bright smile lit up her face and Harriet saw more than a hint of the attractive woman she would one day become. Suddenly the cat ran off down the road with Molly in pursuit while Daisy remained unaware that she had gone.

'Oh dear!' Taken aback, Harriet lingered. Surely the mother would miss the child and go after her. Seconds passed and both cat and child disappeared round the same corner that had swallowed up Squinty. Now Daisy would have no idea where her daughter had gone. Resignedly, Harriet set off after Molly. When she, too, turned the corner she received a nasty shock. Molly was nowhere to be seen. Slowly Harriet walked along the street, peering into doorways and looking over shabby fences and through dusty hedges. A commotion caught her attention.

'Get out of here, you little minx! Go on! Get out!'

From a doorway three houses further down the road, Molly appeared suddenly and a door was slammed behind her. She stood bewildered on the pavement and stuck her thumb into her mouth. There was no sign of the black cat. Relieved to have found her, Harriet watched in fascination as a small drama developed. Molly looked slowly up and down the street and her face fell. As it dawned on her that she could no longer see her mother Molly slid down into a sitting position and started to whimper. The door opened again and a woman stepped out. Taking Molly's arm she yanked her to her feet. 'Go home to your ma,' she told her, exasperated. 'You don't belong here. Hop it!' Molly burst into loud sobs and Harriet hurried forward.

'I know where her mother is,' she explained. 'The girl wandered off.' She held out her hand. 'Molly! It's me, Mrs Lester. I'll take you back to your mama.'

The woman said, 'She come in bold as brass after the cat.'

'I'm sorry. I'll take her back.'

To Harriet's surprise Molly allowed herself to be led back along the street. As they turned the corner they almost collided with Daisy, who looked none too pleased to see them. She grabbed Molly and gave her legs a token slap.

'That's for running away, see! Now you behave yourself.' Ignoring Harriet altogether, she hurried back to her friend, pushing Molly before her.

Hurt and offended, Harriet stared after them, struggling to think charitably about Daisy, and as she turned to go back to Havely House her hopeful mood had vanished. How on earth was she going to turn Daisy's life around?

'To you, I'm nothing but a busybody!' she told the absent Daisy.

At Havely House, Robert had settled himself on a chair in the garden, determined to enjoy the spring sunshine. He was well wrapped up and a small rug lay across his knees. Although he had the newspaper with him it was folded in his lap and he was watching Cummings, who was mowing the grass on the large front lawn. This involved steering the heavy lawnmower, which was pulled by Sam's pony, whose hooves were encased in leather shoes for the duration of the exercise. Robert was a tall, spare man who never mentioned his age but he was Agnes's uncle and she rightly assumed him to be in his seventies. He had never married and had lived alone for most of his life until his nephew George's death. Now, with the family around him, he was enjoying life. He was fond of Agnes, proud of Sam and Harriet and he liked Godfrey well enough.

When at last the grass was cut to the gardener's satisfaction, Cummings reined in the pony and glanced across at his employer.

'Sweating like a pig, I am,' he told Robert and to prove it he pulled a rag from his pocket and wiped his face.

'Gives the pony some exercise.' Robert smiled. 'When Sam's away at school the pony gets too fat. He misses the boy.'

The gardener nodded. 'A fine lad, young Samuel. Kind-hearted. He brought five new stamps for Timmy when he came home from school. Got them from his schoolmates 'cos lots of them live abroad for part of the year. One was from Mauritius, wherever that is. Never heard of it, I told him, but young Timmy was thrilled with them stamps.' He nodded. 'Not many boys would bother for a poor little cripple.'

'That reminds me . . .' Robert fished in his waistcoat pocket and pulled out a crumpled envelope. 'An Italian stamp.' He tore it off carefully and held it out. 'I found it in the waste-paper basket in the library. I daresay Timmy may have one already.'

Frowning, Cummings took it from him. 'So there was one after all!' he muttered. 'Funny that!' Thanking his employer, he tucked the stamp into the band inside his cap for safe keeping. 'Very funny!' He moved round to detach the pony's harness from the mower and took hold of the pony's head-band. 'I'll stable this one, then come back for the mower. Can't leave it out. It'll go rusty.'

Robert watched him go. What was so funny about an Italian stamp? he wondered, then unfolded the newspaper and began to read.

Two

Harriet returned from the town feeling frustrated and angry. Daisy Pritty was obviously determined to go her own way and would refuse advice and help from anybody else. Making her way upstairs to her mother's room, she found Agnes engrossed in a book but, unable to hide her dismay, Harriet interrupted her, launching into an account of her unsuccessful efforts to help Daisy.

'After all we've done for that girl!' she protested. 'She really is a most ungrateful wretch! And what sort of mother is she going to be? That poor child!'

'She hasn't had time to learn motherhood,' Agnes reminded her. 'She's been in prison since before the child's birth. We must give her the benefit of the doubt, Harriet.'

'I do, Mama, but I quite see why nobody else will. Daisy could have come out earlier if she hadn't behaved so badly. If she wanted to be with her child she should have been a model prisoner.' Longing for a child herself, Harriet found Daisy's careless attitude outrageous.

'Well she wasn't.' Agnes shrugged. 'There's no point in wishing things undone, Harriet. We have to help her *now*.'

'But does she *want* to be helped? She made me feel like a meddling busybody!' Harriet stared unhappily out of the window. 'Not a word of thanks to the undertaker for offering her some work. Too intent with finding her partner in crime.'

'You mean Digby Wise.'

'Yes. I sincerely hope she *doesn't* find him. He's a bad influence. If she *doesn't* find Digger she may well resign herself to life in Maybourne. At least she would stand a chance here.'

Agnes nodded. 'Going up to London is a big step and for all her brave words she may baulk at the prospect – especially with a child. They might never find Digger, in which case the two of them could easily end up living on the streets like so many others.'

Harriet sighed, her anger rapidly evaporating at the prospect of Daisy and Molly begging on a street corner for the price of a bed. 'Please God it doesn't come to that.'

Agnes sipped her tea. 'When does Godfrey get home?'

'In an hour or so. I wanted to travel up and down with him but he reminded me that I had the workhouse meeting to attend.' She gave her mother details of the report including the fact that the influenza victim had died.

'The woman has died?' Agnes looked alarmed. 'I hope they take adequate precautions to prevent the disease from spreading.'

'I think they are . . . Oh, yes! Daniel Stick's name was mentioned. Thankfully he seems to have moved on. Nobody has seen him for a week or more.'

'Good riddance! That man's the sort to bear a grudge. He'll never forget that we once had him arrested.' Agnes pointed to the bedside table. 'I've written to Sam. I'm so pleased he is doing well at school. Apart from anything else it is costing so much money but that was George's last wish and the least Sam can do is study hard and make it worthwhile.'

Harriet said nothing. Her father's preference for his son and heir had always grieved her and the trust fund he had secretly set up for Sam's education had caused the family some hardship after George's death.

Harriet rose. 'I must see to the meal. I'm longing to hear how Godfrey's meeting went. Men are so lucky. They have by far the most interesting lives.'

Agnes smiled at her. 'They also carry a huge burden of responsibility. I have never envied their role in life and nor

21

should you. Queen Victoria sets us a wonderful example. She has created the ideal family. She has brought up her children in a—'

'With a great deal of help! Countless servants to do her bidding,' Harriet reminded her sharply, 'and she also has interesting business of state to attend to, which must be fulfilling. Most women don't have such satisfying lives.'

'You have your duties for the workhouse, Harriet.'

Harriet paused. 'Yes, I do . . . and I actually enjoy it more than I ever expected. I was so reluctant at first.' She smiled at the memory. 'But I must get on. I want to have a meal ready for Godfrey when he arrives back from London. I'm going to make some cheese scones for our tea and a bacon roll for supper. It's his favourite. Poor dear will be hungry by the time he arrives.'

By five o'clock most of the scones remained untouched and Harriet was seriously worried by her husband's lateness. She stood looking out across the drive, waiting for the first glimpse of him. Despite her anxiety that something had happened to him, Harriet began to feel angry. He had no right to cause her to worry, she thought resentfully. He'd allowed ample time for his meeting and the midday meal, so why hadn't he travelled back at the promised time? Unless he had had an accident . . . or the train had been delayed for some reason that she could not imagine. Half past five came and then six o'clock. She went upstairs to her mother, trying unsuccessfully to hide her confusion.

'Be patient, dear,' her mother told her with a smile. 'The moment he appears you will forget all this. Whatever the reason, I am sure Godfrey did not intend to upset you.'

Downstairs again, Harriet found Robert waving three letters at her. 'If you would be so kind, Harriet,' he said.

Harriet was accustomed to his tall, gaunt frame and odd ways and she could not imagine life without him. In a way he had replaced her father.

'I've written again to the Pope,' he told her, 'and there's

22

a letter for Samuel. The third is . . .' He frowned. 'Ah yes! The third is a plea to *The Times* asking for fuller reports on parliament. They don't tell us enough.' He glanced at the clock. 'Where's that husband of yours? I thought you expected him hours ago.'

Harriet was about to confide her worries but at that moment they heard carriage wheels on the gravel drive and Harriet ran to the front door and down the steps to welcome Godfrey, home safe at last. Illogically, now that she knew her fears were groundless, her resentment surfaced.

'Where have you been?' she demanded as he climbed down from the hansom cab. 'I've been out of my mind with worry for you! I can't believe you would . . .' She stopped, alerted by something in his manner. His arms went round her and his embrace was unusually fierce but still he said nothing. 'What is it?' she asked. 'Godfrey? Speak to me!' She tried to free herself but he clung to her until at last he released her.

'Please! *Please!*' he cried. 'Don't reproach me, Harriet. Something has happened . . . I can explain if you will hear me out.'

'Something has happened? You mean something *bad*?' Shocked, she followed him up the steps and into the hallway and helped him take off his coat. 'Tell me!' she urged, her mind reeling with terrible possibilities, and as he took her hand and led her into the parlour she was aware that she was trembling. They sat opposite each other and Harriet saw for the first time just how anguished he looked. Pale and distraught. A dreadful thought came to her. 'Oh no! Don't say it! Oh Godfrey – you are not ill, are you?'

At that moment Robert came into the room but his smile of welcome faded as he saw their expressions. After a moment's hesitation, he withdrew without saying a word. In silence they heard his footsteps as he made his way upstairs to the library.

Leaning forward, Harriet clutched at his hands. 'Tell me, Godfrey, are you ill? Is that where you went today – to a doctor? Dear God, I can't bear it! Suppose I lose you!'

She felt cold and empty as though she were already a widow. She thought of her mother's despair when George Burnett had died and the emotional chaos his death had caused her. Harriet's heart was already beating erratically as she waited for Godfrey's answer. If only he could reassure her, she vowed, she would be forever grateful.

He looked into her eyes and looked away again. 'It's nothing like that,' he said. 'It's . . . It's hard to explain . . . You won't understand, Harriet.'

He pulled his hands away and covered his face but Harriet pulled them down again, still trying to read his expression.

'Tell me,' she said. 'Just tell me. I promise that I *will* understand.' In a flash she recognized the elusive emotion she had glimpsed in his eyes. It was guilt. So he had done something wrong – something terrible. Something the police might consider a crime! She fell back against the cushions, staring at him in disbelief. Not Godfrey, she argued. He could never, *never* do something underhand. He was not a criminal – but if he were then he had not intended the crime and she would stand by him.

'You're tormenting me, Godfrey!' she cried, her voice rising. 'For pity's sake, *tell me what has happened!*'

He straightened up and forced himself to meet her gaze and she saw at once that he, too, was anguished.

'I lied to you, Harriet,' he said, 'and I'm so sorry. The truth is I was afraid to tell you. I had a letter which I hid from you. It . . . It was from Amelia.'

She stared at him uncomprehending. 'Amelia? Amelia who?' Her panic had abated marginally.

'Amelia Bianchi, the woman I knew in Italy when I was a student.'

Harriet blinked. Her mind worked slowly. 'You don't mean the married woman . . . Not the one you had the . . . the romance with!'

He nodded.

'But I don't see the connection. You had a letter from her

24

and you didn't tell me. Why not? Why was the letter such a secret? You should have told me . . . I'm asking why you were so late home and didn't . . .' Her expression changed as doubt flickered through her. Horrified, she stammered, 'You . . . you . . . *didn't* go to your publishers. Is that what you're saying?' She felt strangely light-headed.

He nodded again and for a long moment they stared at each other until Godfrey lowered his gaze.

Harriet swallowed hard, attempting to come to terms with the extent of the problem. 'Are you telling me that on the strength of this letter – a letter which you kept from me – you went to London to *meet* this woman? You *can't* mean that. I won't believe it. You *wouldn't!*' Not if you loved me, she thought. Fear had now replaced any other emotion. Her mouth was dry and her heartbeat had increased alarmingly. She covered her face with her hands, then she opened them again and said, 'But *why*? What is this Amelia to you now? You told me it was all over between you. I believed you, Godfrey.'

'You were right to do so, Harriet. It *was* all over. But a few weeks ago—'

He stopped as Harriet put her hands over her ears. 'Stop! I don't want to hear it!' she told him. 'I just want you to swear that you will never, *never* do this to me again. That this woman means nothing to you . . . and that you will never see her again.' She struggled for breath. Nothing in her whole life had prepared her for this and she had no idea how to cope. Reluctantly she went on listening.

He said, 'I can't make such a promise, Harriet. She's in trouble and I can't abandon her. It's my fault. Her husband found some of my letters that she'd hidden all those years ago and . . . and he's learned that we were . . . more than just friends. He's thrown her out of the house.'

'I don't care! I don't see what that's got to do with you. She shouldn't have kept the letters. She must be very foolish to take such a risk.' Or so much in love with Godfrey that she couldn't bear to part with his letters. Harriet wanted to

25

scream or cry or run away and hide but she did neither. She sat frozen to the spot, feeling utterly helpless. Her trembling increased and Godfrey attempted to put his arm round her but she pushed him away.

'Please let me comfort you, Harriet,' he begged.

'How can you?' She stared at him, stricken. 'You have broken my heart and ruined our marriage. You! How can you possibly help me?'

Her words struck home and he pulled back as though she had physically hurt him. Part of her wanted to comfort *him* but her own pain made that impossible. Another thought occurred to her. Her mother would be devastated when she knew what had happened. 'Mama!' she whispered. 'Whatever will this do to her?'

Godfrey rubbed his eyes. 'Does your mother have to know?'

Harriet stared at him incredulously. 'Of course she'll know – even if I don't say a word. She loves me, Godfrey. She'll know something is terribly wrong. She'll ask and I won't lie to her.'

He sat back and regarded her soberly. 'I have to tell you what has happened, Harriet. I have to make you understand. Please . . . listen to me. Trust me. There is no need for this to ruin our marriage. If you listen you will see why I had to do it.'

Harriet didn't answer. She was torn between hearing the details and knowing that her husband's explanation might make things worse.

When she had remained silent for some time, Godfrey took his chance.

'At the time, all those years ago, Mario, her husband, became suspicious of our meetings and challenged her. Amelia insisted that nothing was happening between us but we . . . *I* thought it best to part. She said she still loved him. He was very wealthy and I had nothing to offer. I was broken-hearted but I decided to leave Italy and never see her again. I wrote to her once, months afterwards, but she didn't reply.'

'That was cruel of her!'

He shrugged. 'She was protecting her marriage. Then she discovered she was expecting a child . . . No! Before you ask, it wasn't mine. I'd been gone too long.'

Harriet closed her eyes. The thought that he might have given this woman a child had never entered her head.

He said, 'She lost the child early on and became quite ill.'

'I hope you don't expect me to feel sorry for her!' Harriet heard the edge in her voice and wished the words unsaid but Godfrey simply sighed and went on.

'A few years later Mario took a mistress and made no secret of it. I daresay he was trying to punish her for her betrayal. She decided to try and divorce him but when she threatened to do so he produced my letters. Recently he told her to leave the house and never come back. She had no money and dared not go back to her family, so she came in search of me. She didn't know I was married.'

Harriet let out a sigh of relief. 'And now she does know, she is going to leave you alone. Is that it?' If the worst was over she could somehow bear it. Somehow they could continue their lives.

The silence lengthened. 'She has no money and is desperate. I've given her a few pounds and have found her a cheap hotel room.'

'You have *what*?' She stared at him as new fears surfaced. 'Why, Godfrey? She has no right to expect anything from you. It was all over between you *years* ago! Or so you told me. Did you lie to me?'

'No! It *was* all over!'

Her throat tightened, leaving her breathless. 'You mean it *isn't* over?'

'Certainly it is. I meant that we both knew it was over then but . . . things have changed for her and suddenly she didn't know where to turn. I couldn't simply refuse to see her.'

Harriet focused on her hands and tried to keep them from

27

shaking. She felt a creeping nausea and struggled to remain calm. 'You have a wife, Godfrey, and we are hardly wealthy. You seem to be making yourself her protector! Giving her money and paying for her accommodation! How do you think that makes me feel? How would *you* feel if Marcus Wellbury suddenly came back into *my* life and tried to renew *our* relationship? He has never married and might still be in love with me.' Her voice cracked and Godfrey drew back from her. Harriet realized that she was perilously near to losing control and she did not want Godfrey to see her as a hysterical victim. Somehow she must ignore the pain and humiliation she was suffering and retain some dignity. Somehow she must compose herself and speak rationally. She drew a long, deep breath and then another.

'It's hard for you, I know—' he began.

'You don't know, Godfrey.' She forced herself to stand although her legs trembled with weakness. With an effort she controlled her breathing. 'If you love me at all, Godfrey, you will write to this Amelia and tell her to stand on her own two feet. Tell her that you have a wife and can no longer be responsible for her predicament. If you can't do this for me, Godfrey, then I shall wonder if you ever really loved me. Perhaps all along I was second best.'

'No, Harriet! You were never that.'

'Then don't let her come between us, Godfrey.'

She left the room and somehow struggled up the stairs. She was cold with fright and shivering from the shock. Once in the bedroom she threw herself on to the big bed she shared with Godfrey and wept.

Elsewhere in the town, Eveline was returning from the draper's with a brown-paper parcel tied with string. Inside was a length of dark-brown cloth which she would make into a serviceable skirt. Sam, when younger, had once imagined her as a witch and unconsciously she added to this fantasy by always wearing plain clothes in very sombre colours. A dressmaker might have recommended a more interesting colour scheme but Eveline considered dressmakers a waste of good money and preferred to trust her own judgement. She had long since given up any idea of attracting a husband and found dark colours more serviceable. As she rounded the corner and her house came into view she was surprised to see a child sitting on the step. She was even more surprised, as she drew closer, to see that it was Molly Pritty.

'Molly Pritty!' she said sharply. 'What are you doing on my step?' The child merely glared at her. 'Stand up, child, when you're spoken to – and stop sucking your thumb.'

Molly stood up, removed her thumb from her mouth and said, 'I'm to wait here for me ma.'

'Your ma? Where is she?'

'Dunno.' She glanced hopefully up and down the street and Eveline did the same. There was no sign of Daisy.

Eveline hesitated. 'I think you'd better go home,' she told the child. 'You do have a home, I take it?'

'Dunno.'

'Don't know? Of course you know.'

'The lady said we was to get out and stay out 'cos I wetted the bed.'

'Where did you sleep last night?'

'Down the harbour. In a shed.'

'A *shed*?' Eveline's voice rose.

'It was locked but Ma found a bit of iron and broke the lock. She found some old sacks to keep us warm.' Seeing Eveline's disapproving expression she added, 'Ma said it was fun.'

Fun? Eveline rolled her eyes in despair. It seemed that Daisy was as feckless as ever after her years in prison but what else could anyone expect? Everyone accepted that the system was at fault but nobody knew how to improve matters. After a moment's consideration Eveline decided to wait and see what happened. She had a nasty suspicion that Daisy would not reappear.

'You'd better come in,' she said reluctantly.

'Shan't! I have to wait here. Ma said so!'

'She didn't mean on the step. She meant—'

'She *did*!' The little girl's eyes flashed and she stamped a small defiant foot. 'She said, "Stay right there and don't move!"'

Eveline could picture the scene. 'Sit down again, then,' she ordered, 'and wait for her to come back.' She hesitated. 'Would you like some milk and a slice of cake?'

Molly's face brightened and she nodded. Eveline shook her head at the child's predicament. Full of a growing unease, she produced her key and let herself into the house.

When Harriet ventured downstairs an hour or so later there was no sign of Godfrey and she guessed he was in the library, keeping out of her way and hoping she would talk herself into forgiving him. If only it were that easy, she thought as she set about preparing some cold ham and salad for their supper. The idea of preparing his favourite bacon roll no longer appealed. What was Godfrey planning to do next? she wondered unhappily. There were so many unanswered questions. Had he promised Amelia to be in touch again? Tears pricked again at her eyes. They had been so wonderfully happy and now everything was spoiled. How could it ever be the same again?

She tried to think compassionately about Amelia but it was impossible. She was a threat, pure and simple. And what were *her* plans? Was she determined to take Godfrey away from Harriet? Could she? Godfrey had promised to love Harriet for better, for worse, for the rest of his life. Would he keep his promise or would he be persuaded to leave her? Amelia had been his first love. Maybe in his heart he still loved her. She moved round the kitchen distractedly, picking up pans and putting them down again, unable to concentrate. She tried to imagine the evening meal. They would be trying to pretend that everything was normal but Robert was very sharp still and might well guess that something was wrong. Thankfully her mother would stay in her room.

As she was grating carrots for the salad the front-door bell jangled and she hurried along the passage, wishing that her eyes were not so reddened. Eveline stood on the doorstep, holding Molly's hand. Eveline looked badly shaken.

'I must talk to you,' she said and Harriet groaned inwardly as she opened the door to admit them.

She took them into the parlour. Eveline sat down opposite Harriet and Molly sat on the floor, her thumb in her mouth. Her eyes, too, showed signs of recent tears, Harriet noted.

Eveline said, 'Little pitchers have big ears!' and glanced at Molly.

Harriet said, 'Let's go into the kitchen.'

Once there, she opened the back door. Jasper the cat lay in his favourite place in the back yard. Soon Molly was sitting beside the animal, crooning to him as she stroked him, and Eveline and Harriet could keep an eye on her as they talked in lowered voices.

Noting Harriet's obvious distress, Eveline said, 'I'm sorry if this is a bad time but I do need some advice.' Harriet nodded and she continued. 'I came home from shopping this afternoon to find that wretched child sitting on my doorstep. From what I can understand, Daisy told her to wait there and promised to come back for her. That was hours ago and there is no sign of her. I tried to take the girl into the house but she wouldn't leave the front step. I gave her a slice of cake and a mug of milk and she wolfed it down as though she were starving.'

Harriet rolled her eyes. 'And now you wonder if Daisy is ever coming to collect her. Or ever intended to!'

'Exactly. I'm beginning to think she has deliberately dumped the girl on me and skedaddled!'

Harriet sighed. 'That means, I suppose, that Daisy might be off to London some time soon, in search of the wretched Digger! What will you do with Molly if her mother *has* gone?'

'That's what I want to talk about. I really can't bear to take her back to the workhouse when she's only just left it

31

and when they have cases of influenza. I know this will sound very rash but I thought I might keep the child with me overnight in the hope that Daisy does return. If she will stay, that is. If she takes after her slippery mother, she'll disappear at the first opportunity.'

Thoughtfully they both watched Molly trying to lift the cat into her arms. Jasper, unused to such treatment, wriggled frantically and lashed out with his claws. Molly let out a scream and dropped him. The cat at once fled to the safety of the nearest fence and Molly stood in the yard and wailed piteously.

'Bring her in,' Harriet suggested, 'and I'll find her a biscuit.'

While Harriet made a pot of tea Molly gobbled down three biscuits, her tears forgotten.

Eveline said, 'It's none of my business but I can see something's upset you. If you need someone to talk to . . .'

The kind words undid Harriet and after the first few sobs the tears came hot and fast. Without intending to, she found herself confiding in her friend and found Eveline surprisingly sympathetic.

'I can't claim to know how you feel, Harriet, because I've never been married but I do think you'll feel steadier when you've had a good night's sleep.' Eveline handed her a clean handkerchief. 'Shock has frightened you and you're imagining the very worst. But when you have dealt with it between you, as I'm sure you will, it may make your relationship even stronger. Maybe you could see it as a kind of test. Can you survive it? Can Godfrey?'

'But how will I ever trust him again?' Tears welled up again in Harriet's eyes.

'You'll find a way. You're stronger than you think, Harriet. This woman has placed him in a terrible position and he has to find the way out. That's the problem *he* has to deal with. Yours is to learn to forgive him.' She leaned forward and clasped Harriet's hand. 'My advice, for what it's worth, is do nothing hasty. Bide your time and see what happens next. Remember it wasn't his choice that they met up again. She approached him and made him feel guilty. He blames himself for the breakdown of her marriage and that's a heavy burden. Godfrey probably saw her as a damsel in distress and you know what gallant fools men are! He probably needs you now more than ever before.'

Harriet sighed. Eveline's words had struck a chord. Yes, it was good advice. She had reacted with panic and anger but now she must think matters through carefully. 'You're very kind, Eveline,' she said. 'What would I have done without you? I couldn't talk to my mother for fear of distressing her – she is frail enough already.'

At that moment Molly sidled up to Eveline and tugged at her skirt. 'When's Ma coming back?' she asked plaintively, her small mouth trembling. 'I want my ma!' Tears rolled down her face.

Harriet and Eveline exchanged worried glances.

Awkwardly Eveline patted the child's head. 'I don't know,' she said. 'She didn't say, did she – but there's no need to start snivelling. You'll be quite safe until she does.'

Footsteps sounded then in the passage and Godfrey came in. Startled he looked from Harriet to Eveline and then to Molly.

Eveline said quickly, 'We have an abandoned c-h-i-l-d here, Mr Lester, and your wife and I are discussing the situation.'

'Then I won't interrupt.'

He turned to go but Harriet forced herself to speak naturally. 'Were you after a tray of tea? I know Robert gets thirsty. There's plenty of tea in the pot.' She couldn't bring herself to jump up and minister to him, so there was an awkward silence as he began to collect tray, cups and saucers, milk and sugar and spoons. Molly watched him warily, clinging to Eveline's skirt.

Eveline stood up. 'We must be on our way, Harriet.'

The three of them walked to the front door.

Harriet saw them out. 'Do call in tomorrow and let me know what happens.'

'I will.' Eveline took Molly's hand. 'We'll give you a nice bath,' she promised. 'In the outhouse. And we'll wash your hair.'

Molly scowled. 'Don't want a bath!' she muttered. 'I want my ma!'

Eveline ignored her. 'Plenty of soap will be necessary, I suspect! Then when your ma turns up she'll find a nice clean little girl.' She smiled at Harriet. 'Let's hope she's not averse to warm water! I might need a scrubbing brush!'

Molly, sharper than they expected, let out another scream and Eveline explained hastily that it was just a joke and she had nothing to fear.

Harriet saw them leave and when she returned to the kitchen Godfrey was still there preparing the tray. He turned and held out his arms. 'Please say you still love me,' he begged. 'I've been such an idiot.'

They clung together for a long moment and Harriet reminded herself of Eveline's words. If this *was* a test of their love, they must somehow win through, she thought, and with Godfrey's arms tight around her she knew that anything was possible.

First thing Sunday morning, Harriet went into her mother's bedroom to find her unwell. Agnes had had a restless night and her usually pale face was flushed. When Harriet felt her mother's forehead, she knew at once she had a fever.

'You're burning up, Mama!' she exclaimed. 'I must fetch Doctor Fletcher.'

'Oh no, dear!' Agnes protested. 'Allow the poor man his Sunday. He's due to call in tomorrow. Please don't trouble him – he will want to be at church.'

'He'll want to be looking after his patients, Mama! There'll always be another Sunday and another church service. I shall ask Godfrey to call round to his surgery as soon as he's eaten his breakfast.'

Harriet and Godfrey had achieved a compromise. After a long and somewhat anguished discussion on the subject they had agreed that neither should mention Amelia again. Godfrey had admitted he had been wrong to keep the matter a secret from his wife and Harriet had accepted that he had offered Amelia financial help which would see her through the first few days in a strange country. Now it was up to her, they agreed, to find employment and support herself. If not, Harriet had argued, Amelia should swallow her pride and immediately write to her parents in Italy for help. At Harriet's insistence, they had penned a short but polite note to this effect and had sent it to the hotel where she was staying. Although no more was said on the subject, Harriet made doubly sure that she always intercepted the postman so no more letters from Amelia could slip past her.

Now Harriet decided she would wait with her mother until the doctor arrived and later in the day she and Godfrey would attend the evening service at their church. She scrambled an egg and cut and buttered a thin slice of bread but Agnes complained that her throat hurt and she could only swallow a few mouthfuls.

Putting a hand to her head, Agnes gave a wan smile. 'My head aches abominably.'

'Poor Mama! I'm sure the doctor will give you something to ease the pain.'

Agnes pushed the tray towards her daughter. 'I feel sleepy now after that dreadful night but I must try to stay awake until after the doctor's visit.'

Fortunately Angus Fletcher's carriage rattled up the drive soon after half past ten and Harriet hurried to let him in. He was a big, jovial man with bright-blue eyes and an unruly mop of curls which seemed to resist the presence of his hat. As well as his ordinary practice Angus Fletcher also served on the Maybourne Workhouse for the usual pittance because he felt it his duty to do what he could for the unfortunates housed there. Harriet always felt her spirits lift when she saw him and today was no exception. She led the way upstairs, talking cheerfully.

'Mama, Doctor Fletcher is here. Let me help you sit up.'

She lifted her mother higher on to the pillows and then discreetly withdrew while the doctor made his examination.

When she was downstairs again Godfrey greeted her with an anxious expression. 'You don't think it might be influenza, do you?' he asked. 'If so we must keep Robert away from her. At his age it would be a disaster for him to catch the disease.'

She nodded. 'But it won't be easy. Ever since Papa died Robert has been so solicitous. He reads to her most days and was with her yesterday. We must hope for the best.'

The doctor came downstairs, looking a little less cheerful. 'I think it may be influenza,' he told them. 'Has she been in contact with anybody who might have passed on the disease?'

Harriet frowned. 'Only Eveline Boothby, who makes regular visits to the workhouse where one of the inmates has died from it. Oh dear! I wonder if that . . . But no! That's not possible, because Eveline isn't ill.'

He shrugged. 'Some people don't take it,' he said. 'It seems to pass some people by. There's no rule of thumb with this type of disease. But keep an eye on Miss Boothby also. As for your mother, she's already in the best place – her bed – and has in her daughter a devoted nurse!'

He smiled at her and Harriet thought, not for the first time, that he really was an attractive man.

He went on. 'Keep her warm, plenty of fluids and light food if she can keep it down. She's already feeling a little nauseous and might get worse. I've taken the liberty of closing the curtains in the hope that she might sleep. The gloom will also be kinder on her eyes.' He accompanied Harriet to the front door. 'I'll call tomorrow on my round. If you'll forgive me, Mrs Lester, you do look a little under the weather yourself. Are you feeling at all unwell?'

Harriet looked into the kind blue eyes and suddenly longed to tell him the truth – that she had received a massive emotional shock and still felt as though her secure world was crumbling . . . That, however, would be disloyal to

Godfrey, so instead she forced a bright smile. 'No. I'm very well. A little tired, perhaps.'

'You would tell me, I hope, if your health was giving you concern.'

'I would. Yes, certainly I would.'

He hesitated. 'Or if there was anything I could do to help you . . . in any way at all.'

'That's most kind,' she told him, touched by his concern. 'I'll remember your offer. If I need you . . .'

'I hope you will.' He touched her arm gently. 'You have a lot on those slim shoulders, Mrs Lester. You mustn't neglect your own health while you worry about everyone else. I shall keep my eye on you.'

She smiled. 'That's very reassuring, Doctor.'

Later that day Harriet made her way to Eveline's home, intending to warn her friend that Agnes probably had influenza. To her surprise young Molly was sitting at the table poring over a wooden jigsaw. She glanced up when Harriet entered and said, 'I've done the pig and the cow and I've nearly finished the chicken! Miss Boothby helped me a little bit.'

Harriet made the right noises. 'A farm. What a splendid picture,' she said, 'and what a clever girl you are.' She followed Eveline into the kitchen. 'Still no sign of her mother?'

'She has almost certainly gone to London,' Eveline told her. 'The stationmaster saw her on the platform early this morning. He says it was definitely Daisy. She had a small battered suitcase with her and bought a ticket to Charing Cross. The porter chatted to her and she said she was going to stay with an aunt who lived in Bowden Street.'

'A likely story, but does that mean that's where Digger is?'

'More than likely, I should think. I'm still pondering what to do with the child. Sending her back to the workhouse when they have the influenza there might mean sending her to her death. There's another fatality – an old man. Albert Hawke was measuring him up when I was there this morning.'

'How is Molly behaving herself?' Harriet was curious. The serious spinster and a rumbustious child made an unlikely combination.

'Molly?' Eveline lowered her voice. 'Let us say the word "angel" doesn't spring to mind! She's a very demanding child, to put it mildly. She tells lies and she uses some rather unfortunate language. Her manners are atrocious, she wets the bed, she answers back . . .' She gave an exasperated sigh. 'Does that answer your question?'

Harriet grinned and decided to change the subject. She explained that her mother was now very unwell. 'Maybe you shouldn't visit us for a while,' she suggested. 'Mama is very feverish and her headache is quite severe. Doctor Fletcher came round and is almost certain that it *is* influenza.' She thought how kind he had been and smiled. 'He's a very good man. Very sincere. We were lucky that young Doctor Chisom moved from the town. Angus Fletcher really cares.'

Eveline looked at her through narrowed eyes. 'And your husband? Has that particular problem been eased at all?'

'Ah!' Harriet tried not to appear embarrassed by her friend's outspoken question. 'I think so. I *hope* so! We wrote to Amelia and said Godfrey had done all he could and she must now find work and support herself. We've heard nothing more. That seems to be the end of it.'

'And you are happier now?'

Harriet wished she would let the matter rest but replied, 'It's just a matter of time, I think. We have to let the bad memories fade. I woke in the early hours of this morning with a sense of panic and my heart was racing. But we'll survive.'

'Hmm. Well I hope so. I hope your husband realizes how lucky he is.'

'I'm sure he does. And thank you for your wise words, Eveline. I truly appreciated your advice and we're going to find a way through this.'

Three

Thursday morning dawned bright and clear – a beautiful May morning with a soft breeze that ruffled Harriet's hair as she made her way towards Maybourne Workhouse. She reflected on the circumstances in which the workhouse had been built and was thankful Maybourne had met the requirements of the Act so promptly. The location of the town fell within a day's walk from the nearest workhouse, so that itinerant workers or travellers could be sure of somewhere to stay overnight. Few people now slept rough on Maybourne's streets and for that the residents were heartily thankful. The workhouse had been a godsend to Hannah Wenright, Harriet's birth mother, when she went into an early labour nearly twenty-six years earlier.

As Harriet approached the imposing, somewhat forbidding, building, set back a little from the road, she wondered how many inmates in all would fall victim to the influenza for which the doctors had no certain cure. Live or die – it was in the lap of the gods.

A carriage slowed down as she reached the forecourt of the workhouse and she turned to see Doctor Fletcher reining in his horse. As usual a barefoot boy ran forward.

'Mind your horse, mister?'

The doctor climbed down. 'Morning, young Alf. Can you mind the horse? Yes, you can. There'll be the usual penny in it for you.' He handed him the reins and joined Harriet. 'It seems the monthly report has become a weekly one,' he informed her briskly as they went together up the steps to the large oak door. 'For the duration of the influenza. Give Swift his due – he's a conscientious man.'

Harriet was beginning to feel more at ease with him now that he called daily at Havely House to monitor her mother's progress. 'You also are a conscientious man,' she told him with a smile. She noticed that his boots needed a good polish and the handkerchief protruding from his pocket was crumpled. She knew his mother had died the previous year and if he had taken on a housekeeper, it was clear that she was less than diligent in caring for the doctor's clothes.

'How is your mother?' he asked as they were ushered inside.

'She had a better night's sleep but I thought this morning she seemed a little confused.'

'I'll be along later and I'll see for myself. I might reduce the dose of her medicine.'

The meeting was soon underway. Eveline, still caring for Molly, had sent her apologies for absence but the remaining members of the board were present. Mrs Fenner looked very tired and drawn and Harriet suggested that they take on some temporary help for her but Charles Swift said there was no available money.

'Even if there were some, I doubt we'd find anybody willing,' he explained.

Doctor Fletcher then presented his report, which was short and to the point.

'We now have three inmates in the infirmary – two cases of influenza and a third suspected case. Ivy Weddon died yesterday, God rest her soul. I strongly recommend that any inmates who need treatment for any other ailments be kept in a different room to prevent the spread of the influenza.' He looked at Swift. 'Is there anywhere suitable? The influenza victims should be isolated.'

Swift looked at Mrs Fenner. 'We *could* use the children's dormitory,' she said, 'but then the children would have to be moved to the women's ward. We've only got four children at the moment and all under eight years old. It would be possible.'

Swift said they would arrange this and Doctor Fletcher left to start his round of house calls while Mrs Fenner recorded the exchange in the log book. The Workhouse Master then described an incident which had occurred on Tuesday night.

'Daniel Stick again!' He rolled his eyes despairingly.

Harriet groaned. 'I thought the town was rid of him. Is he back, then?'

Edgar Laycock grunted. 'Unfortunately. The man's an animal! *Worse* than an animal!'

Mrs Fenner shook her head. 'I see myself as a God-fearing woman but there are times I wish Daniel Stick at the bottom of the sea! The wretched man is nothing but trouble wherever he goes. He's a menace to law-abiding folk. He laughs at the police!' She shuddered at the memories of past encounters.

'He arrived after here midnight when everyone was asleep,' Swift told them. 'He was very drunk and Mrs Fenner refused to let him in but he continued to hammer on the door and shout obscenities until he had woken everyone and terrified the more timid.'

'Me included!' Mrs Fenner admitted. 'He made enough noise to awaken the dead and then threw a large stone through the window of the casual ward and tried to force his way in. He was—'

Swift glanced sharply at her and she fell silent, allowing him to finish his account of the incident. 'I was called in to deal with him, by which time one of the men in the casual ward had pushed him back out of the window, causing him to cut his arm on the broken glass round the edge of the window. He then started screaming abuse and threatening to strangle Mrs Fenner with his bare hands! The noise awoke the neighbours and someone went for a constable. Stick was arrested and put in a cell overnight to cool off but the following morning they released him.'

'Released him?' Harriet cried indignantly. 'But why? There must have been plenty of witnesses.'

'According to the sergeant the police are sick of him. He

41

causes so much trouble when he's in the cells. They did a "deal" and offered not to arrest him if he would promise to leave the town and never come back.'

Edgar Laycock snorted with annoyance. 'They've tried that before without success!'

'They say they've banished him.' Swift shrugged. 'If he's ever seen again they'll arrest him on sight.'

'Banished him?' Edgar Laycock glared round at the others. 'That sounds highly irregular. They can't enforce something like that!'

Swift leaned forward. 'If it keeps him away from Maybourne I say they *can*! Let some other town deal with him. We've had our share of the wretch!'

Laycock shrugged. 'I think if they *hanged* him he'd find a way to come back and plague us!'

Time was passing and the meeting proceeded. The next item was Daisy Pritty and her daughter and Harriet brought them up to date. '. . . So Miss Boothby is hoping Daisy will return for her daughter as soon as she returns from London – if she ever does. Molly is quite a handful but it seemed a shame to return her to the workhouse when she has only just left it. Miss Boothby thinks Molly could be quite a pleasant child given the right care. Ideally she should be with her mother.'

Mrs Fenner made no effort to hide her surprise. 'Miss Boothby of all people! A determined old maid!' She caught a warning glance from Swift and hastily modified her tone. 'What I mean is, she's extremely well meaning but what does *she* know? About children, I mean. She has no experience of children whatsoever.'

Detecting a certain unstated criticism, Harriet said quickly, 'I must say Eveline is doing remarkably well in the circumstances. I'm full of admiration for her. Molly looks clean and cheerful and she's bright as a button but she's a very taxing child and Eveline looks tired. Let's hope Daisy reappears soon for both their sakes.'

After a few informal comments the meeting was closed

and Harriet made her way home, diverting along the promenade in order to enjoy a change of scenery and some fresh sea air.

The Covenant Hotel was a small shabby building close to Charing Cross Station. It boasted forty rooms and catered mostly for men who regularly travelled into London on business – men who did not notice the faded wallpaper or limp curtains or the smell of stale pipe tobacco and uninspired food. Room 31 was no better and no worse than the others. It was small and cramped with a tarnished mirror over the small fireplace and a chipped washbasin with a matching jug in a rose-patterned design. Beneath the bed the chamberpot was badly stained.

While Harriet was making her way along the promenade, the woman in room 31 was rereading a letter. In her late thirties, she was handsome in a Mediterranean way – not tall but with strong features and dark gleaming hair drawn into a soft knot at the back of her head. Large brown eyes and a slightly dusky complexion suggested her Italian blood. Amelia Bianchi was studying the note she had received from Godfrey and Harriet. A note she could recite from memory.

> *Dear Amelia,*
>
> *As you know, we are married and although we acknowledge that you needed help initially we feel that you should now be able to take responsibility for your own welfare. You will surely soon find a suitable occupation – you did mention becoming a lady's companion – which would provide both an income and a home.*
>
> *Our sincere good wishes for your future,*
>
> *Godfrey and Harriet Lester.*

Amelia dried her tears. 'Sincere good wishes . . . !' She echoed the formal English bitterly. Her childhood tutors had taught her to speak reasonable English and travels with her father had improved her accent. Dear Lord! What a mockery.

In the past every letter from Godfrey had ended with passionate endearments and rows of kisses – the same letters which her husband had discovered, which had been the cause of her present calamitous situation. This terse loveless letter signed by Harriet and Godfrey added insult to injury. To the absent Harriet she muttered, 'You had a hand in this. I know you did! You're a cold, heartless creature! As for you, Godfrey, perhaps you deserve her.' Her beautiful face, now ravaged by excessive grief, was twisted with anger and resentment. 'Godfrey alone would never write like this to me. Never. He loves *me* and he always will no matter how much he pretends otherwise. He may not know it but *I* know it.'

How, she wondered, could she have been so blind to this possibility? Why had she not even considered that Godfrey might not be waiting for her in England when she most needed him? Because he had once vowed undying love and she had believed him.

'Oh Amelia! You are so stupid to trust a man . . . *any* man!' she muttered. When they met a few days earlier she had been so sure of him . . . but now there was this dreadful wife to complicate the situation. Harriet. Such an ugly name! What had induced him to forget his pledge to her? This Harriet must have bewitched him. She certainly could not love Godfrey the way that *she* did.

Angrily Amelia crumpled the letter and tossed it across the room but she had done that twice before and knew that she would eventually retrieve it. It was one of the few items that still linked them. She thought of her husband, Mario, and her bitterness grew. Mario was at least wealthy and could take care of her. Because of Godfrey she had lost everything and now, encouraged by his horrible wife, he had thrown her to the wolves.

Holding back a sob, she reached out for her purse and counted her few remaining coins. Three shillings and ninepence. She must leave this place on the eighth of May – in two days' time. In the meantime she must eat. She was aware that in the lining of her coat she had sewn her pearls

44

and a gold locket but she had not mentioned these items to Godfrey because it had been essential to present herself as a tragic victim. She would only sell or pawn them if it became necessary, that is if she failed to persuade Godfrey to leave his wife. Meanwhile the jewellery was her safety net.

'But I can no longer afford to eat in a tea room,' she reminded herself. 'Those days are over.' Pulling on her coat, she left the hotel and went in search of the street vendors. Finding a pie man, she bought a mutton pie, carried it into a small park and bit into it hungrily. It was not at all to her taste. The pastry was hard, the filling was brown and lumpy and she could detect nothing remotely like mutton.

'Oh, for a plate of good Italian pasta or a dish of fresh seafood!' she muttered, ignoring the curious glances of passers-by. She knew how strange she must appear to the dull English – an attractive, beautifully dressed foreigner sitting on a bench scattering crumbs from a cheap pie.

'Oh Godfrey! You don't understand what you've done to me!' she said bitterly. How could she find a job? What could she do? In Milan she had had a cook and servants. A dress-maker had made up her clothes and a milliner had created wonderful hats. Women envied her and men admired her. Godfrey had been one of them. He had fallen willingly under her spell and she had found him naïve and so amusing. Now the tables were certainly turned. How was she going to survive? she wondered fearfully. A tramp headed in her direction and she watched him apprehensively. He sat down beside her and gave her a toothless smile.

'Give us a bite, dearie!' he begged and with a cry of disgust Amelia thrust what was left of the pie into his outstretched hand and fled back to the Covenant Hotel. Too desperate to await the lift, she ran up the stairs and along the dim corridor and locked herself inside the anonymous safety of room 31.

She threw herself on to the bed and stared up at the ceiling. Without Godfrey's love she was nothing. Nobody knew her and nobody cared. Without Godfrey's admiration she was a pathetic creature and she would eventually lose her identity in this vast and inhospitable city. For a long time she sobbed despairingly but gradually the urge for self-preservation came to her aid and abruptly she sat up.

'This will not do.' There was a look of grim determination on her face. She slid from the bed and crossed to the tarnished mirror and stared at her ravished reflection. She wiped away tears with her fingers and tidied her hair.

'You are Amelia Bianchi and you do not give in so easily!' she whispered.

'Godfrey must not be allowed to do this – for his own sake! He has made a foolish marriage but you can still save him. One day he will be grateful.' She drew a long, deep breath and some of the fear left her. She traced her dark eyebrows with a trembling finger, pinched a little colour into her cheeks and ran a moist tongue across her dry lips. Already she looked a little better.

'You *know* that he loves you,' she told herself. 'You must fight to win him back!'

Harriet awoke later that night, alert and fearful. What had woken her? She slipped out of bed, lit her candle and padded silently along the passage to her mother's room. There she gave a cry of fear. Agnes lay sprawled on the floor, her face deeply flushed, her hands clutching the air.

'Mama!' Harriet rushed to help her up and felt at once the heat of her skin. Agnes's hair was damp from perspiration and Harriet guessed that the fever had increased alarmingly.

'Come back to bed, Mama, and I'll fetch you some water.' She glanced at the small decanter and saw that it was empty. 'Would you like lemon barley water?' She was shocked to feel how light her mother was as she half-dragged, half-carried her across the room and somehow hoisted her back into the bed. 'You should have rung your bell, dearest! You know it always wakes me.'

Glancing at the bedside table, she saw that the small brass

bell had fallen to the floor and rolled out of her mother's sight. She picked it up and replaced it on the table.

Agnes said, 'I don't want to wake George!' She was breathing very quickly and Harriet realized with a flash of panic that her mother had taken a serious turn for the worse.

'You won't wake Papa,' Harriet told her gently. 'Papa's dead, remember? A long time ago.' She was thinking rapidly. There was no way she could allow her mother to continue like this without medical attention. Her temperature must be excessive if her mind was wandering. 'But you're going to be fine, Mama. First I'll fill your decanter again and then I'll ask Godfrey to fetch Doctor Fletcher.'

Agnes shook her head fretfully. 'I . . . I mustn't wake George . . . '

When Harriet returned to her bedroom, Godfrey was sitting up, running his fingers through his hair. 'What's happening?' he asked sleepily. 'Are *you* unwell now?' They were all hoping not to catch Agnes's disease.

'No, it's Mama!' Harriet told him breathlessly. 'She's much worse. Please fetch the doctor while I try and cool her with damp flannels.'

Five minutes later Godfrey had set off in search of a hansom cab to take him to the doctor's house and Harriet had restoked the fire to provide some tepid water. She soaked a small towel in this and wiped Agnes's face, arms and neck, murmuring encouraging words as she did so. She soaked a second flannel and laid it across her mother's neck then threw back the bedclothes so that Agnes's bare feet and legs could also cool down. Searching, she found a fan and used it to create currents of air around her mother's body.

The minutes passed slowly and the waiting seemed interminable. Harriet found her thoughts wandering and, as usual, she dwelt on her real mother, whose untended grave in the churchyard boasted nothing but a small rusting iron cross with her name scratched on it. Harriet had always wanted to make improvements to it but was afraid that someone would notice the changes and start to investigate. Above all she dared not risk any disclosure of the facts of that day years ago when Hannah Wenright died giving birth to her.

Agnes opened her eyes and looked up at Harriet, then stared past her. 'Oh, there you are, George!' she murmured.

Harriet shivered at her mother's words, aware of a sudden chill. 'I'm here, Mama!' she said. 'It's me, Harriet!'

Agnes closed her eyes again and her speech became alarmingly jumbled and increasingly faint and Harriet was grateful when she heard the front door open followed by footsteps on the stairs. She rushed to open the bedroom door. 'Thank goodness you're here,' she gasped, clutching the doctor's arm. 'Mama is quite delirious. A moment ago she spoke to my father who—'

Doctor Fletcher took hold of her hand and at once his warm, firm grasp steadied her. He said gently, 'Please, Mrs Lester. Don't distress yourself. Take a few deep breaths and then sit in the window-seat, where you will get some fresh air. Meanwhile I'll see to my patient.' He waited until she was seated, then moved to the bed and Harriet saw Godfrey hovering anxiously outside the door. Comforted by his presence, Harriet watched the doctor.

He leaned over Agnes and took hold of her hand. 'It's Doctor Fletcher,' he told her. 'I want you to relax, Mrs Burnett. You need to rest and save your strength. I want you to sleep comfortably. Do you hear me?'

She murmured something. He checked her pulse rate and frowned. Then he listened to her heart and nodded. 'That's fine. Good.' He felt her forehead and raised his eyebrows. Agnes still lay with her eyes closed and her breathing remained fast and shallow.

The doctor sighed and stood up. Harriet stepped forward, trembling. In a low voice she asked, 'Mama's not going to die, is she? Please say she won't die.'

To her surprise he put a reassuring arm around her shoulders, tightened it briefly, then released her. Had Godfrey noticed? she wondered nervously. She hoped not.

'We must put our trust in God,' the doctor told her. 'I

won't lie to you. Your mother is very ill and everything depends on her will to live. We'll rouse her before I go and persuade her to take another smaller sleeping draught. Her restlessness is sapping her strength and we have to calm her. I see you've been cooling her down and that is very important. Can you carry on with that treatment throughout what's left of the night?'

Before Harriet could answer Godfrey said, 'I'll help Harriet. We'll take it in turns.'

'Well said.' He smiled at Godfrey, then turned back to Harriet. 'The fever has reached its peak and hopefully will burn itself out in the next twenty-four hours. If Mrs Burnett survives that period she should make a total recovery. So, plenty of liquids if your mother can manage them. Even a few sips will help. And no need to worry about food.'

Harriet said, ' "Feed a cold, starve a fever." ' *If* Mrs Burnett survives . . . ? She felt as helpless as a child and her legs felt weak.

'Exactly.' The doctor reached for the bottle which held the sleeping draught and Harriet watched, mesmerized by his large, capable hands as he measured out half a spoonful into some water.

Guiltily Harriet tried to concentrate. Together they raised Agnes a little and managed to slide most of the liquid into her mouth.

Doctor Fletcher stood back. 'I'll call round first thing in the morning. If you are frightened at any time, send for me. At any time, Mrs Lester. You can rely on me. No matter how late the hour, I shall come at once.'

He followed Godfrey down the stairs and the bedroom seemed empty without his burly, reassuring figure. Harriet fussed with the bedclothes while Godfrey saw the doctor out and hurried back upstairs to her. He immediately pulled Harriet into his arms and held her close. 'We won't let her die,' he whispered. 'We can save her. I know we can.'

Next morning they broke the news to Robert and warned him to stay well away from Agnes's room. Godfrey also called on Eveline Boothby to issue the same warning. The doctor came as promised but there was no change and the day dragged on, hour after anxious hour.

That same afternoon, a weary Daisy, hungry and dishevelled, was still in London and making her way along Bowden Street, looking for number 70. Squinty had given her an address when she'd finally tracked him down and forced the information from him – not that he had taken much forcing, she recalled suspiciously, but he had been arm in arm with a young woman and had wanted to get rid of her. She'd now wasted several days visiting Bowdon Road, then Bowen Drive, Bordon Walk, Baudwin Road before she'd remembered Squinty has said Street.

She counted breathlessly. Soon she would see Digger again. 'Twenty-six, twenty-eight . . . All even numbers!' So she must be on the wrong side of the street. She darted across, narrowly avoiding a man pushing a barrowful of old furniture who shouted, 'Watch it, you daft dolly!'

Daisy turned on him fiercely. 'Make a nice bonfire, that lot!'

'Bonfire? You cheeky young hussy! I'll have you know these chairs . . . ' Ignoring him, she hurried on. The street ended at number 65 and Daisy cursed under her breath. No number 70. That stupid Squinty . . . or had he done it on purpose? She should never have trusted him. On impulse she went round the corner but that was Lamply Street and the other way it was Hammer Row. Racked with indecision, she went back to number 64 and stood outside, hesitating. She could either give up and go back to Maybourne or she could keep trying. If she wanted to see Digger again she would have to persevere. There was no knocker, no bell and very little paint so she banged on the door with her knuckles. A burly man opened it. His belly suggested too much ale and his nose seemed to have been squashed at some time.

'What d'you want, miss?' he growled and Daisy smelled

onions on his breath. His collarless shirt hung outside his trousers and his feet were bare and in need of a wash but she'd seen worse. Daisy explained her problem.

'What am I supposed to do about it?' he demanded. 'There's no number seventy. You got the wrong number or else the wrong street.'

He tried to shut the door but Daisy was too quick for him and got her foot in the door. 'So have you seen a man called Digby Wise? Thin face, dark eyes, curly hair. In his twenties.'

A sly grin appeared on the man's face. 'Like *that*, is it? Bun in the oven and he's done a bunk!' He laughed. 'Most like he give you the wrong address on purpose! You should have chose more carefully. The man's dumped you!'

Daisy swallowed hard. She, too, was beginning to wonder if Squinty had been *told* to give her the runaround and her hopes were plummeting. She tossed her head. 'At least he was better looking than you, cleaner than you and he didn't smell!' Before he could retaliate she withdrew her foot, darted backwards and ran. Incensed, he lumbered after her for fifteen yards or so but when she glanced back he had given up and was holding his sides and panting heavily.

Maybe she had got it wrong again, she thought. Maybe it was 17 and not 70. With renewed hopes Daisy retraced her steps. Number 17 was marginally neater than number 64. Daisy tried to imagine a cosy upstairs room with a little fireplace and some food and a bed big enough for two. And Digger! She knocked and a girl came to the door and eyed her without much interest. She looked about eighteen, scruffy and unhealthy looking.

'If you're looking for Digger he's not here. Left yesterday,' she told Daisy.

Startled, Daisy stared at her. 'So you know him? He's *been* here?' Her heart began to race. He was all but found! Everything would be all right. She imagined his surprise when he saw her. His face would light up and he'd realize how much she meant to him. He'd throw his arms round her and . . .

'Can't say I *know* him,' the girl told her, 'but he was here for a few days. Like I said, he left yesterday . . . without paying his rent! Looks like my ma was right. She says you can't trust a man with no lobes to his ears!'

Daisy wanted to shout for joy but restrained herself. 'Did he leave an address? Somewhere I can find him? I'm Daisy. He might have mentioned me.'

'He did. He said if you showed up I was to say I'd never heard of him!' She smiled at Daisy's expression. 'Look, if I knew where he was my brother'd be after him like a shot. Give him a bit of a kicking. Knock some sense into him. Buttering me up like he meant it. Rotten little toad! What's he to you anyway?'

Something in her tone made Daisy cautious. 'I'm his sister.'

'And I'm Queen Victoria! Come off it, ducks!'

Daisy shrugged. 'Look, he owes *me* a bob or two as well!' Not that he'd ever admit it after all this time, she thought bitterly, but he did. She'd put him up to a nice little burglary job – easy as pie, in and out. She'd told him where the best pieces were and he'd made a good haul. Sold the stuff and boasted about it but never gave her so much as a penny piece! 'No idea, then, where he is now?' she said.

'No idea at all but if you find him tell him he owes me ma for the rent.'

Daisy's excitement was fading fast. So near and yet so ruddy far, she thought. When was her luck going to change?

The girl moved to close the door but Daisy cried, 'Has he got a job? I might find him . . . '

'He said summat about a job going at the the Grey Nag, a few streets down. Hotel but seedy with it. Know what I mean? Bad reputation.'

Daisy had an immediate vision of Digger dressed in black with a white shirt, looking smart with his hair smoothed down. Digger cleaned up well. He'd look good as a waiter. Not much money but he'd flatter the old ladies and get lots of tips. Her hopes rose, only to be instantly dashed as the girl continued.

'Stable boy. That's what they wanted. Mucking out the horses. About all he's good for, that one, if you ask me!'

The door closed in Daisy's face and she tried to recover from the disappointment. So he didn't want to be found. It was crushing news but Daisy tried hard to see a bright side. He'd most likely forgotten how pretty she was and when he actually *saw* her again it would be a different story. Daisy tossed her head. She would *make* him love her. She would make her dream of happy families come true. With a determined nod she set off once more, in search of the Grey Nag.

On Thursday Harriet welcomed the dawn with relief. Still sitting beside her mother, she continued to cool her with damp flannels but was afraid to open the windows in case it created a draught which might not be so helpful. Throughout the night Agnes occasionally roused from sleep but Harriet thought her less fretful and the confused mumblings had stopped. Gradually her hopes began to rise.

The faint hint of light behind the curtains and the first birdsong alerted a weary Harriet to the fact that the long night was at an end and showed her that her mother looked marginally improved. An even closer look proved that the long days of fever were definitely over. Agnes was pale now with no sign of the flushed cheeks. Her skin was cooler and she seemed to breathe more comfortably. Harriet whispered a short prayer of thanks and rose stiffly to her feet. Her back ached from the cramped position she had maintained and her eyes were dulled by lack of sleep but she did not care. Her mother had survived and nothing else mattered.

Downstairs Harriet coaxed the grey coals back to life, boiled a kettle and made a pot of tea. She was sipping it gratefully when Godfrey joined her. He was still tousled from sleep and he stood in the doorway, rubbing his eyes and smoothing back his hair.

He smiled when he saw her face. 'Your mother's recovered!' He leaned closer and kissed her. 'Thank the Lord – and your devotion!'

Harriet beamed at him. 'Doctor Fletcher will be so relieved,' she said. 'He said he'd call in on us first thing this morning. I can't wait to see him!'

'You sound very eager, I must say!' His tone was somewhat cool, she thought.

'To tell him the good news.' She gave him a sideways glance. Was he *jealous*? If so then he was definitely over the hateful Amelia, which was reassuring. 'He's been wonderfully attentive,' she said innocently. 'I don't know what I would have done without him.'

'He's been a greater support than me, then.'

'Godfrey, he's a *doctor*!' Another glance showed her that Godfrey was definitely out of countenance. Was he sulking?

'You'll miss his visits, I daresay.'

'Don't be so foolish, Godfrey.'

Godfrey poured himself a cup of tea and sat beside her. 'I missed you,' he told her softly. 'Last night in bed.'

'So you should!' She smiled cheerfully.

'The bed was so empty without you.'

She laughed. 'And that's my cue to say that I missed you but the truth is, Godfrey, I thought of nothing and no one but Mama! I thought she was improving but could not believe it. Hour after hour I hoped and prayed. God has been very merciful.'

He nodded and kissed her again.

'What would I do without her?' Harriet whispered.

'You will always have me, dearest.'

The words rang true but Harriet looked sharply at her husband, instantly reminded of the narrow escape they had had. Their world had been shattered briefly by Amelia Bianchi's intrusion but fortunately they had dealt with the situation sensibly and the threatened disaster had been averted. Harriet had forgiven him and she knew that he was doing all he could to make amends. For better or for worse . . . They had passed what Eveline had called the first test.

She stood up and ruffled his hair. 'I'll see if Mama is

awake yet. She'll be very thirsty – and then I'll wash and dress before the doctor arrives.'

Angus Fletcher came just before eight o'clock and was delighted with his patient's progress. Agnes was already awake and had enjoyed a cup of tea. Harriet had washed her, brushed her hair and helped her change her nightdress.

'You look wonderfully refreshed!' the doctor told his patient with a broad smile. 'The worst is over and you must now concentrate on regaining your strength. I'll give Harriet a list of suitably nourishing food that you will be able to digest. Not too much at a time. Small meals but often.'

On his way downstairs he said, 'And you must rest, Mrs Lester. We can't have you tiring yourself out.' He smiled at Godfrey, who was waiting at the foot of the stairs. 'Let your husband help you. We men are not all fools, you know. We can be trusted to do simple jobs around the house.'

Godfrey said, 'I don't think my baking is up to Harriet's standards but I'm very willing to try. I might surprise us both!' He put an arm round her waist possessively. 'My wife is an excellent cook. Have you never considered finding a wife, Doctor?'

He smiled. 'My mother was always urging me to marry but I could never reconcile myself to second best.'

There was a short but awkward silence. Harriet wondered what he meant. Had he been crossed in love? She could hardly imagine any woman refusing him.

Godfrey said, 'Well, we mustn't keep you, Doctor. You have other patients to attend to.'

Harriet nodded. 'And thank you for all your help – and your reassurance. A good doctor is a real treasure. If you ever leave Maybourne I shall "up sticks", as our cook used to say, and follow you!'

The words were said lightly but to Harriet's surprise he seemed startled by them. Suddenly there was an expression in his eyes she could not read.

He regarded her steadily. 'I can assure you I have no plans to leave Maybourne . . . or you. Whenever you need me, for whatever reason, I'll be here.' Just as suddenly his expression changed and he smiled, picked up his bag and closed it. 'Take care of the invalid.'

'I will most certainly. Will you call in tomorrow?'

'If you wish it.'

Godfrey began to say that probably there was no longer any need for daily visits but Harriet heard herself say, 'I do.' She knew at once that she had put too much expression into those words and knew without looking that Godfrey gave her a pained look.

'Then I'll be here around ten o'clock,' the doctor promised.

As she watched him climb into his carriage she felt a ridiculous sense of loss but as soon as he was out of sight she regretted her careless words because she knew she had hurt Godfrey. Her own humiliation was so recent and the memory of the pain so fresh in her mind that she had yielded to the temptation to retaliate. Now she was ashamed of her behaviour. She had been petty-minded. A marriage was not a battlefield, she reminded herself. There were no winners and losers, no attacks and counter-attacks. There was certainly no need to punish Godfrey for his foolishness, especially when he was trying so hard to make a fresh start.

Determined to make amends and to avert further recriminations, she slipped her arm through his and suggested jokingly that he should make good his boast by baking a tray of gingerbread. Fortunately he found it funny and the moment for his possible protest was overtaken by their laughter. Then there were the household chores to do, the pony to be checked and put out to grass. Great-Uncle Robert would be wanting his breakfast and there was shopping to be done in the town. In no time at all Harriet had forgotten all about Doctor Fletcher and the countless cares of the day intruded once more.

Robert was excited by the news of Agnes's recovery and wanted to visit her but Harriet persuaded him to wait a few more days. He agreed and spent the morning in the library writing one of his many letters. This one was to the Speaker of the House of Commons but when he was halfway through it he complained of a headache and went to his room to rest. When Harriet took him up a cup of tea just before three o'clock she found him fast asleep. She tiptoed out with the tea and sent Godfrey up again at four, so she was spared the discovery of his lifeless body. Robert Burnett had died peacefully in his bed.

'I should have been with him!' Harriet wept as she clung to Godfrey. 'If only I'd known . . . Oh Lord! Forgive me!'

'He was a good age,' Godfrey comforted her. 'Much older than most. And he was happy and well loved. He told me once that he was living on borrowed time but he was ready to go whenever God called him.'

Harriet looked up. 'He really said that?'

Godfrey nodded. 'We often talked philosophically. You know how he enjoyed a good discussion. When we moved into this place we changed his life. He told me so many times. And he wasn't afraid of death. He said that as you grow older you become reconciled to the idea.'

She narrowed her eyes. 'You're not saying this to help me bear it, are you? He really did feel like that about . . . about passing on?'

'I swear it, Harriet.' He smiled. 'He was a very lonely man for most of his life but when he offered us a home he gained a family. Between us we made him happy, Harriet. Mourn for him, we all will, but don't blame yourself for anything. He wouldn't wish it, you know. He adored you and Sam.'

'And you, Godfrey!'

'We were good friends. I'll settle for that.'

After more discussion it was decided that Godfrey would wait for the doctor's visit while Harriet went to the undertaker to choose a coffin and arrange the funeral. Just before ten o'clock she threw a shawl round her shoulders and set off.

Four

When Harriet arrived at Albert Hawke's yard she found him in a state of great distress. The little office had been ransacked and Albert had a large bruise on the side of his face.

'Mr Hawke!' she cried. 'What on earth has happened? Your poor face!'

He gave her a painful smile and touched his face gingerly. 'The wretch was in here when I came down, first thing. Smashing up the place. Look! He's even broken the chair! What sort of mind does a man like that have? Mindless thuggery! Nothing less. And all because he didn't find any money because I keep it upstairs overnight.'

She looked around the small room. The much prized photograph of the mayor's funeral had been smashed, she noted. And the curtains had been ripped down and tossed in a corner and even the gaslights had been damaged.

'This is terrible!' she cried. 'I'm so sorry. He was still here, you say? You surprised him.'

'I think it was the other way round! He surprised me. Must have heard me coming. As soon as I opened the door he jumped on me and *whack*! Right on the back of my head. Then he punched me in the face. I was reeling by then. I tried to have a go at him but I was a bit dazed and he got clean away.' He leaned heavily on the counter. 'The constable's just left but they can't do anything. That man's too much for them if you ask me.'

Her eyes widened. 'You know the man?'

'Aye. Donald Stick – or is it Daniel? I've seen him lurching around the town on and off. Usually up to no good.'

58

'Daniel Stick? That horrible brute! We were told that the police had banished him from the town.'

'Did they? They keep trying to get rid of him. Well, he's back!' He straightened up. 'But you're not here to listen to my woes. How can I help you?'

With a pang of guilt, Harriet remembered the sad reason for her visit and told the undertaker what had happened.

'I'm sorry to hear that,' the undertaker told her. Instinctively he had changed his expression and softened his tone in order to assume his usual role of sympathetic adviser. 'A very sad loss. Very sad indeed. He'll be missed, I'm sure.' He smiled sadly. 'And you'll be wanting to send him to his Maker in a beautiful coffin. Rest assured, Mrs Lester. I'll see that you get exactly what you want for your beloved great-uncle. Saying farewell is never easy but laying him to rest in a certain style will ease your pain.'

Harriet nodded. Earlier she had faced the prospect of her mother's death but Robert's passing had taken her by surprise. Her grief was very real for she had grown fond of the old man but deep down she was thankful that God had chosen to take Robert and not her mother. Robert had been granted a long life but her mother was still comparatively young. They had been fortunate to enjoy Robert's company for so many years and had no cause for complaint on that score.

Now the undertaker was talking her through the various choices of wood, design, lining and handles. The coffin she finally selected was reasonably priced. Albert Hawke volunteered his funeral vehicle and she accepted although she wasn't sure whether Robert would have approved. He might have thought it too ostentatious but it did mean that they could transport the coffin more easily.

'Now all we have to do is choose the hymns for the service,' she said with a sigh. 'I'll ask Mama's help. She will know better than I will. I'll speak with the vicar and let you know the date and time, Mr Hawke, and thank you for your kindness.' As she walked to the door she paused uncertainly. 'I feel I should offer to help you with the clearing up. Especially as you . . . '

He was shaking his head. 'No need for that, Mrs Lester, but it was a kindly thought. I shall close the business for a few hours and take a short rest. I'll sort the office out when I feel better. It's rather shaken me up. I'll make no secret of that.' As they shook hands he went on. 'Any news about Daisy Pritty?'

Harriet shrugged. 'There's a rumour that she's gone up to London to try and find that awful friend of hers – the one she calls Digger.'

The undertaker's expression was awkward. 'It was just that . . . I've been thinking and . . . Well, I did wonder whether I might offer her a job as my housekeeper instead of the occasional hours. Her and the little girl. I mean, there's a spare room and a bit of an attic. We could manage something. What d'you think?'

Harriet hesitated. She didn't want to dampen his enthusiasm because basically the idea was sound and for Daisy and her daughter it would be a wonderful opportunity. Her only reservations were about how Daisy would react and whether or not she would take advantage of Albert Hawke's generosity. 'It's a splendid idea,' she began, 'but I think you should realize that Daisy probably has no housekeeping skills at all. The workhouse doesn't teach cookery or money management. Nothing of that kind, to be honest – although she may have spent some time in the workhouse laundry.'

'I could maybe help her at first until she gets the hang of it.' He looked at her eagerly. 'The truth is, it gets a bit lonely at my age – not that I'm not used to it, and me and Snapper do all right. But they'd be a bit of company. Can she read or write? She could help me with the bills and suchlike.'

'She knows a few letters, I think, but maybe—'

'I could maybe teach her enough.'

Harriet was torn. She could be brutally frank or she could help Daisy. On reflection she did not want to encourage this kindly man only to see him bitterly disappointed. 'Daisy might not be too reliable, Mr Hawke.' She spoke with growing reluctance. 'As long as you realize that. She was placed in a very good position some years ago and she . . . she ran away and then helped Digger to break in and rob them. I wouldn't like something like that to happen to you.'

He was not going to be convinced. 'Oh, that's all in the past, Mrs Lester. She's older now and maybe wiser. I'd be willing to give her a chance. *If* she can be found before . . .' he lowered his eyes, '. . . before it's too late. London's a big city, if you see what I mean. Too many people willing to exploit a pretty girl like her.'

Harriet knew exactly what he meant. If Daisy couldn't or wouldn't work she might well end up as a woman of the streets. 'Think it over, Mr Hawke,' she advised, 'before you make a decision. By all means keep the idea in mind and see what happens next. If, perish the thought, she finds Digby Wise and moves in with him there'll be no decision to make!'

Five minutes later, as Harriet walked home, her thoughts reverted to Robert and it suddenly occurred to her that there would be a will. Or *should* be. She stopped so abruptly that a woman walking behind her cannoned into her and Harriet hastily apologized. What exactly would Robert's death mean to them apart from the loss of his company? Would they find themselves homeless again or had Robert left Havely House to Agnes? Or to Sam? She frowned. Did Robert have any other relatives that had never been mentioned? Sighing, she pondered the future. They would know the answers as soon as the will was read and that would be immediately after the funeral. Poor Robert. Her eyes filled with tears as she tried to imagine life without him. Strange now to remember that when much younger she had been afraid of the strange old man. Havely House had seemed a forbidding place, the garden full of sinister, shadowy shrubs and their regular visits to him events to be dreaded. Sam, too, had found Robert daunting. Now of course, life at Havely House had given them the chance to understand him and they had all grown very fond of him.

Sighing, she decided to ask Godfrey to go to Winchester and bring Sam back for the funeral. Now eleven, Sam would be saddened by his great-uncle's death but he would have the pony to fuss over. Her footsteps slowed as she drew nearer home, where she was going to have to break the news of Robert's death to her mother, and suddenly she couldn't face it. She stopped irresolutely, searching unconsciously for an excuse to delay her return. It occurred to her that the situation with regard to Daniel Stick was far from satisfactory. If Mrs Fenner discovered that he was back in Maybourne she would be terrified. Maybe a complaint from a member of the public would inspire the police.

Seizing on this thought, she changed direction and made her way to the police station, where she was greeted by a man she recognized as Sergeant Wiley, a large, red-faced man who was rapidly growing out of his uniform. Buttons strained, the collar of his tunic had been loosened and a large gusset had been let into the back seam of the trousers.

'I'm told that Daniel Stick is back in Maybourne,' she said without preamble. 'How can that be? He was banished quite recently.'

'News to me, miss.' His tone was non-committal.

'It's Mrs. Mrs Lester. Daniel Stick—'

'I mean, news to me that he's back.' In the background a young constable listened with undisguised interest.

Harriet adopted a stern expression. 'It shouldn't be news. One of your constables attended Albert Hawke's yard recently. In the last hour. Stick caused a lot of damage and assaulted Mr Hawke.'

'Well now, Mrs Lester. I don't know anything about any assault. Maybe the constable hasn't come back to report it yet. Most likely still on duty.' He turned away and fussed with some papers, suggesting that the conversation was at an end.

Harriet persisted. 'Well, now that you *do* know, what can you do about it? Daniel Stick is not a small-time villain. He is a fully fledged criminal. He drinks heavily and then he becomes very violent and he could easily do someone serious harm. He recently caused a lot of trouble at the workhouse and Mrs Fenner—'

He turned, affronted by her attitude. 'What can we do about it? We'll do our *job*, Mrs Lester. We'll do *what's necessary*. That's what we'll do! At the proper time. *When we've seen the proper report.*' He was breathing heavily. 'We don't need busybodies telling us our job! *We'll* decide what to do about Daniel Stick.'

'All I'm saying is that Stick is a very dangerous man. If he won't stay away he should be locked up.'

'I'll wait for the report if you don't mind.' The sergeant ran a finger round the inside of his collar. 'Now, Mrs Lester, I've got work to do.'

Harriet eyed him angrily. 'I'd like my complaint noted, Sergeant. The name is Lester. Mrs Lester. Banishing a dangerous man simply means that someone else has to deal with him. He's a local man, he's Maybourne's responsibility and he should be in custody.'

He picked up a pen and dipped it in the inkwell. Reaching for a notepad, he wrote the words 'LESTER' and 'STICK' and held it up for her inspection. 'Duly noted, Mrs Lester!' He leaned forward. 'Now you've had your say, do please get along home!'

Harriet was furious although she knew in her heart that she had overstepped the mark. Searching for a way to retain her dignity, she said, 'I shall put this conversation on record, Sergeant Wiley, and send it with a letter to the Mayor. That way we shall know who to blame when Daniel Stick *kills* someone! Good day to you.'

The summer season in Maybourne did not properly start until the beginning of June and there were very few passengers alighting at Maybourne Railway Station from the London train. A soldier with a kitbag, an old man with a puppy tucked into the front of his well-worn jacket, a young man with a pregnant wife and four children, a large woman in a moth-eaten fur coat – and Amelia Bianchi. She looked totally out of place as she stepped down from the carriage and was immediately aware that most people were looking at her with either admiration or envy. She had pawned the pearls in order to make the most of herself. Her dark hair was immaculate, her clothes fashionable, her luggage obviously expensive. And she was naturally beautiful. A porter rushed up to help her collect her luggage from the guard's van. She gave him a tip, then glanced at the station clock. Five minutes to eleven. Carrying her small suitcase and a round hatbox, she walked towards the gate but when she reached it she hung back to let the last of the passengers pass her. When she was the only one remaining she offered her single ticket and asked for directions to Havely House.

'Never 'eard of it,' the ticket collector told her. 'But I'm not from Maybourne, see. I live four miles away at Bridley. Walk to work and walk back. Keeps you fit. That's what they say. You're from foreign parts. I can tell.'

'From Italy.'

'Italy? My! I've never been across the sea but I've heard about it. They have those boat things – gondolas. I've seen pictures, of them – and that volcano . . . What was it called?'

'Vesuvius. So you do not know Havely House?'

'Havely House?' He scratched his head. 'You'd best ask the stationmaster. He's out there on the forecourt.' He nodded in the direction of a dapper-looking man in railway uniform.

'Thank you. I'll speak to him.'

He hesitated, obviously wanting to prolong the conversation. 'Just visiting, are you, ma'am?'

She smiled enigmatically. 'I have not decided yet. I am – how you say? – exploring possibilities.'

'Ah!' he said, looking uncertain. 'Exploring possibilities. I see.'

Leaving him, Amelia made her way across the forecourt to the stationmaster, who glanced up at her approach, looking pleasurably surprised.

Amelia repeated her enquiry.

He frowned. 'Havely House? That rings a bell . . . Burnett! That who you're looking for? Big house set well back.'

'I do not think so.' Amelia shook her head. 'The name's Lester.'

'Not the Havely House I'm thinking of then. Old man lives there. Been in the family for years. Odd sort of chap. Eccentric. They say—'

'No no! This is a Godfrey Lester. A youngish man.'

'Afraid I can't help you then. I only know one Havely House. Know *of* it, I should say. My grandfather used to be groom to the Burnetts. Dogged by scandal, they were. Suicides. Runs in the family, so he reckoned. Still got the cutting from the paper.'

'How too unfortunate.' Amelia shuddered. 'Then I must make other enquiries,' she told him.

He pointed to the bus that waited nearby. 'That'll take you into the town centre. Just waiting for the up train at eleven twenty, then it'll be off. You could ask at the post office. They should be able to help you.'

Amelia gave him a bright smile. 'No. I cannot wait. Perhaps you would call me a cab.'

'With pleasure, ma'am.'

When it arrived there was a short conversation during which the cab's driver mentioned that George Burnett's daughter had married a chap called Lester and the problem appeared to be solved. Less than ten minutes later the driver reined in his horse outside Havely House, helped Amelia down and handed her the suitcase and the hatbox. She set them down on the front steps and together they stared up at the windows.

The driver crossed himself. 'Drawn curtains! Crikey Moses! Looks like they've 'ad a death in the 'ouse!' He glanced at Amelia as she fumbled in her purse for the fare. 'Come for the funeral, 'ave you?'

'No! I did not know . . .' Amelia pressed the coins into his hand. 'Maybe you'd better wait.' She felt a coldness within her. Please God, don't let it be Godfrey, she thought.

65

Could it possibly be Harriet? That would be heaven-sent. 'Here's another sixpence. Wait for a few minutes and if I don't come out again then go.'

She had planned to send him away as soon as she arrived so that she would be without transport and more vulnerable but now she was unsure what to do next. The driver climbed back into his seat and lit his pipe while Amelia rang the bell. She stared up at the building, taking in the large windows and elegant design. Was this Godfrey's house? she wondered. No. The stationmaster had said it was owned by the Burnett family. So had Godfrey married a wealthy woman? That might be a problem. There was no answer, so she seized the bell pull and tried again. She could hear it ringing inside the house. She stepped back and stared around. The cab driver called to her. 'All at the funeral, mebbe.'

She drew a deep breath. Nothing was working out the way she had imagined. 'I'll walk round to the back of the house.' Then she would have to leave. Perhaps he was right. She imagined all the mourners returning to the house at any moment. Quickly she ran round and saw two men through the shrubbery beside the path. Hurrying towards them, she saw that one was Godfrey and the other a man she assumed was a groom. He was holding the halter of a pony and talking earnestly to Godfrey. They both turned, startled by her sudden appearance, and Godfrey paled visibly.

'Good God, Amelia!'

She stepped forward, relieved to see him alive. 'Godfrey! Thank goodness! I had to see you!'

He mumbled something to his companion and the other man nodded and began to lead the pony away towards the stable. Slowly Godfrey moved towards her. 'What in God's name . . . ! You can't come here! Are you crazy?' He looked badly shocked and Amelia saw none of the delight she had expected.

'Wait, Godfrey. Before you say anything, I can explain,' she told him. She was thinking desperately. Somehow she must strand herself here. She must get rid of the cab. She turned to retrace her steps but he came after her and caught hold of her arm.

'You have to go!' he hissed. 'Harriet will be back at any moment. She mustn't see you here. You've seen the letter. I've told her it's over. I've said we won't see each other again.'

Amelia felt as though he had slapped her face. 'That letter! Pah!' The coward! He hadn't told his wife what they had agreed. 'You promise!' she accused him, wrenching her arm away. 'When we were in London you promise! You say you will tell her that you still loved me but you do not do it! I can see it in your eyes.' She turned to run back to the cab, intending to send it away, but Godfrey ran after her. She waved to the driver. 'Go! Go!' but before he had gathered up the reins Godfrey was shouting to him to wait and he hesitated. They both arrived beside the cab, Godfrey now red-faced, Amelia pale and near to tears. Damn him! He had *promised*!

Godfrey threw her luggage back into the cab and jumped up into it. He reached down, took her hand and, ignoring her protests, pulled her up to sit beside her. Godfrey cried, 'Go as quickly as you can!' and the driver rattled the reins and they rolled down the drive and out on to the road.

Amelia tried to take comfort in the fact that at least they were together but she was not happy about his betrayal. She let the tears gather in her eyes, then turned to look at him. 'Why did you not tell her, my love? You promise you will tell her the truth. That terrible letter. I was wounded. Such cold, hard words.'

'I couldn't tell her, Amelia. I wanted to but when the time came . . . She *is* my wife and I do love her.'

'But not as much as you love *me*! I know it and you know it!'

They reached a junction in the road and the driver said, 'Which way now?'

She looked at Godfrey. 'You cannot abandon me again, Godfrey. I am not going away. I will stay in Maybourne until you see sense.'

Godfrey said, 'Take us into town, please.'

The driver turned to the left. Amelia was fighting hard to control her anger. She must not show herself in a bad light. This was a time for pleading. She snatched up Godfrey's hand and kissed it passionately. 'I was so frightened,' she told him, 'when I saw the closed curtains. I thought you had had an accident and were dead. I thought I would never see you again. Kiss me, Godfrey. Just once. To show me that you still care. Because I know you do.'

'I can't . . . I can't do that, Amelia. We've talked about this and I've given Harriet my word. I won't—'

Amelia twisted in the seat and pressed her mouth against his. She put up her hand to the back of his head so that he could not move away. At last his arms went round her and she closed her eyes.

'Amelia! Oh God! My sweet Amelia!' He was kissing her now, making no effort to push her away. The cab suddenly drew up with a jolt.

'Town centre.'

His words seemed to break the spell. Godfrey drew back hastily and they both stared around them. She said, 'I shall find myself a room. Come and find me, Godfrey. If you do not come to me I shall come back to Havely House.'

Once again the driver helped her down and Godfrey passed down her luggage. She could see the anguish in his eyes.

The driver jerked a thumb. 'The County Hotel's a few 'undred yards thataway. Not too pricey these days. Gone down in the world, you might say.' He looked at Godfrey. 'You going 'ome then?'

Godfrey nodded. He threw a kiss to Amelia and she returned it. As the cab turned and once again headed out of town, Amelia picked up her belongings and turned towards the County Hotel. Her thoughts were chaotic. She still had no idea who had died but it couldn't have been Harriet or Godfrey would have told her. And he *had* returned her kisses. He could be very passionate but he needed the right woman. A sensual woman. She wondered what Harriet was like as a lover. The English were so unromantic. Somehow she must contrive to see her. They had no children, so maybe they were no longer lovers. She smiled at the thought. Some women were frigid. Perhaps Harriet was one of them. Amelia crossed her fingers.

By the time she reached the hotel she had entirely recovered her composure and she swept into the hotel foyer with a firm smile on her face. Poor Godfrey. She would have to be strong for both of them. Her smile deepened at the realization that Godfrey still loved her. He was still hers for the taking.

On the way back home Harriet called in on Eveline to tell her about Robert's death, her mother's recovery and her visit to the police station but she found her friend on the doorstep in a state of great anxiety.

'It's Molly. She's gone!' she told Harriet. 'I took her shopping with me – I bought her a small basket so she can carry some of the lighter items – and the little minx slipped away in the market. Or else was spirited away – although why anyone should want such a difficult, disobedient child, I cannot imagine!'

She glanced up and down the road, her eyes narrowed. Instinctively Harriet joined her, searching the street for a glimpse of the missing child. The area was busy as usual. A washerwoman with a bundle of washing made her way between groups of chattering neighbours. A boy bowled a hoop erratically with loud shrieks of excitement, calling down curses when he veered too close to a horse and cart. From somewhere not too distant a barrel organ was playing and there were bursts of laughter from the children who danced to its jangling music. A dog barked. A door slammed. There was no sign of Molly.

Distractedly, Eveline put a hand to her head. 'I despair of her. When I find her she'll go straight back to the workhouse!' Her voice broke and she blinked furiously.

Harriet said, 'But why would she run off? She's so happy with you.'

69

'I have no idea. Worrying me like this! It's unforgivable.'
She swallowed hard. 'I've searched for her for the best part
of an hour and then I thought she might have made her own
way home, so I came back.' She shrugged. 'It's really very
naughty of her and I'm wondering if I've been too lenient.
I haven't even smacked her although I've been sorely
tempted. Maybe she needs a sterner discipline . . . but she's
so tiny and she looks at me with those big blue eyes!'

'It must be difficult for you,' Harriet agreed. 'I'm sorry I
can't give you any useful advice.'

'Well, of course you can't. How could you? You have no
children of your own,' Eveline said tactlessly.

Stung by the careless words, Harriet bit back a sharp retort.
Eveline was also childless but she would remain so. Harriet
was still hopeful. Seeing how upset her friend was, however,
she let the remark pass without comment.

Eveline fussed anxiously with the beads round her neck.
'I've told her repeatedly to stay close to me. The streets
aren't safe for children any more. I recall that dreadful case
a year or so again. A little boy stolen away and then found
dead. Oh!' She clapped a hand to her trembling mouth. 'It
doesn't bear thinking about! Where *can* she be?'

'Maybe Daisy is back in Maybourne,' Harriet suggested
hastily. 'She might have come across her and whisked her
away. It's the sort of thoughtless thing she would do.'

Eveline brightened a little. 'Anything's possible. But why
simply snatch her? I'm quite happy for her to be back with
her mother. The silly child is nothing to me. Nothing! I
should have let her go back to the workhouse. At least she
would be well supervised there but I kept her with me, so I
alone am responsible if anything bad happens to her.'
Abruptly she darted past Harriet and spoke to an elderly
woman who was passing. 'Have you seen a little girl
wandering on her own? A pretty child with fair curly hair.'

The woman shook her head. 'Don't think so. Kids! You
need eyes in the back of your head these days. I'm thankful
mine are—'

'If you see a child like that – her name is Molly – would you please let me know?'

'You her grandmother?'

Eveline hesitated. 'Her aunt.'

When the woman had gone Harriet said, 'Could she have found her way back to the workhouse?'

'I've asked there. They haven't seen her . . .' She swallowed hard and drew a long breath. 'But what am I doing, keeping you on the doorstep like this? Come inside, Harriet. I'm not being very hospitable, am I? You must forgive me.' She led Harriet into the parlour and they both sat down and Harriet broke the sad news about Robert.

'I'm so sorry, dear,' Eveline said. 'He was a good man but his time has come. Be pleased for him to slip away so peacefully, Harriet. You made him very happy.'

'That's what Godfrey said.' She sighed. 'The vicar wasn't available but I saw the undertaker.' She told Eveline about Daniel Stick and Albert Hawke and the way the police reacted to her visit. 'They showed very little interest – in fact they obviously resented my attitude. Maybe I went about it the wrong way but I do feel they should lock Stick up. He's a menace and their job is to protect the public.'

'The police are a law unto themselves, Harriet – if you'll forgive the pun!' She managed a weak smile. 'But at least you alerted them to his presence and public feelings about him and when the constable reports the attack on Mr Hawke perhaps they will scour the streets for him. One of us had better warn Mrs Fenner. 'She glanced at her clock and her worries flooded back. 'Oh Molly! You naughty little girl! Where *are* you, you silly child?' She closed her eyes but opened them again and gave Harriet an anxious smile. 'I shall give her a severe talking-to when she *does* come home. If she doesn't see the error of her ways I might even give her legs a smack. "Spare the rod and spoil the child!" Isn't that what they say?' She sighed. 'Frightening me like this, it's too bad. But listen to me. You have enough worries, my dear, without bothering about mine.'

'I'm sure she'll come back soon. Give her a little more

time. She's probably sitting on someone's doorstep playing with a kitten or something.'

They both rose. 'Give my kind regards to your mother, Harriet. I'm so very happy for you that she has come through the crisis. You must have had a terrible night and then to lose Robert! Poor Harriet. Tell Agnes that as soon as the doctor says it's safe to do so, I'll call on her. In the meantime take a jar of my lemon curd. I know she likes it and it may tempt her appetite.'

Minutes later they were halfway along the passage when they heard a small tapping sound. They looked at each other and Eveline rushed to open the front door. Molly, grubby but unharmed, beamed up at Eveline and held out a few wilting dandelions.

'Molly!' cried Eveline, with a cry of relief. 'Where have you been, you naughty girl?'

'For you, Aunt Evie!' the child told her.

For a moment or two Eveline struggled with her feelings, then she whispered, 'Oh Molly! What lovely flowers!' She bent down, pulled the little girl into her arms and held her close. Harriet smiled. She suspected that all thoughts of stern discipline had already been abandoned.

As soon as Godfrey arrived home from his meeting with Amelia he hurried through the house to see whether or not Harriet was home and uttered up a prayer of thanks that she had not returned from her trip to the undertaker. Probably called in on Eveline Boothby, he thought. He hurried upstairs to knock on the door of Agnes's bedroom.

She was sitting up in bed and smiled at him. 'I rang my bell,' she said, 'but no one came. Has Harriet gone out?'

'Er . . . Yes, she has.' He remembered in time that Agnes had not been told about Robert's death. 'She . . . popped in to Eveline to tell her you have passed the worst night of your illness and the doctor said you are on the mend.'

Agnes closed her eyes sleepily. When she opened them again she said, 'You didn't come and neither did Robert.

I rang for someone. I wanted some lemon barley water.'

'I'll get it for you.' He was eager to be gone. In his experience Agnes was as sharp as a pin and missed nothing. 'We were both in the garden,' he lied. 'Robert and me. Talking to Cummings about . . . about the pony. That's why we didn't hear your bell. I'm so sorry.' He wondered whether she would mention this to Harriet.

Agnes was studying him and he felt that she must surely read his guilt.

'Are you all right, Godfrey? You look so worried.'

'Worried? No! Not at all. I . . . It's rather warm, that's all. I'll fetch your drink.' Afraid to remain under her scrutiny, he left the room and went downstairs. His mind was full of Amelia. He could still taste her lips but it gave him no pleasure at all. That foolish moment had passed and now, more than ever, he wanted to keep his marriage alive, but Amelia was a serious threat. He remembered now how insistent she had been when they first met in Italy so many years ago and how carefully she had manipulated the situation. Only eighteen, he had been thrilled by her attentions and fallen completely under her spell. He had adored her, hating every moment when they were not together. Hating her husband for his share in her life. Yes, he *had* promised her undying devotion but time had passed. His life had changed. He sighed as he found a jug for the lemon barley water and carefully filled it.

Upstairs he found Agnes a little more alert.

She said, 'Godfrey, I want you to be honest with me. Can you promise to do that?'

He felt the colour rush from his face. Had she heard Amelia's cab draw up on the forecourt? Did she suspect that Amelia had visited? 'I hope so,' he said under his breath. He crossed to the side of the bed, picked up her glass and refilled it with an unsteady hand. What should he say if she challenged him? Suppose she *knew* that Amelia had been to see him . . .

'I know what's happened,' she said, confirming his worst

fears. 'I've been expecting it, Godfrey, and I daresay you have also. You can tell me.'

He put the jug down, struggling for words. If he had to tell anyone it should be Harriet who heard his confession. 'Agnes . . . I don't think . . . That is . . .' He felt sick with fright. He had had no time to plan for this confrontation.

She reached out to take his hand but he stepped back guiltily.

'It's Robert, isn't it?' she said. 'He's caught the influenza from me. He's ill, isn't he?' She waited but when he didn't speak she said gently, 'I understand you don't want to upset me but I've guessed. I heard someone in his room this morning after the doctor had gone. A voice I didn't recognize. You've called in a nurse, haven't you?'

Staring at her, Godfrey felt light-headed as relief flooded through him. Then he let out a long breath. She didn't know anything about Amelia's visit but she *did* know all was not well with Robert. She must have heard the woman from the town who washed and laid out Robert's body. Playing for time he said, 'Harriet wants to tell you herself, Mrs Burnett. Will you wait a little longer, please.'

She nodded, reaching out for the barley water. 'If that is Harriet's wish.'

Thankful, he withdrew from the room but she called him back. 'I hope there's nothing wrong with Sam's pony.'

He stared at her nonplussed for a moment before he recalled his earlier excuse. 'Nothing wrong at all. Something about a new set of horseshoes. What a relief you are on the mend.'

Before she could ask further questions he escaped from the room and ran downstairs two at a time. He needed time to think about Amelia but at any moment he expected Harriet to return. Should he or shouldn't he tell his wife what had happened? That was the dilemma. If he didn't tell, she might well find out for herself. If he did tell, would she understand that he had not encouraged Amelia in any way?

'And she means nothing to me now!' He said the words aloud, practising them. Did the words ring true, he wondered, or would Harriet detect a false note? Amelia still loved him, that was clear, but were his feelings for her really dead? For a moment he recalled the excitement of seeing her again. But was it just a revival of that earlier excitement he had felt as a young man? A passion laced with a sense of danger which was no longer part of his life. Married life was so unlike the thrill of an illicit romance . . .

'No! Stop this!' he told himself. His thoughts were drifting out of control towards the unthinkable. He was married to a wife he loved and he must *not* allow his feelings for Amelia to resurface. To take his mind off the problem he made his way quietly upstairs and went into Robert's room, where the old man was neatly arranged on the bed. The bed linen had been changed and Robert was dressed in a clean nightshirt, his arms folded over his chest in the traditional way. His face was very pale, his hair brushed back in an unfamiliar style and a penny piece had been placed on each closed eye. A tall candle burned on the bedside table.

'I'll miss you, Robert,' he whispered. 'Havely House will be a different place without you. Rest in peace, old friend.' He rested his right hand lightly on Robert's shoulder and then glanced round the room. A book beside the bed lay opened at the last page that had been read and his clothes were draped neatly across the armchair by the window. Below them his shoes had been set side by side but they still showed the shape of their wearer and Godfrey found himself blinking back tears. With a last glance at the still figure on the bed, he made his way out of the room and closed the door. Glancing through into Agnes's room, he saw that she was asleep again and went downstairs.

Still Harriet had not returned. Godfrey stood in the hall, thankful that his trip into Maybourne with Amelia had passed undetected. Perhaps fate was on his side. Had he forgotten anything? 'The gardener!' he exclaimed. He had told Agnes that he and Robert had been in the garden talking about Sam's pony. He would make sure that his story was secure.

He hurried outside and found Cummings in the old green-house with the watering can.

'Mr Cummings, I'd like a quick word,' he said. 'I had to tell Mrs Burnett a lie this morning. The doctor thought she was too weak to stand the shock of Mr Burnett's death, so when she asked to speak to him I pretended he was in the garden with me and you, talking about Rollo.'

'Ah! Right. I've got that, Mr Lester. We was all talking about the pony.'

'No! Not *all* of us. Just you and me. About some new horseshoes. Good man.'

Cummings frowned, suddenly nervous. 'Is she coming down to ask me, like?'

'Good Lord no! She can hardly get out of bed, poor soul. But . . . If the matter comes up at all with anyone . . .' He smiled. 'You know what to say.'

'Right you are, sir. I'll remember.'

'What I mean is, we *are* talking about the pony, aren't we. Now.'

'I suppose so.' He looked thoroughly confused.

As Godfrey walked back to the house he had the uneasy feeling that he had made matters too complicated.

Just before seven that same evening Harriet made her way into the back garden and caught Cummings locking the potting shed in preparation for his walk home. 'Mr Cummings! I'm glad I've caught you.' She smiled although her heart was hammering.

'I was that sorry to 'ear about the old man dying. Very sad that. Very sad indeed.'

'Yes. We knew it was going to happen before long but it's still a dreadful shock.'

'Oh aye!' The gardener drew a quick breath. 'I said as much to him and Mr Lester,' he said in unnaturally meas-ured tones. 'When he come down 'ere to talk about the pony and the horseshoes. Just him and me. Today like.'

Harriet frowned. 'Not today, Mr Cummings, surely. It must

76

have been yesterday because Mr Burnett died during the night or early this morning.'

Cummings licked his lips. 'Did he now? Ah! Well, maybe it *was* yesterday but I thought Mr Lester said it was today. That's what he said. On account of your ma, like, not knowing he was dead. We was talking about Rollo.'

'What about Rollo?'

Panic touched his eyes. 'I don't rightly know, to tell you the truth. I'm . . . I'm a bit fuddled to be honest. You'd best ask Mr Lester. He knows more'n I do.'

He's lying, thought Harriet, cold with fear. Godfrey had rehearsed him in the lie. Not that it mattered. 'Thank you, Mr Cummings. You be on your way. We'll see you in the morning.'

He touched his cap, nodded and walked hurriedly away. Harriet watched him go, her mind full of doubts. Her mother, drowsy from a heavy sleep, had told Harriet how many times she had rung her bedside bell in vain. Now Harriet knew for certain that Godfrey had been away from the house. He had left her mother alone in the house with Robert's body and this was a pathetic attempt to cover his tracks. Which meant that it *had* been Godfrey she had glimpsed in the hansom cab, sitting with a beautiful dark-haired woman, who *had* to be Amelia Bianchi. Sick at heart, Harriet decided against an immediate confrontation. Godfrey was deceiving her and there was no point in pretending otherwise. A moment's reflection caused her to reconsider. She would let him think her unaware. She would say nothing and do nothing – except watch and wait. Perhaps he would confide in her of his own free will. There just might be an innocent explanation.

Five

Daisy had to wait several days before she could see the owner of the Grey Nag because he was away from London seeing his brother buried. When he returned, Daisy was sent through into his office in the rear of the premises. Bert Fry was a large burly man with a pockmarked face and fists like hams. His belly protruded over his leather belt and his neck hung over his dirty collar. He slouched in his chair and his feet were on the desk, which was littered with papers and crumbs.

Daisy forced a smile. 'I heard you might have a lad working here, name of Digby Wise. Friend of mine.'

'What if I have?' He reached for a penknife, opened it and began to clean his fingernails with the end of the blade.

'I've been trying to find him. I've . . . I've got a message from his old mother.'

He gave a scornful laugh, which turned into a revoltingly chesty cough that left him redfaced and breathless. When he'd recovered he said, 'A message from his ma? Now where have I heard that before! Old mother be damned!' he said. 'He's put you in the family way, hasn't he? You girls are all the same! Chasing after the fellers, then moaning when they catch you.'

Daisy maintained her pleasant expression with an effort. 'So does he work for you? In the stables is what I heard. Mucking out.'

'Digger, you mean. Lazy good-for-nothing! Yes, he's out there. Go on!' He jerked his head towards the back door of the office. Daisy was almost there when he called her back.

'Want a job? I need another barmaid. The customers like a pretty face. Let's see your legs, doll.'

Daisy's spirits rose. Her and Digger working at the same place. That would be a right turn-up. She hitched up her skirts to knee height but Bert Fry waved his hand. 'Up a bit! Come on! What's the matter with you?'

She pulled her skirt right up and he nodded. She said, 'The scar on me ankle – that was a dog bite years back. Perishing animal! Belonged to an undertaker.' Without waiting for permission she lowered her skirts. 'Who's going to see me legs, anyway? I'm not a dancer.'

He grinned. 'You'd be surprised what a feller can see if he's a mind for it and a bit of cash to go with it. Some of my customers need a bit of loving, know what I mean?'

'No, I don't!' She did but wasn't going to admit it. 'You said a barmaid.'

'And I meant it but you can make a nice little packet if you play your cards right.' He examined the nails he had cleaned on the right hand and began on the other hand. 'Mel, that's Melissa, one of our girls, has a nice little nest egg under the floorboards! Yes siree! She's too bright to turn away good money, is our Mel. You two would get on just fine.'

'Well, I just want to talk to Digger.'

He risked another laugh. 'You'll change your mind. They all do.'

'In a pig's eye I will!' she muttered as she closed the door behind her. Bert Fry began to cough again and she wrinkled her nose in disgust.

Outside, at the rear of the property Daisy saw a row of rundown stables and a large barn where presumably carriages were kept overnight. She hurried towards it and saw that most of the stables were empty. By nightfall, she guessed, it would be a different picture as the available rooms would be let out to travellers, and their carriages and horses would be accommodated here. As she went she saw what looked like a familiar figure and shouted, 'Digger! *Digger!*' It *was* him. Her heart soared. 'It's me, Daisy Pritty!'

At the sound of her voice, he bolted into the shadows at the side of the stables and, mortified, Daisy stared after him. She headed for the shadows but a young red-headed man stepped out to bar the way.

'Daisy Pritty? Who's she when she's at home?' he demanded. He was thin as the rake he was carrying and had a twisted ear.

'Where's he gone?' she demanded. 'I know it was Digger. I *saw* him.'

'You saw Digger?' He shook his head. 'No. Couldn't have done 'cos he's not here any more. You just missed him. Will I do instead?'

'I *saw* him,' she insisted. 'He went round the side there and . . . Oh, there you are!' Her heart steadied as she saw him come round the corner of the stables and she smiled with unrestrained delight. 'I knew it was you!'

No wonder he didn't want to be seen, she thought. He was filthy. Boots splattered with mud, moleskin trousers stained and damp with the splashes from the dirty work he was doing. He, too, carried a rake and behind him she saw a steaming pile of horse manure. Looking at the dark eyes and the thin face surrounded by tousled dark curls, she felt the familiar longing. She knew he was a devious devil but she loved him anyway. More than anything in the world she wanted to be with Digby Wise. But he needn't know that. Quickly wiping the smile from her face, she said, 'You owe me money, Digger and I want it. Now!'

He looked astonished. 'Me owe you money? Don't know what you're talking about.' He glanced at his companion for support. 'I don't see the woman for years and she comes asking for money!'

The redhead grinned. 'Just like a woman. They're all the same! You should have stayed out of sight!'

Daisy ignored him. 'You know it's true, Digger, so don't try and wriggle out of it.' She wondered why he *had* showed himself. Maybe he couldn't resist seeing her again. Her hopes rose.

Digger leaned on his rake, a sly smile on his face. 'Ah! But can you prove it? You can't! Anyway, even if you could I've got nothing. D'you think I'd work in this stinking place if I didn't have to?'

Why, thought Daisy despairingly, do I love this lying hound? He doesn't deserve me. 'We have to talk about it,' she told him.

He turned to his companion. 'Women!' and they both laughed.

Daisy glared at the other man. 'You mind your business! This is private, so hop it!'

He shrugged and sauntered off, whistling.

Daisy turned back to Digger. If they didn't come to an arrangement now he might disappear again and the prospect frightened her. It was now or never and she must swallow her pride. 'Look,' she said, her tone more conciliatory. 'I want us to be together, Digger, so what say I forget about the money and we talk about you and me. You know you miss me. We could find a room and I'd cook for us and—'

'I've got a room – up there.' He pointed to the loft above the stables. 'Not a room exactly but a space of my own and a bit of a bed. Straw mattress. Table and chair. Can't swing a cat but it goes with the job. There's no room for you.'

'Then we'll find somewhere else, something better. Say yes, Digger. We could be good together.' She crossed her fingers.

'I can't afford a room let alone a woman. How much d'you think I earn in this dump?'

'I bet you get your meals free.'

'So?'

'I'll be earning. He offered me a job, Bert Fry I mean, working here as a barmaid.' She stifled her doubts. 'He says I can make good money. We'd be rich!' Suddenly she realized he was wavering.

He ran the rake backwards and forwards over the dirty cobbles. The screeching sound set her teeth on edge but she ignored it. Behind him the solitary horse sneezed. Daisy waited. She sat herself on a convenient bale of straw and managed to hoist her skirts to reveal her ankles. Give him a reminder, she thought, of what was in store.

He narrowed his eyes. 'Where's the kid?'

'Maybourne Workhouse. At least that'd be my guess. I left her on old Ma Boothby's doorstep. She'll have handed her back.' Daisy looked at him steadily but her heart began to beat faster. There was a decision to be made and this was the moment. She knew suddenly that she wanted her daughter. Molly had to be part of the deal. She swallowed. 'But she'll join us.'

He scowled. 'No fear! She's not mine. Anyway I hate kids. Always whining, snotty noses, wet beds. Not the kid. Not ever.' He was eyeing her ankles.

Daisy moved her knees, drawing her skirts up a little higher. 'Old Fatty Fry says I'll be very popular with the men. Says I'll soon find meself a feller. He took a bit of a shine to me himself. Is he married?'

'Was. She scarpered.'

Daisy nodded cheerfully. She mustn't let him see how much she loved him. Nor how important Molly was to her. 'What about your mate with the funny ear? I like men with red hair.'

He glared at her. 'Toddy? God! You don't want the likes of him! He's a dobbin, he is. Doesn't know his arse from his elbow!'

Daisy had missed nearly four years of her daughter's life and she wanted a family. A big happy family like normal people. Her and Molly and Digger. Then maybe Digger's heart would soften towards Molly and they would have a child of their own and he would . . .

Digger said, 'Mel makes a fair bit but she isn't just a barmaid. Not just waiting at tables. She says yes more than most women!' He was watching her expression.

Daisy frowned. 'Not to you, I hope!'

'Not to me.' He shrugged. 'Just warning you. It's rough

but there's money in it. I was just thinking. About your Molly. If you was earning enough – earning good money like Mel, say – I might consider having her with us.'

Daisy's eyes widened with surprise. Did he mean what she thought he meant? 'What, you mean the three of us? Like a family?'

He shrugged. 'Only if you was to earn enough, and you could. You're prettier than Mel. The men would pay 'andsomely for a bit of what you've got to give! It's up to you, Dais. If you're ready to go for it, then Molly comes to us. Otherwise the kid stays where she is – in the workhouse.'

Daisy was racked by indecision. Ideally she wanted to save herself for Digger but she also wanted Molly back. She said cautiously, 'But what about us? You and me. We'd be together, you mean. I'd be like your wife. Is that what you're saying?'

He grinned. 'Couldn't 'ave put it better meself. But I'd want to look after the money, Dais, because I'd pay all the bills. You'd hand it over to me and I'd do all the worrying while you're busy with your clients.'

Clients? He made it sound almost respectable. 'But Fatty Fry would want a cut, wouldn't he?'

'Course he would but not much. I'd sort that out for you. Wouldn't want you worrying your pretty little 'ead about that stuff.'

Daisy thought about it. It wouldn't be too bad, she told herself. She'd been with a few men before she met Digger. She could bear it if it meant Molly joining them.

'I'll do it!' she announced. She slid from the straw bale and threw herself into Digger's arms. Her heart was so full there were tears in her eyes. She had found the man she loved and he wanted the three of them to be together. She would make Digger deliriously happy and everything else would fall into place.

He kissed her and then held her at arm's length. 'Better go and tell Fatty Fry you'll take the job,' he told her. As she turned to go he patted her bottom and Daisy grinned. Things were definitely looking up.

Robert's funeral went as planned although there were few mourners – not because nobody had liked him but because so few people had known him.

Agnes had been told of his death but was not fit enough to attend the church service. She was, however, well enough to be left alone at home for the length of the funeral but Godfrey, Harriet, Sam and Alfred Cummings were joined at the church porch by Dr Angus Fletcher, Eveline and Molly.

When the service was over the vicar expressed disappointment and surprise at the number of mourners but Harriet explained Robert's problem.

'Robert was a solitary man. He also outlived his brother by many years and had no wife or children. We were his only family these last few years – and my mother, of course, who is recovering from influenza and unable to leave her bed.'

At that moment Angus Fletcher came up to them and said, 'A very nice service, vicar.'

Harriet nodded. 'Will you come back to the house for some refreshments?'

The vicar shook his head. 'I'm afraid we have another service shortly – a christening.'

As the vicar hurried back into the church Godfrey rejoined Harriet and took hold of her hand but she pretended to need her handkerchief and freed it again. Eveline joined them, holding Molly firmly by the hand. The doctor said, 'Young Molly was very well behaved,' and Eveline coloured with pleasure.

Alfred Cummings hovered nearby and Harriet invited him back for refreshments and the small party set off to walk back to Havely House, where Harriet had earlier prepared a simple meal. They were halfway through this when the solicitor drew up outside. Harriet ushered him up to the library where the will was to be read. Agnes was unable to attend but she would see the will for herself later. Godfrey, Harriet and Sam went upstairs to join the solicitor.

The will itself was short and precise. The house and land were left to Sam as the remaining male member of the Burnett family and he also inherited Robert's library of books. He would inherit when he was twenty-one and Agnes would act for him until then. There were several bequests – a small one for Cummings and one for Godfrey's mother, Doris, who had earlier been Robert's housekeeper for many years. There was a larger bequest for Harriet and for Sam and a very comfortable sum for Agnes. Godfrey had not been forgotten either. He had a small bequest and Robert had left him his chess set.

Overcome with emotion Harriet wept. Sam scuttled away to fuss with his pony, unable to deal with his sense of loss and embarrassed by the tears of the family. Eveline took Molly down to the stable to see the pony and Sam volunteered to look after her for half an hour. Cheered by having something to distract him, he gave the little girl a ride on Rollo's broad back and then found her some polish and a cloth and the two of them settled down to polish the four leather 'boots' which Rollo wore when he pulled the lawn roller.

By five o'clock the family had waved goodbye to the last of the guests, Eveline and Molly had departed and the doctor had left to start his evening surgery. Harriet was washing up the crockery and cutlery and Godfrey was upstairs in the library when Sam came into the kitchen. He sat down and stared at the remains of the salad. When Harriet suggested he pick up a tea towel he ignored her.

He said, 'What's the matter with Godfrey? He's not the same.'

'Isn't he?' Harriet tried to sound surprised. 'In what way is he different?'

Sam picked up a small lettuce leaf and ate it thoughtfully. 'He doesn't say so much and he looks sort of different. He hardly ever comes down from the library.'

'I expect he's busy sorting through Robert's books and papers. Somebody has to—'

'Is it to do with that lady that came to the stables this afternoon?'

Harriet dropped a cup and it shattered on the tiled floor. Harriet closed her eyes. 'Which lady?' she whispered, picking up the broken china with an unsteady hand.

'She wanted to talk to Godfrey but I wouldn't fetch Godfrey. I said he was too busy. I didn't like her. She was bossy.' He kept his eyes averted and Harriet was swept by a deep dismay. Sam was a bright boy and at eleven he was old enough and perceptive enough to draw his own conclusions. Swallowing hard, she dropped the pieces of broken china on to the table and sat down heavily. 'What was she like?'

He shrugged. 'Dark hair. She just appeared. One minute she wasn't there and then she was. She said, "Please fetch him for me," but I didn't. I don't know why. Who was she?'

'I . . . I suppose she is an old friend of Godfrey's. He has some friends I've never met.'

'Then why didn't she come to the front door?' His tone was belligerent but Harriet recognized the fear.

'I don't know, but you did the right thing, Sam,' she said in an effort to reassure him. 'She shouldn't have tried to interrupt a funeral.'

He stood up abruptly. 'She sounded like a foreigner and her name was Amelia. I hate her.' Before she could answer, he dashed for the back door and, from the window, Harriet watched him run down to the stables. Her own pulse was racing and she, too, was filled with a dangerous mixture of shock, fear and anger. How dare Amelia come to the house as bold as brass? The time for watching and waiting was over, she decided. She would tackle Godfrey immediately.

She ran up the stairs and burst into the library and Godfrey looked up startled. 'Harriet! What on earth—?'

Harriet faced him, white-faced with anger. 'I thought you'd like to know, Godfrey, that your wretched Amelia had the gall to come into our garden this afternoon and ordered Sam to fetch you to speak with her! I'd like to know exactly what is going on between the two of you – and before you tell me any more lies, I *saw* the two of you together in Maybourne on Thursday, looking very cosy in a hansom cab!' She stopped to draw breath and was pleased to see that her accusations had shocked him into silence. In fact, Godfrey looked as frightened as she was. The silence continued as he struggled to find words which might help the situation.

'Harriet, I'm so sorry. Believe me, I didn't want her here and I certainly didn't invite her. Thursday, when you saw us together, I was taking her back into the town because she came uninvited and didn't want to leave. She wanted me to tell you . . .' He closed his eyes, searching for the right words.

'Tell me what?'

'That I was leaving you but I wouldn't agree.'

Harriet fought hard to keep her gaze steady. 'What made her think that you *might* leave me?'

'I don't know! She is determined to . . . '

'To win you back!'

He nodded unhappily. 'She won't accept that she is nothing to me now.'

Harriet closed the door and leaned back against it. Her legs felt weak and she longed to sit down but felt that she appeared stronger standing. She said, 'Nothing to you? I can't accept that either, Godfrey. From the way she's behaving I can only assume that you must be encouraging her in some way.'

'I'm *not* encouraging her, Harriet!' His voice rose. 'I don't want to leave you and I don't want to lose you. I can't make her understand that things have changed.'

After a long moment Harriet pushed herself from the door and walked slowly across to the window. The worst of her anger had abated, leaving a cold feeling in the pit of her stomach. 'So she came here while I was out on Thursday and she came again today. You didn't invite her and neither did I. She's trespassing, Godfrey.' She turned. 'If she comes here again we could have her arrested for trespass! Do you think you could get that idea into her head?'

'I'll tell her, Harriet.'

'No you won't, Godfrey. You won't go anywhere near her. *I'll* tell her! You tell me where she is staying – and *don't* pretend you don't know! You've told me enough lies and I don't want to hear—'

'She's staying at the County Hotel but I don't think you should see her, Harriet. She's my problem.'

Harriet stared at him. 'You don't think she's also *my* problem? Are you crazy, Godfrey? Amelia is *our* problem. She has made it perfectly clear that she wants to break up our marriage. If we want to prevent her, then we have a shared problem. Do you want to stay married to me, Godfrey?' It was pointless to appear weak against a woman who was so strong. Amelia had come to England in search of a former lover and, discovering that he was happily married, still persisted in her pursuit. Harriet must be equally determined – *if* Godfrey still loved her. She said, 'If you want to be with Amelia I might as well know now!' She watched him closely and thought she saw uncertainty flicker in his eyes but then it was gone in a welter of protestations of good faith.

Finally he pulled her into his arms and held her close. 'I want to be with you for ever, Harriet. I was a fool to lie to you. I should have trusted your understanding. Now that you know what is happening we'll fight her together.'

Harriet left him to write another letter to Amelia and when she had amended it to her satisfaction Godfrey again offered to deliver it to the hotel.

'No, Godfrey! That is too much of a risk. She might see you there and we have agreed that the two of you won't meet again.'

'Don't you trust me?'

'I don't trust *her*! I'll ask Cummings to take it down late tomorrow morning and hand it in at the desk. That way neither of us need see or speak to her.'

To her relief Godfrey agreed without further protest and Harriet felt greatly relieved.

* * *

The following morning when Sam appeared with a friend of his from the town she was able to greet them cheerfully.

'Teddy says there's going to be a gymkhana,' Sam told her excitedly. 'May I enter Rollo. It won't be a race and I won't jump him over the hurdles. The poor old dear would never manage it, but there's a prize for the best-turned-out horse and Teddy and I could make Rollo look very smart!'

Teddy said, 'There's a cup to be won and two guineas. Sam says we could share it if Rollo wins.' He was a little taller than Sam but only a month older and he had no horse of his own. The two boys had attended the local school together for several years before George Burnett sent Sam away to boarding school. Teddy's parents were farmers who rented land from the Wellburys.

Harriet smiled. 'It sounds like a wonderful idea. I assume it takes place before Sam has to go back to Winchester.'

Sam nodded. 'It's on the Saturday before I go back. We'll have to smarten up all the harness and the saddle as well as Rollo and we'll give him a few rides round the paddock because he's looking a bit tubby.'

Teddy produced a form and asked Harriet to sign it so that Rollo's name could be officially enrolled for the competition. 'And it costs a half-crown to enter,' he added.

Harriet signed and promised the money and the two boys rushed back to the stables in high spirits. Harriet smiled, pleased that, for Sam at least, the gloom of the funeral was over and he could enjoy the rest of his week at home.

Upstairs, Doctor Fletcher was examining his patient, who was making slow but steady progress. He came downstairs and Harriet offered him a cup of tea or a glass of elderberry cordial. Accepting the latter, the doctor sat with her in the parlour and Harriet suddenly realized how much she had been looking forward to his visit. Her mother's illness had meant that they spent more time together than before and because of this she now felt more relaxed in his company. Today she watched him unobtrusively and found herself intrigued. How did doctors make friends, she wondered, when every relationship was of necessity a formal one? The doctor/patient relationship was finely balanced with boundaries to be observed. In a way they were rather like vicars.

'I think she needs a change of scenery,' he was saying. 'Perhaps she could spend time in the garden and later you could hire a bath chair and take her along the promenade. There's a lot to see with the summer season beginning and it would give her something to talk about. It's too easy for her to stay in her room and withdraw into her shell.'

'That's a good idea. Thank you, Doctor. I'll certainly see what we can do.'

Was he lonely? she wondered. How could he begin a friendship if everyone treated him simply as a professional man? With an effort she concentrated on what he was saying.

' . . . and I don't think the cost would be too high but I have to say I don't know whether your financial situation has changed with Mr Burnett's death. If you were in straitened circumstances—'

'No, Doctor Fletcher. Quite the opposite, in fact. A careful study of the will shows that there is money available for the maintenance of the property, for instance, which we can now call on. And I was left a generous legacy. The house, naturally, passes to Sam when he comes of age but it's with my stewardship until that date.' She smiled. 'Great-Uncle Robert was a wealthy man, although none of us realized it because he lived such a frugal life. He has actually given us a measure of security which we have never known before. We have so much to be grateful . . . for . . .'

She faltered to a stop, aware that he was leaning forward and staring at her intently. Was he actually listening to her? Close to, she could see just how blue his eyes were. She could imagine what a handsome child he had been. Slightly chubby, perhaps, but mostly jolly . . . And now *she* was leaning forward. Hastily she sat back, picked up her cup and saucer and sipped her tea.

Abruptly he straightened in his chair. 'I'm sorry. I was . . .' He seemed disconcerted. 'I was miles away. At least, not miles away but thinking about . . .' He gave an embarrassed laugh. 'Forgive me. Let's just say that I was distracted for a moment.'

'Even doctors are allowed to be distracted.' She smiled and changed the subject, telling him about the gymkhana and then he asked about Eveline and Molly and the awkwardness passed.

When it was time for him to leave, he took Harriet's hand in his. 'I know how proud Robert was to be the protector of the family and I'm sure you miss him in many ways. Please remember, however, that if you ever need help you can call on me and I will do all I can for you.' He paused. 'Life can play some horrid tricks sometimes and we all need good friends.'

Surprised, she smiled her thanks. 'You're very kind,' she told him. 'I'll certainly remember.'

Later that same morning Alfred Cummings walked into the the County Hotel feeling very important. He had never been into the hotel before and he found it awe-inspiring. It would be good later in the day to tell his wife about it, he thought, as the uniformed doorman held open the door for him. Impressed by the dark maroon cloth with its braided cuffs and gold buttons, Alfred gave the man a nervous smile as he stepped inside. The interior was even better than the exterior – cool and elegant with dark-brown walls and buttoned leather chairs grouped round low tables. He did not register the shabbiness of the hotel. Velvet curtains had been faded by the sun, there were unemptied ashtrays on the tables and the carpet had been worn thin in certain well-used areas. He *did* notice that the flower arrangement on the reception desk was not as fresh as it might have been, with a few half-dead roses and shrivelling leaves.

A man behind the reception desk caught his eye and asked, 'Can I help you, sir?'

Alfred wished he had been able to wear his Sunday suit but he had made an effort, scrubbing the mud from his boots and brushing dead grass from his jacket. He had rubbed at his teeth with a rag and washed his hands and face under the tap by the stable, but a glance in a shop window earlier had shown up serious deficiencies in his appearance and the man behind the desk was regarding him with suspicion.

'Er y-yes, you can,' he admitted and moved to the desk. On his right a young man in a smart blazer and straw boater was collecting a key. An attractive woman to his left was asking for her mail. 'I've to give you this,' Cummings explained, fumbling in his pocket for the envelope which he handed across the counter.

The manager looked at it. 'Mrs Amelia Bianchi? Right, sir, we'll see that she—'

The attractive woman turned sharply. 'I am Mrs Bianchi.' She held out her hand for the letter, then glanced at Alfred. 'Should I know you?'

'I'm the gardener, ma'am, at Havely House. Alfred Cummings.'

Her expression underwent a sudden change and Alfred was dazzled by the brightness of her smile. 'Mr Cummings! Of course. We met briefly. You look rather thirsty. Would you like a cup of tea?' Without waiting for his reply she said, 'Tea for two – and some biscuits, please!' and the man behind the desk said, 'Certainly, Mrs Bianchi,' and rang a small bell.

They sat at one of the low tables and Alfred perched warily on the edge of his armchair. Mrs Bianchi opened the letter and her expression underwent another sudden change. Her smile vanished and her mouth tightened and Alfred wondered what was in the letter. She closed her eyes, crumpling the letter fiercely in her hands and glared at him.

'How dare they!' she hissed. 'How dare they write to me like that! My God but he'll be sorry!' She thrust the letter into his hand and rose to her feet. For a moment she seemed about to say something else but then she muttered in a foreign tongue, turned on her heel and swept away.

Stunned, Alfred watched her approach the lift and vanish

inside. He glanced nervously around to see if anyone had noticed the exchange but everyone else seemed busy about their own affairs. He looked at the crumpled letter. No point trying to read it for he had left school at eleven and had never quite mastered reading. So what should he do with it? He stuffed it back into his pocket as a waitress arrived beside him. With a brisk smile, she set down a tray. Two cups and saucers, a teapot, milk and small cubes of sugar and a plate of iced biscuits. 'The w-woman,' he stuttered. 'She's gone. I mean I don't know if she's coming back.'

'Why not help yourself, sir?' she told him and winked at him. 'She's in a fine old tiz! Serve her right, hoity piece! She won't be back. You tuck in, sir. I would.'

'But . . . I 'aven't much money on me.'

'It's going on her bill. She ordered it. You enjoy it.'

So he poured milk and tea and stirred it and added three sugar lumps and stirred it again. It was hot, so he added more milk and, because it had all been paid for, he added another few sugar lumps and ate all seven biscuits.

He went back to Havely House feeling very pleased with himself and after he had finished for the evening he went round to see his nephew, who was bright and who could read, and gave him the crumpled letter. The boy found some of the words a challenge but he persevered, delighted to be the centre of attention. After a few false starts he was able to read the entire message.

Dear Amelia,

We are sorry you have obviously failed to understand our situation and seem determined to visit us unannounced and uninvited. We have been happily married for nearly four years and are very much in love. We both feel that your intrusion into our lives is intended to cause us distress. We have nothing further to say to you and hope you will leave us alone in the future. Your future is in no way linked to ours. Please

understand that. If you do call at our home again we
shall be forced to notify the police and sue you for tres-
pass . . .

    Godfrey and Harriet Lester

Alfred scratched his head. 'Well I'll be damned!' he muttered.

The boy said, 'But what does it mean, Uncle?'

Alfred ruffled his hair playfully. 'Blessed if I know, lad,' he lied but he thought he now understood why Amelia Bianchi had left in tears. 'Bless my soul!' he said. 'Sue you for trespass! Now there's a thing!' and remembering the tea and biscuits the woman had bought him, he began to laugh.

Six

It was nearly eleven o'clock two days later when the hansom cab pulled up on the promenade and the cabbie and Harriet lifted Agnes down and placed her in the hired bath chair. Harriet settled the fare and glanced up and down the promenade. Eveline had decided to join them with Molly and already Agnes was looking flushed with excitement and the change from her old routine. Looking at her, Harriet blessed the doctor who had recommended the fresh sea air. It was a balmy day but Agnes wore a shawl around her shoulders and had a tartan rug over her knees.

'Here they come!' cried Agnes and Harriet turned to see Molly dancing towards them with Eveline in hot pursuit.

Eveline stopped thankfully, holding her side. 'A stitch!' she explained with a smile. 'A certain someone cannot walk. She has to run, skip or dance along!'

Agnes smiled at Molly, who was staring at her curiously. 'Do I see new shoes?' she asked and Molly lifted a small plump leg to show off the red-buttoned shoes.

'How are you, Agnes?' Eveline asked. 'It's so good to see you out and about again – and on such a perfect day.'

They set off with Harriet pushing the bath chair and Eveline trying unsuccessfully to keep Molly within sight. In mid-May there were hundreds of Londoners holidaying in Maybourne and others arriving hourly for the day. It was pleasant to be strolling beside the sea, watching the frolics on the beach and the satisfaction of being part of the happy crowd. Eveline and Agnes waited on the promenade while Harriet took Molly for a donkey ride.

'I can ride,' the little girl told her as they waited on the sand in the small queue. 'Sam gave me a ride on Rollo. I love Rollo. He's the bestest pony.'

Harriet smiled. 'Sam thinks so, too! Ah! Here we go.' A free donkey was led back and Harriet parted with sixpence and helped Molly into the saddle. As the donkey man urged the animal forward, Harriet held Molly securely and found herself wondering if Daisy's childhood had ever encompassed such excitement. Perhaps the Board of Guardians should take out the few children who remained in the workhouse. A day at the seaside would be such a treat. They could have a picnic on the sands and an ice cream as well as a donkey ride. Offhand she couldn't recall how many children there were in the workhouse at the present time but made a mental note to ask Mrs Fenner.

At the end of the allotted walk the driver turned the donkey and led him back. Harriet watched Molly and wondered where Daisy was and how she was faring in London. They rejoined Eveline and Agnes and they all moved on in the direction of the pier, where they were in time to watch a Punch and Judy show. By this time Agnes was tiring and Harriet decided to take her home.

Eveline smiled. 'We'll stay a little longer in the hopes that a certain little miss will tire herself out! After her midday meal I like her to take a nap.'

'Don't want a nap!' Molly tossed her fair curls and stamped her foot.

Harriet hid a smile. 'If you keep stamping your feet you'll wear out your nice new shoes!'

Molly looked stricken and then crouched to examine them. Finding nothing wrong, she lost interest and began to hop to and fro until she fell over a passing poodle and hurt her knee. She let out a shriek and Harriet grinned.

'Time to go, I think, Mama!'

After hasty farewells she waited for a gap in the traffic. Tramcars, motor cars, vans and waggons careered past but at last Harriet was able to wheel Agnes across the road.

The impatient scuffle of horses' hooves indicated the position of the cab rank and Harriet signalled to the first one. The driver jumped down and they manoeuvred Agnes up into the cab, Harriet climbed up beside her and as her mother settled contentedly against the seat, they set off for home.

On the way Agnes said, 'I worry about Eveline and that child.'

'So do I, Mama. She is much too fond of young Molly. If Daisy returns for her . . .'

Agnes nodded. 'I imagine it's hard for Eveline to remain detached, because she's never had a family and Molly is an oddly bewitching child. At first I thought it would only be for a day or two but time's passing.'

Harriet looked at her mother and smiled. 'How long did it take for you to be bewitched by me?'

Agnes took hold of her hand. 'Less than an hour!' she confessed. 'I know that what Eveline does is not strictly our affair but I very much fear that she is setting herself up for a broken heart.'

Thursday night. Eleven o'clock in the casual ward of the workhouse. Mrs Fenner entered as usual to read the roll-call before closing and locking the outer door. Most of the men had called in earlier in the day to reserve an overnight place but a few had arrived between ten and eleven. There were now thirteen men present and each one answered his name as it was read out.

'Stanley Harris, joiner . . . ?' Mrs Fenner glanced round. She liked to put names to faces, she had told Harriet. In case of trouble.

'I'm 'ere!' An elderly man raised himself up from his 'bed' and nodded at Mrs Fenner. He was small, hollow-cheeked and very pale. He began to cough and almost choked. Mrs Fenner hesitated. Perhaps he was consumptive and needed treatment but Mr Swift insisted there was never enough money available and wanted it kept for the permanent inmates. If Harris could make it to the next workhouse *they* would have to help him. She hardened her heart.

'Tom Biddley?' This was a new name.

'Yup!' Stocky, middle-aged, she thought, memorizing the details. Sometimes it was the most innocent-looking men who caused the most aggravation.

'Andy Blow—' She peered at her own hasty handwriting. 'Candlestick maker?'

He raised a large head which was tufted with greasy hair of an indeterminate colour. 'Summat like that!'

She gave him a suspicious look but he slid further down under his thin blanket and she continued. 'Sid Tommason?'

'I'm here! Leastways I reckon so!' He chuckled at this witticism but a surly voice cried, 'Grow up, Sid!'

Mrs Fenner said, 'You look better than you did last time you were here.'

'I had a bout of new ralgia,' he reminded her. 'Something chronic, it was. All up me neck and into me jaw.'

Someone quipped, 'You shouldn't talk so much, you dozy devil!'

Mrs Fenner ignored them and went on with her list. When she'd finished she glared round the room and made her usual announcement. 'No fighting, no smoking, no swearing, wash outside in the yard first thing, breakfast at seven. Any bad behaviour and out you go!' She hoped she sounded more confident than she felt. This was the worst part of the job. The unknown element. Reaching up, she turned off the gaslight, plunging the room into sudden darkness, then went out, closing and locking the door behind her. One night, one of the casual men had found his way into the women's dormitory. She had no intention of allowing such a thing to happen again.

For a moment after she left there was silence. Then a cough or two and the scuffling sound of various bodies trying to make themselves comfortable.

From the darkness a disembodied voice growled, 'Wash, she says! There was no ruddy soap last time I was 'ere!'

'Stop moaning!'

Another silence descended.

Then another disembodied voice. 'I was in Dover couple of days ago. They give you a bit of a pillow – stuffed with straw, like.'

'Shut up and go to sleep!'

Someone sat up and peered through the gloom at his companions and the moonlight shone on his fair hair. The men's eyes were becoming accustomed to the gloom and they could see that he was about thirty, thin and wiry. He had taken off his shirt and rolled it into a makeshift pillow.

He said, 'I saw Dan Stick yesterday. Still fuming, he is. The police banished him and he's smarting! Told him never to set foot in the town again but he's back. They just look the other way!' He laughed. 'He says he knows who to blame and he's going to get even.'

Tom Biddley sat up. 'Who does he blame?'

'Didn't say. Just tapped the side of his nose!'

'Mrs Fenner, most like. She reported him to the police. Said he was a troublemaker. But so did Mrs Lester – the woman whose father shot himself.'

'Dan *is* a troublemaker. A real nasty piece of work. A dyed-in-the-wool villain!'

The fair-haired man said, 'Most likely got a chip on his shoulder.'

'Chip? More like a log, that one!'

They all laughed.

Stanley Harris sat up. 'Mrs Fenner's decent enough. Who'd have her job? I wouldn't.' He fumbled in his pocket and produced a clay pipe, filled it with tobacco and lit it. He looked at the fair-haired man. 'You a friend of Dan's, then?'

'Me? No. Don't even know the man.'

'Daniel Stick doesn't have friends! Just enemies!'

They all laughed. Andy Blow climbed out of his bed and perched on the end of it. Inspired by the first smoker, he also lit his pipe.

Someone said, 'No smoking! You lot deaf or something?'

99

They turned to him and with one voice said, 'Go back to sleep!'

'But it's regulations. Might burn the place down.'

'Good riddance to it!'

The fair-haired man said, 'Where'd we be tonight without it?'

From a darkened corner the first snore made them giggle but a moment later another man fell asleep and one by one they reluctantly settled down and night fell at last on the casual ward of Maybourne Workhouse.

Godfrey sat alone in the library he had recently shared with Robert and stared at the pages in front of him without seeing anything except Amelia's image. He knew exactly how she would feel when she read the latest letter which he and Harriet had written. Her face would crumple and tears would flow but then she would be angry. Amelia was not the sort of woman to take a blow lightly. She would want to retaliate. Her strength in adversity had always been something he admired but now he feared that Harriet would be hurt and he wanted to avoid that at all costs. He still loved her deeply – that was the problem.

'Oh God!' he groaned. *Two* women were in love with him and that would please most men but for him it was an impossible situation. What he wanted was the security and love that marriage had brought him, with the added excitement of an illicit romance.

Around him the daylight was fading and he could no longer see what was written on the pages of the book he had propped up in front of him. He should light a candle but what was the point? he asked himself. He had lost all interest in his translating and found it impossible to concentrate. All he could think about was Amelia and he was forced to acknowledge that his longing for her was intense. Knowing that she was only miles away and not in London created a fierce desire to see her again. If he was honest he wanted to sleep with her and wake with his arms around her. He recalled her face in repose, surrounded by those long dark tresses.

'For God's sake, Amelia!' he muttered desperately.

When she first appeared in Maybourne he had prayed for her to return to London and stay there but now he feared exactly that. The thought that she was so near thrilled him and he dreaded that she would disappear from his life. Suppose he went in search of her tomorrow and she had gone from the hotel. If she had failed to leave a forwarding address he might never see her again.

Abruptly he pushed back his chair, stood up and strode to the window. Staring out over the darkening garden, he decided to find a way to see her. Tomorrow – otherwise he might be too late. He would talk to her and see if there was any way they could remain lovers. It would be dangerous but he would take the risk. All it needed was great care and Amelia's agreement that she would never show her face at Havely House again. Harriet must never know.

The next day was bright and sunny with a few wisps of cloud and Harriet thought this was probably a good day to put Doctor Fletcher's advice into practice and take her mother outside into the garden. Initially Agnes was apprehensive but eventually she agreed and Harriet went in search of Godfrey to help carry Agnes down the stairs and on to the terrace, from which she could enjoy the view.

Agnes sighed as they settled her in her favourite chair and arranged a footstool to support her legs. Beside her on a small table Harriet had placed a tray of tea and biscuits and Agnes smiled with pleasure.

'You're too good to me, Harriet,' she protested. 'I feel guilty sitting here while everybody else is busy. Whatever shall I do?'

'I could fetch your book,' Godfrey suggested.

'Or you could watch the wildlife,' Harriet suggested. 'Squirrels, blackbirds, wood pigeons. Maybe you could make a few sketches.'

Agnes smiled at her. 'I haven't sketched for many years. I should probably hold the charcoal upside down!'

At that moment Sam came in and began to tell his mother about Rollo and the gymkhana. Harriet and Godfrey slipped away and left them to it.

Godfrey said, 'I shall have to go into town again this morning. Cummings has reminded me that we need more hay and feed for the pony and I must call in at the farrier's to arrange for a new set of horseshoes later in the month. He's always so busy at the start of the summer.'

Harriet hesitated. 'Perhaps I'll come with you.'

'Oh no! I mean . . . that really won't be necessary, Harriet. You have so much to do here.'

'I could make some time to come with you.'

'But why? What is so interesting about the farrier's or the corn merchant's?'

He sounded irritable, she thought, and at once she was suspicious. She said, 'We could take a stroll on the prom together. We haven't done that for such a long time. I can spare an hour or so and Mama will have Sam for company. I think it's important that we spend more time together, don't you?'

'Certainly, Harriet, but not today. To be honest I don't feel like wasting time.'

The words stung her. 'Since when has being with me been a waste of time?'

'I didn't mean it like that and you know it, Harriet! All I meant was . . . a walk on the prom—'

'I know, Godfrey. I'm sorry.' She turned away, swallowing hard, willing herself to think carefully. If she pressed the point they might well end up quarrelling and that would be disastrous. He had behaved very well over the last letter they had sent to Amelia and she knew she must learn to trust him again but the constant fear that he might still be deceiving her weighed heavily on her. She had slept badly and had awoken to unhappy thoughts. If only she could confide in her mother . . . but that would mean burdening Agnes with unnecessary anxiety. Hopefully she and Godfrey had dealt with the problem and if that were so, all that was needed

102

was love and forgiveness plus the elusive ability to forget. Somehow they had to recover the feelings they had for each other before Amelia had reappeared in their lives.

Godfrey left half an hour later on his various errands and Harriet watched him go from an upstairs window. 'Don't go to her!' she whispered. 'Please don't go to her!' Fear flooded her and she felt tears pressing against her eyelids. If only she could talk to *someone*, she thought. Suppose she made a quick visit to Eveline . . . But no. She regretted confiding in her earlier. Surely the fewer people who knew about Amelia the better. And surely she, Harriet, was old enough to deal with her own problems? She was not the first woman to have an unfaithful husband and would certainly not be the last.

Downstairs she busied herself with the household chores, choosing to deal with the weekly bills and expenses, which usually demanded a high level of concentration as figures were not her strong point. It was a relief not to have to count every penny since Robert had left the household well provided for in his will. In fact, she realized, it would now be possible for the family to take a holiday. The doctor had suggested that Agnes might benefit from a week or two in Deauville once she was strong enough to make the sea crossing. If they could get right away from Maybourne she and Godfrey might have a better chance of repairing the damage Amelia had caused. She was still considering this when someone rang the front bell and she hurried to open it.

'Are you Harriet Lester?' the woman asked.

Immediately Harriet knew that this strikingly beautiful creature was Amelia Bianchi and her heart almost stopped beating with shock.

'You're . . . you're Amelia,' she stammered. 'What do you want? How dare you come here after . . .' Had her mother noticed her arrival? she wondered.

'I think we have a need to talk. The three of us.' Amelia looked entirely confident and Harriet realized that she must be expecting to see Godfrey also. Amelia assumed she would have an ally. She noted the woman's expensive clothes and compared them to her own everyday garments. She stared at Amelia, wondering what to do. If she invited her inside she might still be here when Godfrey returned. If she turned her away Amelia might meet him in the town.

'We've nothing to say to you,' she managed, beginning to shake with fear and anger. 'We've told you how we feel. Why don't you leave us alone?'

'I only know what you have written in your foolish and insulting letters but I know how Godfrey feels for me. He would never have written like that to me unless you had guided his hand.'

'You knew him years ago!' Harriet cried. 'He was younger and more vulnerable. He's more mature now and I'm his wife and I'm sure I understand him better than you do.'

'Shall we let him speak for himself, Harriet?' Her thin smile was confident. 'I would like you to tell him I am here.'

'He's not here. He has some errands . . . elsewhere.' Even as she spoke, Harriet recognized another problem. If she refused Amelia admission she might well wander about the grounds waiting for him to return and if she did she would stumble upon Agnes. With an effort Harriet tried to control her rising hysteria.

While she hesitated Amelia said, 'I pity you, Harriet. You cannot understand this relationship I have with your husband. He and I—'

'You no longer *have* a relationship with Godfrey, Amelia,' Harriet cried, her voice rising. '*You* cannot understand that you are simply someone he loved long ago when he was a young and impressionable young man. I know all about it. We have no secrets from each other.' Abruptly she opened the door a little wider. 'You'd better come in and wait for him. Then he can tell you himself.'

Amelia made no attempt to hide her triumph and swept through the doorway into the hall. Harriet prayed that Sam would remain outside with his mother.

As Harriet led the way into the drawing room she decided

against being too hospitable. She would *not* offer tea and biscuits to this hateful woman.

Amelia crossed to the window and looked out across the garden. 'You have a very attractive house.'

'It belongs to Sam. It's our family home.' She wondered how long Godfrey would be. Feeling it impossible to spend longer than necessary in this woman's company, Harriet said, 'I have things to do. You must excuse me. When Godfrey comes back, *if* he wishes it, the three of us will talk. If not I'm afraid you will have to leave.' Feeling rather pleased with this, she turned to go but, hesitating at the door, she asked, 'Why do you think you have the right to break up our marriage? You had your chance years ago. You could have left your rich husband for a penniless student but you didn't. You waited until he threw you out. That's how Godfrey explained the situation to me and it does you no credit.'

Amelia's face hardened. 'Didn't he tell you about the child?'

Harriet felt a deep coldness seize her entire body and clutched at the door handle for support. 'A *child*? No . . . *No!* You mean *his* child?'

Amelia nodded. 'So he *does* keep secrets from you.'

Harriet was aware that the other woman was watching her closely for a reaction to the shattering news and knew she must not allow Amelia to see how shocked she was. She left the room, closing the door quietly behind her. Her stomach churned and she ran into the kitchen and poured herself a glass of cold water, then sank on to a chair before her legs gave way. Breathing deeply, she fought against a feeling of nausea as a wave of faintness swept through her. Five minutes later she was still in a deep state of shock when Godfrey appeared at the back door.

'Where is she?' he asked, ignoring Harriet's obvious condition. 'Your mother says Amelia is here.'

Harriet lifted her head and stared at him as though at a stranger. 'You didn't tell me there was a child!' she gasped.

105

'I thought . . . You allowed me to believe . . . You've lied to me, Godfrey!'

His face paled. 'It was her husband's child. It meant . . . You can see what it meant. Both of us. She was . . . sleeping with both of us!'

Harriet longed to believe him but Amelia had been very convincing.

She shook her head in total despair. This was the end, she told herself. There was no way back from this point. 'She wants the three of us to talk things over. If I come with you what are you going to say to her?' Her voice was hoarse with emotion. 'If you are going to . . . to choose her I don't want to be there. Just pack your belongings and go.'

'Harriet! I just can't . . . That isn't the way to deal with this. I need time to think. We all do.'

'Amelia has already done *her* thinking!' Harriet said bitterly. She rose to her feet on trembling legs. 'We'll talk now, Godfrey. If you need time to think then you don't love me.' She turned and made her way along the passage and heard Godfrey run after, calling her to wait. Ignoring him, she pushed open the door to the parlour and Amelia rose to her feet.

Harriet waited until Godfrey was also in the room, then closed the door. Amelia rushed into Godfrey's arms and began to sob hysterically. He held her awkwardly but Harriet saw his distress and knew that she would take that picture to her grave. Godfrey, her husband, with his arms around his former mistress. Or was it Godfrey with the woman he loved? She watched as Godfrey tried to calm Amelia, smoothing her hair and murmuring urgently to her.

Over Amelia's head he caught Harriet's gaze and quickly disentangled himself. Clumsily he pushed Amelia on to the sofa and turned to Harriet.

'Let's all sit down,' he suggested. 'We can be sensible about this.'

Harriet hesitated and then obeyed. Although she felt weak with fear she was also curious in a fatalistic way. Somewhere

106

deep inside her, she recognized that she was about to witness the break-up of all that she held dear. Godfrey remained standing until Amelia tugged at his jacket, indicating the seat beside her. He almost sat but then realized the implications and remained standing.

With an effort, Harriet tried to take control of the situation. If she allowed Amelia to dominate the proceedings, she, Harriet, would be lost.

She said, 'Amelia tells me she had a child by you, Godfrey. If that's true then—'

He turned to Amelia. 'The child was not mine! You know that and so do I!'

Suddenly Amelia looked vulnerable. 'I thought it was yours. My husband—'

'You know it couldn't have been mine! The timing . . . '

Harriet looked at Amelia, who was now dabbing at her eyes with a flimsy handkerchief, and said, 'Where is this child?'

Godfrey gave his handkerchief to Amelia, who nodded her thanks. He said, 'The baby died a few days after her birth.'

Harriet looked at him. 'So how does this concern me? Or you?'

'It doesn't,' Godfrey said quickly. To Amelia he said, 'I was on my way to see you but our paths crossed. I was—'

Harriet gasped. 'You said you were going to the farrier's and the corn merchant. Now it seems you were going to see Amelia, so you lied again!'

Amelia smiled. 'Oh, Godfrey lies when it suits him – don't you, my love? But I always forgive him. We have never stopped loving each other. If you don't believe me, ask Godfrey.'

For Harriet the encounter was becoming a nightmare. Only Amelia was in control of herself. Harriet and Godfrey were floundering helplessly. Briefly Harriet closed her eyes and uttered a silent prayer for help. She heard Godfrey say, 'Amelia, I will always love you but I have a wife. I have Harriet and I love her also.'

107

Suddenly furious, Harriet opened her eyes. 'So you will always love Amelia!'

He paused, then nodded.

Amelia's smile broadened triumphantly. 'Thank you, Godfrey! You have finally told her the truth. So, Harriet, now you understand. I am sorry, but you must accept that you take second place in Godfrey's heart.' She stood up and tried to wrap her arms around him, but nervously he edged away.

'I . . . didn't say that exactly,' he protested. 'I said—'

'It is what you meant, Godfrey. We both know that but you are too weak to admit it. You should never have married. Poor Harriet. It was so unkind when you knew you were in love with me. You told me that you would never love anyone else.'

'*I* said that? I don't remember.'

He looked guilty, thought Harriet. He *did* remember.

Amelia watched Harriet's face as she went on. 'We were on the ferry crossing Lake Garda. The first time that this shy young man said that he loved me.' She touched his arm in a possessive way. 'You *do* remember! I know you do.'

While he protested that he had no such recollection Harriet watched them both. Now they seemed almost to have forgotten her presence. Harriet tried to imagine how it would be if by some miracle Amelia went away for ever. Godfrey would always carry the guilt and Harriet would never trust him again. Whether Amelia stayed or left no longer seemed important. If Godfrey stayed with Harriet, Amelia knew that their relationship would never totally recover. Their bright, innocent joy in each other had been fatally tarnished.

Abruptly Harriet stood up, unable to bear the situation a moment longer. In a low voice she said, 'Get her out of my house, Godfrey, and go with her. I refuse to fight for you.'

'But Harriet!' Stricken, he looked at her, his face ashen. 'I don't want to leave you.'

Amelia stood up quickly. 'You do, Godfrey. That's exactly what you want!'

Harriet gave her an icy look. 'I think Amelia has made your choice for you, Godfrey. Take a few things and later you can come over *alone* and collect the rest. And don't think you will change my mind. Our marriage is over.' The words sounded so unreal that Harriet could hardly believe she had uttered them.

Godfrey regarded her speechlessly, his mind apparently frozen.

Amelia said, 'And you'll divorce him?'

'Maybe. I'll speak to our solicitor in the morning.'

'But if you will not do this, he and I can never marry!'

Harriet shrugged. 'That is not my problem, Amelia. It is yours.'

Godfrey turned to Amelia. 'Amelia, this is all wrong. It's happening too fast! We have to think everything through carefully. You and I . . . we must talk.'

Amelia stepped closer to him and slid her arms round his waist. 'My dearest Godfrey, we have done with talking. We now have what we always wanted – freedom to be together.' She glanced back at Harriet. 'Your wife knows that this is the only way. She has given in gracefully. At least you should show that you appreciate her sacrifice.'

Harriet shook her head. 'It is no sacrifice to reject a man who doesn't love me the way I thought he did.' She looked at Godfrey. 'I truly thought we were meant for each other but I can see I was wrong. You were meant for Amelia.'

'No!' he cried. 'That's not carved in stone, Harriet! There's room for . . . for discussion.'

Somehow she steeled her heart. 'Godfrey, look at Amelia and tell her you don't love her.'

They all waited. Amelia slid her hand over his chest and ran her fingers round his neck and up into his hair. In spite of himself, Godfrey closed his eyes, relishing her touch. Amelia gave a little laugh. 'You can't resist me, can you, my love!'

Harriet looked at Amelia. 'I think you'll live to regret what you've done today! I certainly hope so!' And with eyes brimming with tears, she stumbled from the room, fled upstairs and locked herself in the bedroom.

Later, when Godfrey and Amelia had gone, Harriet and Sam carried Agnes back into the house and up the stairs to her room. When Sam had returned to the stable and his beloved Rollo, Harriet went to her mother and broke the news as gently as she could.

As the realization sank in, the colour fled from Agnes's face and she clutched at her heart. 'Oh my poor darling girl!' she whispered. 'I could kill him! Truly, Harriet, I could strangle him with my bare hands!' Tears filled her eyes but she brushed them away. 'Thank God for Uncle Robert. His legacy means we can manage without Godfrey. That's what matters, Harriet. We can manage without him. Let him go to his stupid woman.'

Harriet held her hands and her own tears came, but in the face of Harriet's distress her mother was surprisingly resilient. 'I shall never mention his name again!' she said with a fierce nod of her head. 'What a fool! Oh God, Harriet! He will live to regret his stupidity. Men! *Men!*'

They talked for a while until gradually Harriet's own courage returned and she knew she was over the worst of the shock. She leaned forward and hugged her mother. 'Thank you for saying the right things, Mama. I don't know what I would have done without you.'

Agnes kissed her. 'You're stronger than you think, Harriet. Women are. Now go and tell Sam while you are feeling positive. Then, I think, I would like a pot of tea.' As Harriet turned to go she added, 'Don't forget the doctor is coming this evening. It might be wise to tell him also. Deal with today, and then tomorrow will be a fresh start!'

Still buoyed up by her mother's encouragement, Harriet walked round that evening to break the news to Eveline. As soon as her friend opened the door, Eveline put her finger to her lips and pointed to the drawing room.

'It's Daisy Pritty. She—'

'Daisy's here?' Harriet brightened. Daisy had come home at last. The prodigal daughter, she thought irreverently. 'Some good news at last.'

'I fear not. She's come to take Molly to London.'

At once Harriet's delight faded as she understood Eveline's distress. Although nothing had been said during the past days, it was obvious that Eveline was becoming attached to the little girl and was hoping to keep her indefinitely. With an effort, Harriet pushed her own tragedy to the back of her mind as she followed Eveline through the house. Daisy was esconced in an armchair while Molly played on the floor with a set of wooden animals. The child glanced up, unsmiling, but said nothing, appearing unfazed by the situation developing around her.

Daisy smiled at her. 'Mrs Lester! 'Ow's things?' She looked confident and happy and Harriet's hopes rose, then fell as she studied Daisy. Her clothes were the same but she wore a 'new' crimson bonnet, and a red petticoat peeped from below her black skirt. Her lips had been coloured and there was rouge on her cheeks. Harriet felt a chill around her heart. In some indefinable way, she felt that Daisy had taken a step away from her – a step into an alien world where Harriet could never follow. They were going to lose sight of Daisy for ever. She sank back in her chair, then remembered Daisy's question. 'I'm very well, thank you, Daisy,' she mumbled. 'How about you?'

Daisy's smile broadened. She crossed one leg over the other in order to show off the frilled petticoat. 'I'm as happy as a pig in muck!' she laughed. 'I've found Digger, bless him, and he and me are setting up house together. I was just telling Miss Boothby. We've got a little room and we can use the yard to hang out our clothes, and Molly can play out there. Course, we haven't got much furniture at the moment – just a few sticks – but we'll do better. We've both got a job, so we're feeling rich.'

She was so obviously happy that Harriet didn't know what

to feel. How much of Daisy's story was true? she wondered uneasily, then reproached herself. Wasn't this what she had wanted – that Daisy should be happy? But not with *him*, she thought desperately. There was no way she could trust Digby Wise to care about anyone but himself.

She heard herself say, 'That's wonderful, Daisy. I'm so pleased.'

Daisy would go to London and she and Digger would disappear into the tangled alleyways of that great city . . . Harriet was trying to maintain her smile but it was difficult.

Eveline said, 'It was a shock but I'm happy for them. A child should be with her mother.' She could not look anyone in the eyes and Harriet knew what a strain she was under.

Harriet smiled at Molly. 'How exciting for you – going to London with your mother.'

Molly said, 'Don't want to go!'

Shocked, all three adults stared at her.

Daisy looked mortified. 'Course you want to go!' she snapped. 'You'll love it in London – and you'll have a pa!' She rolled her eyes. 'Kids!'

Molly said, 'Want to stay here with Aunt Evie.'

'Well you can't, so there! And she's not your aunt!' Daisy glared at her. 'You want to have a nice pa, don't you? You might have a baby brother, too. How about that? All little girls love their baby brothers – and their pa! He'll give you a piggy-back and buy you an ice cream if you're good. You like ice cream.'

'Don't want one!' Molly looked up, her face reddening. 'Want to stay with Aunt—'

Daisy leaned down and cuffed her lightly round the ear. 'Stop saying that, Molly! You're not staying here and that's that. Tut! All I'm putting up with so you can be with us and all you say is—'

'Putting up with? What do you mean, Daisy?' Harriet exchanged a quick glance with Eveline. 'You don't mean Digger . . .' She hesitated.

'What? Treats me bad?' She glared at Harriet, bristling with indignation. 'No! It was his idea, if you must know. I mean I wanted Molly and he says yes. Go ahead. Fetch the kid. Long as I earn enough money and that's fair enough.' She gave them a defiant look.

Harriet said, 'So you've got work already. What do you do?' Were they interrogating the poor girl? she wondered guiltily, but she had to know the worst.

'It's none of your business what I do!'

Molly glanced up quickly, alerted by the change in her mother's voice.

Daisy went on. 'I'm going to earn real good money and Digger's over the moon with me. He says I don't have to do anything I don't . . . That is, it's not . . .' She took a deep breath and forced a smile. 'Beggars can't be choosers! I . . . I work in an alehouse. The Grey Nag. Wait on tables. Satisfied?'

A silence fell, broken by Molly, who threw a wooden elephant across the room and followed it with a kangaroo.

'Want to stay with Aunt Evie!' she shouted, scrambling to her feet. She clung to Eveline's skirt and buried her face in her lap.

Daisy jumped up and pulled her away. 'Stop that nonsense!' she shouted. 'You'll do what I say and I say you're coming back with me.' She shook the child but Molly continued to struggle and kick until Daisy slapped her legs.

Eveline cried, 'Don't frighten her! She doesn't understand what's going on. She's—'

'She's my kid and I'll do what I like!' Daisy glared at her. 'Now. You giving me those clothes or what, 'cos we're going?'

Harriet could see that Eveline was on the verge of tears. 'You must give us your address, Daisy,' she suggested as calmly as she could. 'Then we can come up to visit you.'

Molly was sobbing quietly and Daisy pulled her close and cuddled her awkwardly. 'Stop grizzling, Molly, for Pete's sake! Stupid kid!' She looked up at Harriet and her mouth trembled. 'I'm her ma, aren't I?' She blinked back tears. 'You come to visit? I don't know about that. See, it's up to Digger now we're like, married, and anyway . . . I might be busy.'

Eveline left the room with a parting glance at Harriet, who asked, 'What hours do you work?'

Daisy hesitated then shrugged. 'Any hours I'm needed.'

'And it's good money? I didn't know you could earn much in . . . '

Daisy rolled her eyes. 'You don't understand, do you. I'm pretty and the men like the pretty ones. They tip well if they like you. You have to – you know – flatter them. Butter them up a bit. That's what barmaids do. Nothing wrong in that.'

'And that's all you do to earn the good money?'

There was a short silence. 'What's it to you?' Daisy looked sulky. 'I can do what I like. Anything with anyone! Anyone steps out of line – anyone lays a finger on me – Digger'll sort them out! He looks after me.'

'Why should anyone hurt you?'

'They don't.'

'You said that if any of them lays a finger on you . . . '

'Men can get funny. Go too far.' She tossed her blonde curls. 'Anyway that's my business. You ask too many questions.'

Harriet longed to shake some sense into her. 'I've always tried to help you, Daisy. I thought I was your friend. I wouldn't like to see anything bad happen to you. I just want you to be happy.'

Daisy had the grace to look ashamed but said nothing. Harriet regarded her uneasily but finally let the matter drop. She changed the subject. 'Miss Boothby has been very good to your daughter. It's only fair she should be allowed to visit her from time to time.'

Daisy shrugged. 'No one asked her to keep the kid here.'

'You left her on the doorstep. Remember?'

'What if I did? All she had to do was dump her back in

the workhouse until I could collect her. Making all this fuss of her . . . Poor kid! It's gone to her head. Turned her into a proper little madam. No wonder she's chucking the toys around the room. She's been spoilt something terrible!'

'For heaven's sake, Daisy! You should be more appreciative,' Harriet told her, her tone sharpening. Her patience was wearing thin. 'Surely it was better for Molly to live with Miss Boothby instead of in the workhouse. Which would you prefer if you were in her shoes?'

'I suppose so – but nobody gave me a choice.' Daisy shrugged. 'I'll ask Digger,' she offered, 'but he'll be none too pleased. He hates interfering busybodies.'

This unkind remark struck home and Harriet felt her face flush. An interfering busybody! Was there any truth in that? Deeply dismayed, she looked at Daisy. If only she could give her a hug. If only she could convince her that she had her best interests at heart but, looking at Daisy's beautiful but furious face, she could see no way back to their earlier friendship. She wanted to say, 'I've failed you, Daisy,' but even that was out of the question.

Eveline reappeared with a small bag and a wicker basket. 'These are her clothes, and her toys and books are in the basket.'

'Books?' Daisy blinked.

'She can't read them but she likes to look at the pictures.'

'Right then. We're off. Got to get the train back to London.'

Harriet kept out of the way until the flurry of last-minute activity was over and Daisy and Molly had been waved off. Eveline came back inside and sat down, fighting back tears.

Harriet said, 'I'm so sorry, Eveline. I know how you feel about the child.'

'And I know how you feel about Daisy. Neither of us wanted this to happen.'

Eveline covered her face with her hands, not trusting herself to speak further, and they sat in silence for some time while Eveline composed herself. When at last she uncovered her eyes she looked at Harriet and her eyes widened.

'*You've* been crying!' she said. 'Oh Harriet! Here's me feeling sorry for myself and you've got troubles too. It's not your mother, is it?'

'No, thank the Lord!' Harriet reassured her. 'It's Godfrey and Amelia. The Italian woman. She came to the house.' Briefly she explained what had happened then drew a long breath. 'I told him to leave me. I told them both to go.' Her voice shook. 'I've told Mama and she was very brave but I keep wondering if I've been too hasty. He wanted to stay and talk about it but what was there to say? I can't share him with Amelia!'

'I should think not! The man's a fool. Let him go, Harriet, and count your blessings.'

'My *blessings*?!'

'You have no children, Harriet. You can let him go. If you had a family you would feel obliged for their sakes to give him another chance.'

Harriet sighed. 'Perhaps it would have been better if I *had* children to consider. Now I have nothing.'

Eveline swallowed. 'Children can be a heartache, too. I feel bereft and Molly wasn't even my own child . . .' There was a long silence. 'What did you think about Daisy? This job of hers.'

'I hardly dare think!'

'Exactly. Our worst fears . . .' Eveline lowered her voice. 'Something immoral?'

'I fear so. Poor Daisy. I wonder if the awful Digger coerced her. I don't think she is really that kind of girl. Do you?'

Eveline shook her head. 'No. Wild, scatterbrained but not *bad.* Not in that way. Circumstances, maybe? I knew a woman once who turned to – to that kind of thing when her husband died. Scandalized the family, of course. She didn't need the money.' Eveline shook her head. 'Simply went mad with shock, the doctors said. Poor soul ended up in an asylum.'

Startled, Harriet could think of nothing to say.

Eveline went on. 'I hope we're wrong about Daisy.'

Harriet decided to say nothing of the conversation she had

116

had with Daisy while Eveline was out of the room collecting Molly's things.

Eveline's face crumpled. 'Oh! How can the good Lord allow these things to happen? I cannot bear to think about it. And poor little Molly. She was so happy here. But this won't do. We must stay cheerful and positive.'

Harriet agreed wholeheartedly. There was nothing else they *could* do.

Seven

When she returned to Havely House, Harriet found Doctor Fletcher outside on the drive with Sam, who was telling him all about the gymkhana. For once she was not pleased to see him. He would be sympathetic and she was afraid she might break down and cry. She hoped she might slip into the house unseen, but Sam waved to her and reluctantly she made her way towards them across the gravelled drive. To make matters worse Sam at once made his excuses and hurried off, leaving them together, and Harriet knew at once, by the doctor's expression, that Agnes had told him of her plight. She decided she would plead a headache and leave him before the conversation could develop. By way of proof, she put a hand to her head and frowned slightly as she reached him.

'I want you to know how sorry I am, Mrs Lester,' he told her. 'I have to admit I'm at a loss to understand your husband's behaviour.'

'Doctor Fletcher, I have a slight—'

He went straight on in a flood of words. 'To abandon a woman like you! He must have lost his senses! To give up such a wonderful wife for a woman like that? I never took him for a fool, Mrs Lester, but now you must forget him and pin your hopes on the future.'

Harriet found his positive attitude bracing and forgot the feigned headache. 'I don't know what I should hope *for*,' she confessed. 'Nothing can be undone and I think that nothing could be the same between us even if he wanted to come back to me. He should never have married me, because his heart was still Amelia's. Maybe he convinced himself it was otherwise but . . .' She sighed deeply.

The doctor's kindly face was full of concern. 'He should have been more honest. He's wronged you, Mrs Lester, and that is unforgivable. You are worth a dozen Amelias. I know her type. Extravagant and shallow and selfish to the core.'

Harriet, staring down at her nervously clasped hands, accepted the compliment silently and was ridiculously grateful for his scathing assessment of Amelia. In her present state such comments were like balm to her wounded spirit and important for her lost confidence. She forced herself to look up at him. 'I daresay you think I've been overhasty to send him away but—'

'Not at all. Any woman would have done the same thing!'

'The truth is, I panicked,' she told him. 'I couldn't imagine how we could inhabit the same house while Amelia was nearby, waiting patiently for the moment when he left me. Foolish pride, no doubt.'

He shook his head. 'No! You did the right thing. You acted decisively and that's the best you could do in such terrible circumstances. I worry now that you will find it impossible to sleep. Your mother is so anxious about you. Your father killed himself and that haunts her. She doesn't want you to follow his example.'

Harriet was shocked. 'Poor Mama! I must reassure her. Such a thought has never entered my head. I have too much to live for. Mama and Sam, the workhouse and my friends.'

He smiled. 'Remember what I said to you not so long ago – that life sometimes plays horrid tricks?'

'And this is one of them!'

'It certainly is. And make no mistake, a betrayal is a serious shock to anyone. Worse, in my view, than being widowed. You have lost the man you love but he has also robbed you of your self-esteem. If you are not careful you will find yourself taking the blame for what happened.'

Harriet was startled by his perception. She had already begun to wonder what she had done to make Godfrey value her so lightly.

He regarded her earnestly. 'You are not to blame for your husband's infidelity, Mrs Lester. *You are not to blame!*' To her surprise he held his hands over hers in a gesture of reassurance. 'I can help you through the worst of this if you will allow me to. I could leave you a sleeping draught – just for emergencies . . . Ah!' He rolled his eyes. 'I can see from your expression that you don't like the idea.'

'I'd like to see if I can manage,' she told him. 'If I need help I'll come to you. I promise you that.'

Together they walked back to where his horse waited patiently. Gathering up the reins, he said, 'I should say that I hope your husband returns a wiser man but I can't. I hope he stays away, for your sake.'

'Oh, but surely . . . '

'A man who could treat you in that cavalier way doesn't deserve you. And you deserve a bright, new future and it will come, Mrs Lester. Believe me it will come.'

As Harriet watched him climb up into the pony trap she felt strangely restored by their brief conversation. He had said what she needed to hear and she felt strengthened by his positive words. He was a wonderful friend, she reflected, as she waved him off. Not only an excellent doctor but a very decent, caring man.

Somehow she survived the next few days. There was no sign of Godfrey and no unwelcome letters from either him or Amelia. The house seemed empty with both Robert and Godfrey gone but Sam was there and she found his cheerful chatter helpful. She was wondering how she would cope on Saturday with the gymkhana. Determined to accompany the two boys, she wondered how far news of Godfrey's absence had travelled in the town and whether she would encounter curious stares or clumsy expressions of sympathy. At last she invited Eveline to accompany them, on the assumption that there was safety in numbers and in the hope that the riding events would take their minds off their various problems.

Rollo had been groomed until he looked as good as the

boys could manage and certainly the best that Harriet had ever seen him. His hooves had been polished and his coat gleamed. His long golden tail had been brushed and combed and his pale mane was tied in small bunches with narrow red ribbon. Sam and Teddy fussed over him like mother hens while Rollo stood calmly, staring around with only an occasional shake of his head to indicate possible excitement.

The gymkhana was taking place in a large field on the outskirts of the town and near enough to enable them to lead Rollo instead of transporting him in a horse box. The field was bordered by trees and many of the horses were tethered in the shade. Horses and owners milled about excitedly, while their family and friends offered advice. The spectators wandered around, admiring horses of all shapes and sizes. A large ring had been marked out in the centre of the field with the use of ropes and stakes and a man with a megaphone kept up a running account of instructions for the competitors and information for the spectators. On the far side of the field there were trestle tables manned by people selling horsey items – riding gear, brushes and curry combs, saddlery, horse brasses and much more.

Sam, in his element, studied his programme for the hundredth time. 'Half an hour to go!' he told anyone who would listen. Teddy nodded importantly but Harriet and Eveline were watching an eleven-year-old girl taking her chestnut pony over the jumps. When she had finished the round there was loud applause. She had lost no points and was the current winner. They watched as the trophy was awarded and, smiling broadly, she led her pony back to the edge of the field to unsaddle him. Her proud parents followed at a respectful distance and Harriet crossed her fingers that Rollo would at least earn good marks. The other ponies waiting their event seemed younger and mostly larger than Rollo but none had his placid temperament. Some skipped about, tugging their young owners with them while others tossed their heads and showed the whites of their eyes. One kicked back at anybody who ventured too close.

121

Eveline said, 'Rollo should win a prize for best behaviour!' and earned a dazzling smile from Sam.

He said, 'Only twenty-five minutes to go!'

Harriet grinned. 'A good thing horses can't tell the time or he'd be as impatient as you are!'

Event number nine was a parade of the miniature ponies and these entered the ring with their young owners while the mothers, aunts, uncles and grandparents clapped until their hands were tingling.

Eveline said, 'Molly would have loved this!' and Harriet squeezed her arm consolingly. She had come to realize over the past two days that Eveline's loss of Molly was almost as painful to her as Harriet's loss of Godfrey. Losing someone you love changed your perception of life, she thought sadly, and no one can really help you through the darkness. Climbing into the double bed at night awakened in Harriet a great depth of longing for the love and companionship that Godfrey had given her. With a sigh she tried to shake free from the memories and concentrate on the coming event.

At that moment Eveline gasped. 'Harriet! It's Godfrey!' She was staring over Harriet's shoulder and Harriet turned to see Godfrey hurrying towards her, his face set in deeply troubled lines. Her instinct was to turn and run but instead she faced him, her throat dry. Tactfully Eveline moved away to watch Teddy and Sam saddling Rollo.

'Harriet, I have to talk to you,' he said, his voice low. 'I spoke to your mother. She—'

'You spoke to Mama? How did you get into the house?'

'I still have my keys. Harriet, I have things to say. You must listen to me.'

Harriet stared up into his eyes, expecting a rush of emotion but found herself unmoved except by embarrassment. 'This isn't the time or place!' she hissed. 'Please leave us alone.'

'Then say you'll meet with me.'

'With you and Amelia, you mean! No, Godfrey!'

'No. She needn't know. You and I—'

Harriet glared at him, incensed by the suggestion. 'So now

you are going to deceive *her with me*! Well, I won't be a party to it, Godfrey, and more to the point I have nothing to say to you.' She frowned. 'Did you let yourself into the house?'

'I had to.'

'You had no right!'

'But you weren't there and your mother is unable to walk.'

Harriet held out her hand. 'I'd like the keys, please, Godfrey.'

'But I haven't got all my belongings together yet.' Reluctantly he dropped the keys into her hand. 'Most of my books are still there, my chess set, the trunk in the attic, several framed pictures . . . '

'Write to me with your address and I'll have them all sent to you by carrier.'

'But Harriet . . . '

'No "buts", Godfrey. This is Sam's big day and I don't want you to spoil it, so please don't let him see you here. It will upset him and this event means a lot to him.'

'But I have an idea . . . '

'Are you . . . are you living with Amelia?' She saw by his expression that he was.

'We're sharing a room, yes, but—'

'As I expected. We have nothing to say. Please go away, Godfrey. Your presence is embarrassing for me.'

'I just want to make my peace with you.'

But Harriet turned on her heel and moved quickly away, her heart racing, her eyes aching with unshed tears. She joined Eveline, who whispered, 'Are you all right?'

Harriet nodded then whispered, 'I'm not sure!' and then smiled at Sam and Teddy, who were leading Rollo into the ring. Was she all right? she wondered. Would she ever be all right again? Would she ever enjoy the bright future that Angus Fletcher had hinted at?

As the judging continued Harriet smiled and chatted, refusing to turn and look for Godfrey. Had he left the field or was he lurking somewhere, planning another attempt to talk to her?

Twenty minutes later the two boys led Rollo out of the ring with broad grins on their faces. The pony had won third prize. The small triumph was enough to drive out all thoughts of Godfrey, and tired but happy they all settled down to enjoy the rest of the day's excitement.

Later that night, however, as Harriet lay awake, she was obsessed by the thought that she had done the wrong thing by sending her husband away. Eveline and the doctor had supported her decision that a clean break was the only way but maybe they were wrong. Neither of them had married, so were they competent to give advice?

'For better, for worse,' she whispered. A mouse skittered across the attic above her head and she slid further down the bed. Tomorrow she would have to go up into the attic with a couple of mousetraps. Godfrey had always undertaken that task, but no more. She would also have to chase the spiders from the bath. She shuddered.

She turned over, seeking a more comfortable position in the hope of falling asleep but it was no good. Unhappy thoughts fluttered through her mind like dark birds. She had promised to love and cherish Godfrey through good and bad times but at the first hurdle she had fallen. So much for promises, she thought unhappily. Perhaps in her hurt and bewildered state she had been too hasty. Too strong, in fact. She had played right into Amelia's hands by making it impossible for Godfrey to stay with his wife.

'But he said he will always love her!' she whispered. That was a situation she could never tolerate. No wife would, surely. If only she knew what Godfrey really wanted, but she didn't. He said one thing in front of Amelia and another when he was alone with his wife. If he wanted Amelia then the marriage could not survive and now was the time to end it but if he wanted to stay with his wife, sending him away and refusing to discuss the problem was not the solution. She was still unsure what to do when at last she fell into a deep and troubled sleep.

* * *

Several days passed. On Sunday Harriet and Sam went to church and Harriet prayed for guidance but returned home feeling none the wiser. On Monday she travelled to Winchester to take Sam back to school. Agnes's health continued to improve and Harriet, still beset with doubts, tried to pretend that everything was normal. On Tuesday a letter arrived from Godfrey.

> *My dear sweet Harriet,*
>
> *When I saw you on Saturday I realized that I had been stupid and weak in the extreme to allow matters to come to this. How can you ever forgive me? Probably you never will but at least I owe you an explanation . . .*

Harriet sat down on the nearest chair and closed her eyes. She hoped quite desperately that his explanation would make it possible for her to see the situation in a better light. She wanted to read the letter and then know that they could come together again and repair the damage Amelia had done but she feared the worst and read on, feeling sick with apprehension.

> *My reaction to Amelia's reappearance in my life dates back to the way we parted. She told me she was expecting a child which was mine and I immediately panicked. I was just twenty and an almost penniless student and the thought of being trapped in an impoverished marriage was a frightening prospect. I insisted that the child must be her husband's and abruptly left Italy and fled back to England. Very cowardly, and I have felt deep guilt ever since. I shall never know if the child was mine or not but I do know that I abandoned Amelia. At the time I was deeply in love with her and I did sometimes dream that she might reappear in my life and we could spend our lives together. Now she has come back I was at first swept away in a*

125

tide of longing for her and a desire to make up for my
earlier behaviour. I betrayed you and I am so sorry. I
would like to stay with you, assuming that you would
forgive me and take me back . . .

'I would!' Harriet whispered. 'And I think I could forgive you!'

. . . but Amelia refuses to let me go. She claims she still
loves me and sadly I believe she does. She is a passionate
and excitable woman and insists that she will never
leave Maybourne. If I come back to you she threatens
to continue to visit Havely House and write to me and
complicate our lives so that we will never be free of
her. Sadly, again, I believe her. What can I do, Harriet?
She will never allow us to live except in her shadow.
How would our love survive such a burden?

Harriet closed her eyes, shocked to the core. Yes, she thought. Amelia could and would do that. The woman would ensure that they were never free of the ghost of Godfrey's past. Her love for Godfrey would ruin them. She forced herself to read the last few lines.

It would be unfair to expect you to live that way – you
deserve so much after what has already happened in
your life. I think I must move away with Amelia and
leave you to make a new life without me. You are a
sweet and beautiful woman and I envy the man who
will take my place in your heart.
Yours ever . . . Godfrey

Harriet drew a deep breath and struggled to draw another. It was over. Amelia had succeeded – and how cunning she had been. She had made it virtually impossible for Godfrey to have any chance of winning back Harriet.

'Very, very clever!' Harriet whispered. For a moment or

two, she tried to imagine their life, never knowing when Amelia would arrive on their doorstep to cause a scene. Always fearing to see her in the town whenever they ventured out. Dreading the postman for fear of another letter addressed to Godfrey in that distinctive handwriting. Slowly, line by painful line, Harriet reread the letter. Poor Godfrey. And poor Harriet.

What was it the doctor had said? That she deserved a bright, new future. He was right. Perhaps he had known that the marriage was beyond repair. Certainly he was trying to prepare her for the need to make new plans. She thought how kind he had been that day on the drive and found herself smiling. He had said she was worth a dozen Amelias!

'Doctor Fletcher, you are a dear man,' she whispered. He really cared, she thought.

And then she thought the unthinkable. Just how much *did* he care? He had expressed no regret that Godfrey had left her except for *her* sake, and he had been very determined that she should never take him back. Was he . . .

'No!' she cried. 'Stop this foolishness, Harriet! He was understanding and sympathetic and he said comforting things. That is all.'

She rolled her eyes, annoyed with herself. Her husband had left her and already she was trying to replace him. Before she looked for that bright new future she must somehow come to terms with the dark past. Only then could she find a new direction.

Many miles away, Daisy Pritty's life was already beginning its new direction. That same Tuesday evening she was busy in the bar of the Grey Nag, staggering from table to table with jugs of ale and nips of brandy and back again to the bar with the empties. It was a large inn and there were three other barmaids. The noise was terrific and the room was full of smoke from dozens of clay pipes. Overhead, a green parrot in a large cage cackled endlessly as it recited a small repertoire of phrases to which very few customers paid any attention except to shake the cage and curse. On the counter a tattered tabby cat stretched lazily, while in a corner an elderly man sawed enthusiastically at a violin.

Daisy, hot and flustered, was wearing a new skirt and blouse which Bert Fry had provided and was well aware of the pleasing image she presented. The low-cut camisole was flimsy with ribbons and bows and the full skirt of cherry-red satin flattered her neat waist. She was bombarded on all sides with what passed for cheerful banter but in fact the noise made her head ache and a glance at the clock showed her that it was only ten o'clock and she still faced several more hours of it.

"'Ere, lovey! Get us another drink!'

'Same again and look lively!'

'Come on, doll! Look nippy. I'm dying of thirst 'ere!'

She kept a fixed smile on her face and wished Digger wasn't watching her so closely. She would like to have answered back but Mel had explained that she had to please the menfolk and a snide reply would not go down at all well.

'What's your name, then, sweetheart? I'm Hal, at your service!'

'That's a pert little bottom you've got there!' A boozy face leered into hers and she swerved quickly.

Smiling, she said, 'Get away with you, you saucy devil!' and that made him laugh. Laugh yourself sick! she urged him silently and twisted from a podgy hand that was pinching her upper arm.

A sailor lay sprawled across one of the tables but he raised his head when he saw her approach. He had a young face, round with blue eyes.

'You're lovely!' he mumbled.

'Thank you kindly, sir!'

He sat up as she collected empty mugs. 'I've got a day's shore leave. Want a bit of fun?'

Daisy hesitated. Melly had told her to be choosy with the men. 'You ask *them*,' she had said. 'Then you get to choose who you go with. I turn down the fatties. They squash you

128

half to death! And forget the old uns. They take too long. I go for the young uns.'

She looked at the sailor. Nice-looking, young and slim. 'What sort of fun?' she asked, her head on one side at a provocative angle. 'Some fun costs. Know what I mean?'

He grinned. 'Just got paid, haven't I, *and* I've got a room in a lodging house less than half a mile from here! Your luck's in, ducks! What d'you say, eh?'

Daisy winked at him and whispered, 'Tell you later, sailor!' and whisked away with a flounce of her skirts. She went straight to Melissa. 'That sailor's after a bit! What d'you reckon?'

'That's Greg Banner. He's fine. You'll be OK with him.'

'Thanks, Mel.' She glanced across at Digger and he nodded and gave her the thumbs-up. It was all surprisingly easy, thought Daisy. Things were looking up.

She left Greg around midnight and walked back to the room she shared with Digger. She glanced at once at her daughter, who was asleep on the floor, with her thumb in her mouth. The moonlight played across her tangled curls giving her a deceptively angelic appearance.

Digger, also in bed, propped himself up on one elbow. 'Back safe and sound, then!'

'Looks like it!'

Daisy had hoped for a bit of appreciation and her mouth twisted disconsolately as she unbuttoned her boots. Light from the window lit up the tawdry room and cast flattering shadows across the few sticks of furniture they had been able to buy. A wobbly table, two chairs, a bed with a lumpy mattress. They had nowhere to cook but managed with cheap food bought from the many street vendors. Next, Daisy planned to buy a truckle bed for Molly. At present the child was sleeping on a pile of old blankets covered in newspaper. They also needed a cheap rug to cover the floorboards and a cupboard to keep their pots and pans in. It was a low attic room with a small window but Daisy promised herself that, given time, she could make it the sort of place Digger would like – the sort of place Molly would be happy in.

'How'd it go?' he demanded.

She shrugged, unwilling to talk about it before she had become reconciled to the idea. A strange man watching her undress had not been too awkward but the money side of it had bothered her more than she expected.

'What?' Digger narrowed his eyes. 'He hurt you?'

'No!' She frowned. 'Why should he hurt me?'

'What then?'

'I don't know really . . . It was funny. Not *that* sort of funny but strange. I kept wishing it was you.'

He grinned with relief. 'Don't be daft, Dais! That's different.'

She pulled off her clothes, tossed them into the shadows and slid into bed.

'Tell me then,' he urged. 'What happened?'

'Nothing much. He . . . you know, did it . . . and then he fell asleep. Never even said thank you or nothing!'

'But he paid you up front? You know what I told you.'

'He paid me, yes. A tanner. Fatty Fry took half. All I've got is a mingy threepence.'

'Put it in the purse like I showed you. It's not much but it's a start. Who told Banner it was only sixpence?'

'Don't ask me!' She snuggled closer, pulling his unresponsive arm around her neck. 'Banner said, "How much?" and I said, "The usual."'

Digger laughed. 'You soppy dolly! Next time say, "How much you got?" Cheeky like. Like it's a bit of a joke. If he says sixpence you laugh and tell him to think again. Stuff like that, Dais. Jolly them along. Get them to pay a bit more.' He laughed kindly. 'But you did fine for the first time. Don't worry about it, see. I'll look after everything.' He kissed her, turned over and settled himself down, taking most of the threadbare blanket with him.

Within minutes he was asleep and snoring but Daisy lay awake thinking about Greg Banner and all the men like him

130

who would come into her life. Sixpence. She sighed. Not much, but the poor man was lonely and far from home . . . She smiled into the darkness and whispered, 'Think again, Mr Banner!' It sounded all right. 'How much you got?' Easy enough, but would she ever get used to it? She didn't think it would ever feel right but Mel seemed happy enough. She had confided in Daisy that she was waiting to find a rich man who'd take a shine to her and would pay her much more just to keep her all to himself. It sounded rather tempting but then Mel had no man of her own and Daisy had Digger. A sailor was hardly promising and the rest of the customers were rough and ready but as time went on a rich man *might* come into the Grey Nag. Or might not. It was a seedy place. Mel might have a long wait, Daisy reflected, then frowned as a new thought surfaced. She had been secretly hoping Digger would be jealous of Greg Banner, but he didn't seem to care. She sighed. If Digger didn't care, why should she . . . ?

The next day, in the Maybourne Workhouse, Mrs Fenner glanced up from her writing, glad of the interruption to her labours. She was writing a report on what she thought of as 'the comings and goings of the inmates', a job she hated. She called, 'Come in!'

Albert Hawke entered and she laid down her pen and smiled at him. A little male company, even if it was only the undertaker, was always welcome.

He at once removed his black top hat. 'Come to measure a Stanley Harris – joiner,' he reminded her. 'I said ten o'clock but I'm a bit late. Sorry about that, ma'am. A lady came in just as I was leaving to book a funeral for her brother who died of a fit as he sat reading a book and only thirty-three. Dropped the book and fell sidewards, his arms flailing, his mouth frothing.'

'Frothing! Ugh! What a dreadful thing!'

'But known for it, seemingly. A shock for the family, nonetheless. But not short of money – the family, that is.

131

Chose a mahogany casket. Brass handles, satin lining on a mattress of bran.' He nodded happily. 'It's going to look very good.'

Indicating a chair for him, Mrs Fenner smoothed her bodice and tidied her hair. 'How are you now, Mr Hawke? I was shocked to hear about that unfortunate business with Daniel Stick. Are you quite recovered from your injuries? I said to Mr Swift, "The poor man might have been killed!"'

'That I am, I'm glad to say. Recovered, I mean. Mostly bruises. Nothing broken.'

'And your premises? The office?'

'Back to rights, Mrs Fenner, ma'am. Back to rights.' He smiled, nervously twisting the rim of his hat. 'I was wondering, while I'm here . . . Wondering about Daisy Pritty and her daughter. I mean, where are they? Does anybody know?'

'As far as we know, they are in London, together.' Mrs Fenner signalled her disapproval at his interest by adopting a cold tone. 'Daisy descended on Maybourne without a word of warning, collected the child from Eveline Boothby and took her back to London. She claims they're going to live with Digby Wise in "a lovely little flat". One big happy family!' She sniffed. 'She also claims to have a regular job as a barmaid. The Grey Nag, I think the place is called. All we can do is pray that it works out for her. Poor Miss Boothby was very upset. She was very fond of the child.'

The news seemed to chasten the undertaker and he sighed. 'I always reckoned she could be saved,' he admitted. 'You know, given a decent chance.'

Mrs Fenner stiffened. 'Daisy Pritty *has* been given chances, Mr Hawke. More than she deserved and she resisted them all. The workhouse found respectable work for her but she stole from her employers! She is an impetuous, ungrateful girl and if she ends up in the gutter she has only herself to blame. I, for one, have had enough of her.' Mortified by his interest in the wayward young woman, Mrs Fenner gave the undertaker an icy look. Why were men so easily impressed by outward appearances? she thought bitterly. 'Don't allow yourself to be influenced by a pretty face and a neat pair of ankles, Mr Hawke. That young woman is *trouble!*'

'I daresay you're right.' He shook his head, drew a tape measure from his coat pocket and draped it around his neck. 'So – back to business. Where is the deceased?'

'In the infirmary. I'll come up and let you in. We keep the door locked when there's a body in there.'

'Cause of death?'

'Consumption. Harris came in as a casual a week ago for one night but by the next morning he had become too ill to move on, so he was granted indoor relief.' So much for her hopes of escaping a further drain on their finances, she reflected. Doctor Fletcher had attended him. She smiled faintly at the thought of him. Angus Fletcher was a very eligible bachelor and if she were twenty years younger, she would have found him an interesting challenge. He had never been married but that was because his mother had been an invalid for years and he had had to cope with her as well as with his doctor's practice.

'The doctor was very kind to him,' she told the undertaker. 'He brought round a few eggs for him but the old chap was too weak even to eat, though I didn't have the heart to tell the doctor, so I said how he'd enjoyed them.'

In the infirmary she led the way to the bed on which Stanley Harris had been laid out in a clean nightshirt with two pennies over his eyes and waited as the undertaker muttered a short prayer.

He glanced up at her. 'I doubt that he had many sins, poor soul, but I always ask the Lord to wipe the slate clean, so to speak. It's the very least we can do for them. I suppose it's the *only* thing.'

So Albert Hawke had a generous heart. Mrs Fenner thawed a little towards him. 'My grandmother used to tell of *her* grandmother who used to bake a little cake full of currants when someone died. A soul cake it was called. The currants were the sins, you see. Then someone would eat the cake and take all the sins "unto himself", as she put it. The deceased would be judged guiltless and assured a place in Heaven.'

The undertaker smiled. 'But what of the one who took on all the sins?'

'Someone would bake a soul cake for him when it was *his* turn to go!' She laughed. 'I can still see my grandmother on her deathbed. A tiny doll-like thing she was. No bigger than poor Mr Harris.'

They both looked down at the wizened form of the erstwhile joiner.

'I'll leave you to it,' said Mrs Fenner reluctantly and went back to the office and her report.

Eight

Miriam Downs opened the front door of their modest flat and gave a cry of delight. 'Angus! This is a surprise!' She reached up to kiss him then drew him into the house. 'We don't see enough of you. Now come in and make yourself comfortable.'

Miriam Downs, a plump woman in her late twenties, was like her brother in some ways (but undeniably more homely) with the same curly brown hair and bright-blue eyes. She was happily married to a much older man who was now in failing health and her days were spent in caring for him. She settled Angus in a chair and then bustled out into the small back garden to tell her husband, Humphrey, that they had a visitor.

With an ease born of practice she wheeled him back into the house and the three of them exchanged greetings and news and Angus enquired after Humphrey's rheumatism while Miriam hurried into the kitchen to butter scones and make a pot of tea.

When the tea had been poured and a suitable gap occurred in the conversation Miriam turned to Angus with a smile. 'Now tell me – to what do we owe this pleasure?'

Angus had the grace to blush. 'Is it so obvious?' he asked.

'Obvious? Most certainly it is! We rarely see you although we live in the same town.' Her words were softened by a smile but Angus shook his head.

'Guilty, m'lud! I'm so sorry, Miriam. Pressure of work is my only excuse, I fear.'

Humphrey, a thin, frail man, recognizing his brother-in-law's embarrassment, reproached her. 'Don't tease him,

Miriam. He's a doctor, remember. Show me a doctor who isn't working too hard and I'll show you a charlatan! If Angus needs us, let us be thankful. Go ahead, Angus, and have your say.'

'I have a favour to ask you, Miriam,' he said. 'I want to invite a friend, a young woman, to dine with me. I shall also invite her mother but she is almost bedridden and may not wish to leave her home.'

'The mother – is she a patient of yours?' asked Humphrey.

'Yes. They are both on my list but at present Harriet is fit and well. Naturally I cannot invite her to dine with me alone without some impropriety so I thought . . .'

He paused and Miriam felt a flutter of excitement. Was this what she had been waiting for? Was her brother actually considering taking a wife?

Angus looked at her and her excitement was followed by a frisson of unease.

'Before you raise your hopes, Miriam, I must tell you that the young woman in question is married.' He ignored the sudden anxious glance that flashed between his sister and her husband. 'But her husband, Godfrey Lester, has abandoned her. He has run off with another woman.'

The following silence was finally broken as Angus went on to explain the circumstances of Harriet's situation and they listened intently as he described the favour he was asking. 'I wondered if you, Miriam, would bake a large game pie for us if I provided the ingredients, and then join us for dinner – with Humphrey, of course. I think I could provide a simple salad and strawberries, since they're in season.'

Miriam conceded, 'I'll bake you a pie with pleasure but . . .' She glanced at her husband, then back at Angus. 'Are you . . . This woman, this Harriet, is she someone you might care about?'

'Indeed she is, though I have never given her the slightest hint of my feelings. She is now alone but her husband's desertion is quite recent . . .' He threw out his hands in a gesture of frustration. 'I only ever see her when I call at the house to

136

check on her mother's health. Fleeting visits. I can never speak freely and therefore I have no idea how she might feel about me and anyway it is much too soon to broach the subject.'

Miriam looked at him indignantly. 'You're a fine, good man. She should think highly of you. She should be flattered but . . . Oh Angus, do they have any children?'

'Fortunately not.'

'Thank the Lord for that!' She wondered why but dared not ask. 'Oh dear! Should we dine with you?' She pressed three fingers to her lips. 'For myself I'd accept the invitation but is it wise?' She frowned. 'What can come of it, Angus? There would have to be a divorce and think of the . . .' She bit back the word 'scandal'. 'Suppose she gives you encouragement and later her husband sees the error of his ways and decides to return.'

'Little chance of that,' said Angus. 'The other woman, Amelia, is an Italian – a ghost from his past. According to Harriet's mother, he is besotted with her.'

Miriam felt a frisson of envy. Humphrey had been a good but dull husband and the word 'besotted' could never have been used about his feelings for her.

'Is she beautiful, this Amelia?' she asked, a trace of wistfulness in her voice.

'Apparently so. Very Italian. A dark beauty.'

Miriam took an immediate dislike to both Amelia and Godfrey but she was still filled with doubts. 'Harriet might still love him. She might try to win him back. It might all end in heartache for you, Angus. Is there no other woman who might make you a good wife?'

Angus rolled his eyes and Humphrey said, 'If there were such a woman your brother would have wed long since! Do think what you're saying, Miriam.'

'I'm sorry.' Anxiously she twisted her apron, then glanced at her husband. 'You decide then, Humphrey! You are much wiser than I am.'

Angus turned to his brother-in-law and waited. Miriam watched her brother unhappily from the corner of her eye.

She had waited years for him to choose a bride and now she was bursting with curiosity about Harriet Lester. Years earlier Angus, with his medical background, had insisted that Miriam move with Humphrey into a home of their choosing, insisting that he would stay with his mother in the family home so that he could supervise her health. Now he was free to consider his own future but this new situation was fraught with difficulties. What was this Harriet like? Miriam wondered. She had never expected any sister-in-law of hers to be a divorced woman – in fact she did not even *know* any divorced women – and wondered uneasily what her friends would think of such a union.

She glanced at Humphrey, who was recovering from the idea that his wife thought him wise. He looked pensive for a few moments, then nodded sagely.

'For my part I'll risk anything for a slice of one of Miriam's game pies. I think the idea very pleasant and I look forward to meeting Harriet. It will only be a first step and since Angus is prepared to risk later disappointment, we should support him.' He looked at Miriam for her approval.

'Wonderful!' cried Miriam, happily absolved of all responsibility. 'That's exactly it! Nothing ventured, nothing gained! I'll make a pie and we'll dine with you, Angus. Now all we need is for you to fix a day and me to decide what I shall need for the pie. Duck, for sure . . . maybe a guineafowl and most certainly some good lean bacon . . . '

The next day was Wednesday and Harriet received a letter in unfamiliar handwriting. It was from Doris Lester.

Dear Harriet,
*   I am in such a state as my dear mother has died and now I am shaken by the dreadful news from Godfrey. To think that my only child could treat his wife so badly. I am at my wits' end to know what to say to you, let alone help you. I haven't met this wretched woman but they are coming to Dorset in the near future so that I*

*may meet her, which I would prefer not to do, but I
cannot turn away my own flesh and blood. I had believed
that his affair with her was long dead and I still love
you as a daughter but what will happen now? . . .*

'Who can tell!' muttered Harriet. The letter was unsettling
in more ways than one. It showed just how far the ripples
were spreading and that was depressing. She could imagine
Doris's distress and had delayed writing to her in case her
son had not yet broken the news. She read on.

*I am all at sixes and sevens and last night had very
little sleep. How are you bearing up? It is so sad.
Godfrey is and always has been a little weak and I
suspect Amelia is a strong character to have torn him
away from a wife he loved dearly. Do write to me and
let me know if there is any way in which I can help
you. God bless you, dearest Harriet.*
> *Yours ever,*
> *Doris Lester*

Harriet was becoming accustomed to the commiserations
and pitying glances of friends and acquaintances. In some
ways it helped to be offered understanding and comfort but
it brought home to her very clearly how changed her life
had become. It showed her, too, what Agnes had gone through
when George Burnett killed himself. Scandal and tragedy
marked out the innocent as victims and Harriet was finding
it an uncomfortable feeling.

She took the letter in to Agnes, who was propped up
comfortably in bed with Jasper the cat curled up beside her.
She took the proffered letter and read it thoughtfully. 'Poor
Doris,' she said when she had finished it. 'You must write
something cheerful in reply, Harriet. As his mother, she is
feeling needlessly guilty but she is not to blame in any way.
You might be able to reassure her.'

Harriet stood at the window staring out. 'I wonder how it

will all end,' she said. 'Will they stay in England or go back to Italy? I rather hope they do go abroad. It is so unsettling to know, or to assume, that they are nearby. How fearful to meet them in the street!'

Agnes looked alarmed. 'You think they are still in Maybourne?'

'I don't know, Mama.'

'If you *should* happen to meet them, Harriet, give a polite nod to Godfrey and then move on with firm steps and a calm expression. Let *them* be the ones to feel embarrassed by the meeting. You have nothing to be ashamed of.'

Downstairs again, Harriet was polishing the table in the dining room when the front doorbell rang and she hurried to answer it. To her astonishment she found herself staring into the face of Marcus Wellbury, the man to whom she had once been betrothed.

'Marcus!'

He removed his hat. 'Harriet. If I may have a few words.'

He had aged in the five years since their last meeting but so had she, Harriet thought wryly. His hair was greying a little and the bloom of youth had finally left his face but his eyes were as kindly as she remembered. She opened the door, a smile of welcome on her face. She had always regretted the fact that they had been unable to remain friends even though their planned marriage had been firmly discouraged by his parents when her father took his own life.

Marcus followed her into the drawing room and they both sat down: it seemed fleetingly that the past years had not existed. He was such a familiar presence and had been so much a part of her life before she met and fell in love with Godfrey.

'You're looking well, Harriet,' he began, 'considering the . . . the events . . . What I mean to say is . . . '

It was strange to see him so ill at ease, she thought, but she nodded. 'I know exactly what you mean, Marcus. My husband has left me but I am trying not to let it ruin my life. It's not the first time a man has deserted me – Oh!'

Immediately she regretted the careless words for she had not intended them to be a reproach. 'I didn't mean it to come out like that,' she apologized.

Despite the kind words, Marcus looked chastened. 'Could you bear to hear me out?' he said haltingly. 'I do want you to understand what happened then, but have never had the chance to tell you.'

'I can bear it,' she told him, although her pulse had quickened.

'You always have been strong, Harriet. When your father died . . . you were very brave. I let you down badly but you made a good marriage. Oh!' Appalled by his mistake, he stared at her in confusion. 'Now *I've* said something tactless.'

She smiled. 'It seemed a good marriage at the time.'

He leaned forward, clasping his hands nervously, as he rested his elbows on his thighs. He was so close that Harriet recognized the familiar smell of the soap he always used and found it slightly disturbing.

'When news reached us of your father's suicide, my parents were terribly distressed and my mother almost hysterical. You know how much store she sets by the family reputation.' Harriet nodded but said nothing. 'She was terrified by the way the tragedy would affect the Wellburys. My father became so concerned, he sent for the doctor to sedate her. I told them I wanted to go ahead with our marriage but Mother was adamant that it was out of the question. Father wrote to you without my knowledge and—'

'You also wrote.'

'A brief note, that is all. What I intended was to let some time pass, to give my mother a chance to recover, and then to visit you and ask that we delay the marriage a few months to let the scandal die. Somehow the weeks turned into months and when I finally did suggest it to my parents my mother astonished me by saying there were rumours that your name was being linked with another man.'

'Godfrey.'

'Yes. It was a dreadful shock and I didn't know how to

141

react. Since I had apparently abandoned you I could see your argument. Obviously you were under the assumption that I no longer loved you. I was shocked but too proud to beg you to give me another chance.'

She stared at him, astonished. 'Are you saying that you *do* still love me?'

'You were *married*, Harriet, before I realized what had happened! My mother said you couldn't truly have loved me or you couldn't have switched your allegiance so quickly. I didn't know what to think. During the past five years I have never been interested in any other woman so . . .' He shrugged. 'When I knew what had happened – that Godfrey Lester had left you – I decided to talk to you. No waiting this time.'

Harriet was silent, thinking rapidly. She appreciated that he had come to see her, risking a cold reception or angry reproaches, and she felt she owed him nothing but the truth.

She said carefully, 'I wasn't sure that I was in love with you, Marcus, but I was sure that I wanted to marry you. It seemed the right thing to do.' She shrugged. 'In a way I had grown up *expecting* to marry you because my parents took it for granted and never suggested otherwise. Nobody ever asked me if I loved you. You were offering me security and love and I wanted a family.'

'But?' He frowned. 'There's a "but", isn't there?'

'Yes. Looking back, I think I was very young and inexperienced, Marcus, and I wanted something more exciting.' She smiled faintly. 'To be honest, I found myself envying Daisy Pritty – for her freedom and for the exciting life she was leading. Or seemed to be leading. I suppose I was fascinated by the eventful life she led.'

Marcus raised his eyes. 'I would hardly call her life exciting. As I recall, her life was one disaster after another!'

'Of course! With hindsight I see how ridiculous I was but at the time it unsettled me. I wanted *romance*, Marcus.'

'Oh dear! Poor Harriet.'

'I fell hopelessly in love with Godfrey. It was very sudden.'

His expression became anguished. 'Were you ever hopelessly in love with me?'

'No,' she said gently. 'I wish I had been.'

There was a pause.

He asked softly, 'Do you now regret your feelings for Godfrey?'

Harriet knew she could soften his pain by pretending that she did but chose to be honest.

'I can't regret loving him, Marcus. We've been very happy – until now. Good years . . . and if it hadn't been for Amelia . . .' She avoided his gaze.

'Harriet!' He was staring at her in shock. 'Are you saying you *still* love him after what he's done to you?'

She swallowed, her throat dry. 'I don't know any more. I'm so confused, fearful and angry that my heart seems to beat at a different rate. Do I still love Godfrey? Sadly, I think I might, Marcus, but we have no future together.' Tears filled her eyes but she brushed them away impatiently. 'I want to be able to say I have stopped loving him, but that may not be the truth and I won't deceive you.'

'This other woman . . . Amelia, is it?' She nodded. His expression changed. 'I have to tell you, Harriet – I saw them together a few days ago at the train station. I was meeting Father's old friend and they came on to the platform opposite where I was standing.'

'She's very beautiful, don't you think?' Harriet twisted her wedding ring, thinking how little it had meant to Godfrey.

'Yes she is beautiful. Strong women often are. It's the source of their power.'

There was a silence as she gathered her courage to ask the next question. 'How did they seem to you, Marcus? Together, I mean.' She closed her eyes, waiting for anything she could cling to.

'They seemed very much in love, Harriet. She had her arm through his. Everyone was staring at them, including me. She appeared quite unperturbed by the murmurs of disapproval from some of the women.'

'The men were fascinated by her, naturally!'

'It was quite blatant, I'm afraid. As for Lester – I wanted to punch the man for what he did to you but then I realized that I had treated you no better when your father died. I daresay neither of us deserves you, Harriet, but I would ask you to think kindly of me if you possibly can. And to consider . . . whether or not you would give me another chance.'

He took her hands in his and it felt entirely natural. He leaned forward and kissed her cheek and the years seemed to roll away. That was a time of safety and a calm, ordered existence – the very calm she had so despised, the ordered existence she had tossed away. Harriet closed her eyes and, relishing the memory of a secure way of life, made no attempt to pull back from him.

'Marcus,' she said gently. 'I can't promise you anything. It would be unfair to deceive you. If Godfrey stays with Amelia, and I believe he will, I shall try to divorce him but it won't be easy especially if they return to Italy. And it will take months.'

'At least it will give you time to recover from the hurt, Harriet, and to think about a new life.'

She smiled faintly. 'I enjoyed the life I had.' Her voice shook and Marcus suddenly stepped forward and pulled her to her feet and into his arms. Holding her close, he kissed her hair and she made no protest. In her present state her bruised heart welcomed any show of affection and for a long time she clung to him.

At last he released her and regarded her soberly. 'Promise me you will think seriously about what I have said. I still want to marry you, Harriet. I'm prepared to wait until you can see more clearly where your future lies.'

'Thank you, Marcus. I promise I'll think about it.'

'In the meantime can we at least be friends?'

She looked at him affectionately and smiled. 'I'm sure we can,' she said.

* * *

That afternoon Cummings helped Harriet to bring Agnes downstairs and the two women sat together in the garden while Cummings cleaned out the stable and groomed the pony. Harriet was feeling lethargic and out of sorts although she made no complaint. It was hardly surprising in the circumstances. She stared across the lawn to the shrubbery, where as always one or two squirrels dashed to and fro. She was waiting for the right moment to tell her mother about the conversation she had had with Marcus but Agnes gave her no chance.

'About Cummings,' Agnes began. 'I do think we might give him a rise. He is now so much more than just a gardener and we do rely on him for various jobs. He's also been with the Burnett family long before you and I moved to Havely House. We can afford it now. What do you think?'

'A good idea, Mama. I'm sorry I didn't think of it myself. He does deserve more money. What do you think would be fair?' Harriet was still unused to the idea that there was money available to them.

'I think another shilling a week – or maybe a shilling and sixpence. He'll be pleased with that.'

Harriet nodded. 'And perhaps we should promise to review his wages every three years. Then he has an incentive to stay with us and work hard.'

Agnes sipped her lemonade contentedly. 'I've had a lot of time of late to think about Havely House. We should ask professional advice about the maintenance of the building. With all respect to dear Uncle Robert, he has neglected repairs and we should put this right.'

'Anything in particular?'

Agnes held up her right hand and ticked off the repairs. 'The outside paintwork, especially on the weather side. Some guttering needs replacing, the summerhouse floor needs a few new planks. Inside the house, the kitchen walls need freshening up. The steam from the cooking and the soot from the stove have wreaked havoc with the distemper.'

At that moment they heard the rattle of harness and saw

the doctor's trap roll into the driveway. Harriet waved and walked slowly over to meet Angus.

'Do join Mama,' Harriet told him. 'I'll find Cummings to take your horse into the stable while I fetch an extra chair.'

By the time Harriet rejoined them her mother and Angus were deep in conversation and Agnes was laughing delightedly at a joke the doctor had made. As soon as Harriet set down the chair she returned to the house for a fresh jug of lemonade and another glass.

Angus looked from one to the other and Harriet fancied there was a gleam in his eye she had never seen before.

He said, 'I've actually come to invite you both to dine with me next Sunday.' Both women stared at him in surprise and he added, 'My sister, Miriam, and her husband, Humphrey Downs, will also join us.'

Agnes recovered first. 'How very kind,' she said. 'I really don't know if I will feel able to venture so far, Doctor Fletcher, though I thank you most sincerely for the invitation. But I'm sure Harriet would like to be there. Wouldn't you, Harriet?' She gave her daughter a meaningful look.

Harriet, still thinking about Marcus, had been taken off guard by the invitation. Whatever did it mean? she wondered. They had never been invited to dinner with their family doctor before and she wasn't sure even that she wanted to meet his relations. But her mother was giving her a look that could only mean 'Say yes!', so she did. 'I'd be delighted, Doctor Fletcher.'

'I'd . . . be honoured if you'd call me Angus,' he submitted expectantly. 'Both of you. If, that is, you won't consider it an impertinence. Since you are to be my guests . . .'

'How kind!' said Agnes. 'We'd be delighted. Does that mean we should call you Angus or Doctor Angus?'

They all laughed.

'Just Angus would suit very well,' he told her. 'I have to tell you I have no cook – just a woman who comes in once a week to do the housework but Miriam has volunteered to bake us a pie and she is an excellent pastry cook. I'm sure we shall have an excellent meal.'

When he had left them, an hour or so later, they looked at each other.

'Wonders will never cease!' said Agnes. 'But an invitation to dine! I'm so pleased for you, Harriet.' She narrowed her eyes. 'What is it? You look less than enthusiastic.'

Harriet told her about her conversation with Marcus and Agnes's eyes widened. 'The nerve of the man! After all this time. Mind you, I did wonder that he had never married.' She regarded her daughter thoughtfully. 'So the treacherous Marcus still wants to marry you!'

'Mama! Don't call him that. He has done his best to explain how difficult it was for him.'

'You're making excuses for him.'

'We both thought well of him for many years and that was his only mistake.'

'A very big mistake!'

'But now he wants to make amends. It couldn't have been easy coming here today.'

'I suppose not.' Her mother's expression softened. 'So how do you feel about him?'

Harriet sighed. 'To tell you the truth, I'm not at all sure. I daresay we could be friends and nothing more.'

'Until he announces his engagement to someone else!'

'There you have me!' Harriet confessed with a smile. 'And now the doctor is inviting me to dine! I'm wondering now whether I made a mistake in accepting his invitation. What do you think, Mama? Have I done the wrong thing?'

Agnes looked troubled and for a moment or two made no answer. Eventually she said, 'Since you are now a woman without a proper husband I suppose you are as free as air. I should say the more suitors the merrier! Can you see yourself marrying again?'

After a moment's hesitation Harriet said quietly, 'I want a family, Mama. I want a child or children before it's too late.'

Her mother patted her hand. 'I'm sure it will all happen. In a few years from now this heartache will all be forgotten. You will have your children, Harriet. I'm certain of it.'

147

Still amazed by the day's events, Harriet eventually went in search of Cummings to ask for help to take Agnes upstairs again – and to break the news of the imminent increase in his wages.

Friday morning. Daisy sat at the table with Molly in the other chair. On the table in front of them there were three oranges. Molly reached out for one but Daisy slapped her hand. 'Wait, Molly! What did I tell you? You have to get it right first.' She took two of the oranges and hid them in her lap. 'Now, how many oranges can you see?'

'One.'

'Good girl! Very clever!' She added a second orange. 'Now how many can you see?'

'Two.'

Daisy added the last orange. 'And now?'

Molly covered her face with her hands and peered through her fingers. 'Three oranges!' Lowering her hands, she looked at her mother expectantly.

Daisy glowed with pride. 'Clever girl! Wait till I tell Digger.' She handed one of them to her daughter, put one aside for Digger and began to peel the third one, watching with amusement as Molly's small fingers scrabbled at the peel. Fruit was a treat and Digger would complain, thought Daisy, but Fatty Fry had found her a better source of income. Sunday night, after the Grey Nag had closed its doors, she would go upstairs with a man whose name she was not allowed to know. Not a regular, Fatty had told her, and not your ordinary sixpenny job. This man was going to pay her two shillings! But why, she had asked?

Bert Fry glared at her. 'Because he's rich, that's why, and don't ask so many questions.'

'But *two shillings*!' she repeated, astonished.

'Just do what he says and don't argue. Got it?'

That means she would take home a whole shilling, which would please Digger. Feeling rich, she had bought them each an orange on the way home. She looked at Molly, who had wrecked the orange and scattered scraps of peel all over the table and the floor. She was stuffing the fruit into her mouth and juice ran down her chin. 'Good?' Daisy asked fondly. It was working out, she thought. Digger wasn't complaining – at least, not much – and Molly seemed to be settling down. Daisy had seen a second-hand bed for sale for a shilling in a shop in the High Street and had given the man threepence to keep the bed until she could pay the rest off. True, it had one broken leg but she would prop it up with something. Smiling, she imagined Daisy sleeping in it, her fair curls spread across the pillow. This is what she had always wanted. A proper family in a proper home. There would be no more workhouse for *her* daughter.

Digger came home, filthy as usual, and threw off his clothes. He tossed three pennies on to the table and grinned. 'Geezer gave me that when he come to collect his horse! Stupid old fool! He should have seen the rubbish his horse was fed this morning.'

Daisy stared at him. 'Isn't it proper food then?'

He shook his head. 'Course it's not. Costs too much, doesn't it. Fatty Fry's not as daft as he looks.'

Daisy said, 'Molly's been a real clever girl today, haven't you Moll? She can count to three. Cross my heart! She can count those pennies. You just watch her!'

'Later, Dais. I'm dying for a cup o' tea and a wash.'

'Oh!' She looked at him guiltily. She had been so busy with Molly she had forgotten to go down to the yard for a bucket of water from the pump. She flew down the stairs, bucket clanking, filled it and staggered up again. She poured water into a big bowl and while he splashed his hands and face, she put the kettle on and told him about the mystery man Fatty Fry had found for her.

'He's rich!' she told him as she spooned tea into the pot. 'If he likes me he might come back for more. That's what—'

'Course he'll like you.' He turned to look at her. 'You're young and pretty and if you do what he says, whatever it is, he'll come back for more.' He reached for the threadbare cloth that served as a towel and rubbed himself dry. 'Tell you what, when you've got the shilling you can buy yourself a pretty ribbon for your hair. How's that?' He beamed at her.

'Thank you, Digger, but I'd rather pay a bit off that bed I told you about for Molly.'

'And I told you she doesn't need a bed. She's all right where she is. She sleeps fine in her corner.'

Daisy hesitated. She hated arguing with Digger but she had set her heart on the bed. 'She's not all right. She's a kid, not a dog, and she needs a proper bed!'

It was his turn to hesitate. 'Look, if you must have a bed, you tell the shop owner that you won't give him more than ninepence 'cos that's all you've got. He'll take it, believe you me!'

'D'you think?'

'I'm *telling* you. And ask Fatty Fry for the money for a bit of ribbon. Tell him you want to look your best for this friend of his. He'll go for it.'

Daisy relaxed. It would turn out for the best. Digger was on her side again. She grinned at him. 'I'm wondering what he'll ask me to do, this rich man. Extra, like. I can dance a bit but if he wants me to sing he'll be disappointed.'

She laughed but Digger gave her a strange look.

'Whatever he wants, *whatever*, just do it, Dais. I can't explain it. Men can be funny but they don't mean no harm. See?'

Daisy wasn't sure that she did see but she smiled and turned to Molly. 'Coo! Look at the state of you! What a mucky pup you are.' She picked up the towel and gave her daughter's face a quick rub round. *Whatever* he wants he will get, she told herself. This was her family and she was going to do her best for them.

Nine

Sunday morning, on the way to church, Harriet bought two roses and made her way into the graveyard at the rear of the church. She laid the first one on her father's grave – a small undistinguished plot with a small wooden cross instead of a headstone. This was in recognition of the fact that he was sinner in the eyes of the Church – a man who had shot himself through the head when he learned that his 'daughter' was actually the child of a woman who died in the Maybourne Workhouse. The Church had shown no mercy to a man crazed by anguish and shocked to the core by the terrible revelations.

'It's me, Papa,' Harriet whispered. 'I hope you rest peacefully. This rose comes with love from us all. Pray God, you have forgiven Mama.' She kissed her fingers and pressed them against the wooden cross, then straightened. Quietly she moved further on to a similar wooden cross that marked the grave of her birth mother.

'I've brought you this rose,' she told her, then impulsively knelt beside the plot. She whispered to her mother, telling her about Marcus, the doctor, Daisy and Eveline. 'So you see I am a little at sixes and sevens!' She smiled. 'But I am determined to survive my difficulties. Watch over me, please.'

After church she hurried back to Havely House to check on her mother and to see if the rabbit stew she had prepared was simmering nicely. Eveline had agreed to spend Sunday with Agnes while Harriet was dining with the doctor and his family.

Eveline regarded her critically.

'You look pale,' she told Harriet. 'Are you well?'

'Perfectly, thank you, but very tired. I'm still not sleeping very well and my dreams are full of visions of Amelia hovering like a dark angel!'

'I was asking your mother if there was any news of Daisy and the child but she says not. We must hope and pray they are safe and well. Not that I have high hopes for Daisy – she's a reckless, wilful creature – but Molly shows a glimmer of promise . . .' She sighed. 'But you must be on your way, Harriet. You mustn't keep that nice Doctor Fletcher waiting!'

Moments later Harriet left them and began her walk into town. The sun shone and she had her parasol up and was determined to stay calm in the face of what she thought of as 'the unknown'. In other words, Mr and Mrs Humphrey Downs. If they were as nice as Angus, she would like them, she told herself, but would they like *her* or would they be secretly disapproving? She slowed her pace for she *did* feel weary and was unwilling to arrive looking flustered or fatigued. Agnes had lent her a beautiful lace blouse and she had teamed it with an olive-green skirt made of heavy silk. A soft shawl covered her shoulders and she had taken special care with her hair.

When Angus opened the door to her she saw by his expression that her efforts had not been wasted. His face brightened perceptibly as he held out his hand in greeting.

'We're all on tenterhooks waiting for you,' he admitted. 'Do, please, come in.'

Harriet was impressed by the doctor's house. She had never been further than the waiting room and small surgery before and she was surprised to see that the rest of the house appeared reasonably spacious. From one of the windows she glimpsed a pleasant garden. Angus took her shawl and led her into the parlour, where his sister and brother-in-law waited. Miriam, Harriet thought, was very like Angus, but the husband was much older and apologized for being unable to rise when he greeted her.

'Chairbound!' he told her humorously as he shook her

152

hand. 'Beastly rheumatics! You'd think with a doctor in the family . . .' He rolled his eyes.

Miriam said, 'Get along with you, Humphrey! Even a doctor cannot perform miracles, and anyway you love being waited on!'

Harriet sat down, aware that Miriam was eyeing her speculatively. Angus offered her a glass of sherry and she said, 'A small one would be very acceptable.' Hopefully it might help her appetite, she thought.

Miriam said, 'I've made a game pie, Mrs Lester. It's Angus's favourite but I don't know whether you like pastry.'

'Most certainly! I usually . . . I mean I do enjoy my food – more perhaps than I should.'

Humphrey said, 'Then I hope you have a hearty appetite, for my wife has never learned how to make a *small* pie. They are always enough to feed half a regiment.'

Harriet smiled her enthusiasm but in fact she was not in the least hungry. She had awoken feeling a little off colour and had felt unable to face her usual bowl of porridge. Now the sherry made her feel slightly light-headed but she went on smiling and nodding, waiting anxiously for the effects to wear off. Humphrey asked about her involvement with the workhouse while Miriam darted in and out of the kitchen to keep an eye on the famous pie. By the time the topic of the workhouse had been exhausted Miriam announced the meal and they moved into the dining room.

Angus seated them. He was at the head of the table with Harriet on his right and Miriam and her husband opposite Harriet. The pie looked perfect with a warm golden crust decorated with pastry leaves and at the sight of it Harriet's appetite *was* restored. Thankfully she would be able to do justice to the meal. To her relief the conversation flowed effortlessly with none of the awkwardness she had feared and she learned a lot about the family. Miriam and Humphrey had one daughter, Philippa, now grown up and married, and Angus spoke fondly of his mother, which endeared him to Harriet. Harriet talked about Sam and the pony and the gymkhana. Nobody mentioned Godfrey, and Harriet suspected it had been agreed before she arrived that nobody would refer to her unhappy situation. The strawberries came with sugar and cream and soon disappeared and the little party returned to the parlour. By the time Harriet felt she should take her leave, she realized just how much she had enjoyed the company and how far Angus had risen in her estimation.

His family were staying on to help clear up but Harriet was refused permission to help. Angus sent for a cab to take her home and as they waited on the steps of the house for it to appear he asked casually, 'My sister worried that you looked pale when you first arrived.'

Harriet explained that she had eaten no breakfast and the walk had tired her.

'But you have had no other symptoms?'

'None at all.' She frowned, surprised by the questions.

'No . . . nausea? Nothing like that?'

She shook her head and looked at him anxiously. 'Is there an infection in the town? Don't tell me the influenza continues!'

'No. Not to my knowledge – and I would be one of the first to know!'

'That's a relief. Ah! Here comes the cab.'

He helped her up and she thanked him again for his hospitality.

Brushing her thanks aside, he said, 'You must tell me, Harriet, if you *do* have any fears . . . of any sort. I hope I'm more than simply a friend but I'm certainly your doctor.'

Looking down into his good-natured face and, as always, held by the blue eyes, it dawned on Harriet that he was becoming *much* more than a friend. More, in fact, than a *close* friend. Angus Fletcher was becoming important to her happiness. The revelation shook her and for a moment she almost lost her composure. She stammered, 'Angus, you are so much . . . I mean that . . . certainly you are much more than a friend. Please believe me, I value your friendship . . . Perhaps I depend on you too much. It is hardly fair . . .'

154

His expression silenced her by its joyful intensity and she was at once afraid that she would go too far. Godfrey had deserted her but he was still her husband and she had no right to encourage another man. Marcus, she thought, was different because the two of them had a history together. Perhaps Angus was falling in love with her but how could she allow it when she could offer him nothing in return?

'You could never depend on me too much, Harriet,' Angus told her. 'I know your situation and I . . .' He drew a long breath. 'It's early days, Harriet. You have a deal of heartache to survive but I'll still be here if you are ever prepared to . . . to test our friendship further.'

'Thank you, Angus.' Her voice shook. 'You must know how I appreciate that.'

'Then I'm allowed to hope?' He said it lightly and with a smile.

Recovering, Harriet said, 'Most certainly you are!'

Her last glimpse of him left her slightly puzzled. He certainly looked happy but she sensed, rather than saw, an anxiety for which she could see no explanation.

As soon as the front door closed behind Angus, Miriam was halfway up the passage, her kindly face creased by a frown. 'Oh Angus! You're not thinking what I'm thinking, are you? Don't say she is!'

'Is what?' He avoided his sister's eyes and made his way along the passage saying, 'I think Harriet enjoyed her visit. It was a superb pie and she . . . '

'Angus! Don't try that nonsense with me. I'm your *sister*, remember. I've known you all your life! I'm asking about Harriet's condition. Her husband has left her but he may have . . . Oh Angus! You saw her. Pale and wan is the best way to describe her when she arrived. I recognize that vulnerable look. It has to be a possibility, doesn't it?'

He nodded without speaking.

Miriam sat down, still watching him. 'Sometimes a woman knows subconsciously before there are signs . . . I was like that with Philippa. I knew and yet I didn't acknowledge it.'

155

Angus, at the kitchen window, stared out blankly. Humphrey looked from one to the other, baffled by the coded conversation.

'What's happened?' he asked. 'Have I missed something?' Nobody replied. Angus was cursing his own stupidity. How could he have failed to take this possibility into consideration? he asked himself. A young married woman . . . most certainly she might be with child. Godfrey Lester could easily have left her pregnant without realizing what he had done and Harriet was so naïve that she still had no idea.

Humphrey said, 'What on earth is happening? Is it me? Have I said something?'

'Oh, do be *quiet*, Humphrey!' Miriam turned on him. 'How could it possibly be *you*? It's Harriet. Angus and I are wondering whether she might be in a . . . a delicate condition.'

He blinked. 'With child, do you mean? Oh dear!'

Angus turned. 'That would be the most cruel twist of fate!' He knew that Harriet had wanted a child for the past four years and it would be ironic if the moment the wretch abandoned her she discovered she was carrying his child.

Miriam eyed him unhappily. 'She'll know soon enough if she *is* with child. The problem is, what on earth will she do? Who would want to take on another man's child?'

Humphrey brightened. 'The fellow might come back when he knows. I mean, look on the bright side, Miriam. If the father—'

'Humphrey!' Miriam glared at him.

'I'm simply looking on the bright side, dear!' he protested. 'It might be a turning point for the marriage! They might be reconciled. It would give him the perfect excuse to toss the other woman aside. Most likely he would!'

Miriam gave her husband a withering glance. 'It's not what Angus wants, Humphrey! Haven't you understood *anything*?' She laid a hand on her brother's arm. 'Take no notice of him, Angus. Men don't understand these things.'

Too late. Humphrey's words had added to Angus's frustration. He had been so busy trying to imagine Harriet's reaction to the possibility, he had given no thought to Godfrey's reaction. The last thing *he* wanted was for Godfrey to return to his wife, but was that what Harriet wanted, deep down? He said, 'I think Godfrey and Amelia were going to Italy. If they've lost contact he might never know.' Chilled by his doubts, he stared round the room, seeing nothing but Harriet's face as she had been driven away. She had *almost* said she might one day love him – unless he had read too much into her words. Perhaps he had misunderstood. The doubt grew, casting a dark shadow over his mood. He had started the day with such high hopes but all that was of no consequence if Harriet were to bear Godfrey a child.

He looked from his sister to her husband as the full implications of the situation came home to him. 'Poor Harriet!' he murmured. 'No sooner has she survived one disaster she is about to be plunged into another!'

Bert Fry awoke Monday with a start and sat up in bed with his heart thumping. There was hammering on the door downstairs and his first thought was that the police were after him. What had they discovered? he wondered as he heaved his heavy body out of the bed and staggered to the window. He sometimes allowed his biggest cellar to be used for dog-baiting and he often short-changed his drunken customers and watered down the ale when no one was looking. So had someone finally betrayed him?

'I'm coming! I'm *coming,* damn you!' He pulled on a pair of breeches and tucked in his nightshirt, then hurried downstairs in his stockinged feet. 'Hold your fire, can't you? I'm coming as fast as I ruddy well can!' If it was that poxy Sergeant Hodge he'd never get another free mug of ale, that's for sure. Frightening the hell out of him before he was half awake! Enough to bring on a fit!

Cursing and grumbling, he made his way through the shambles of his bar. The revels of the previous night were everywhere. The tables were awash with spilt ale and the odd gobbet of chewing tobacco while several chairs lay on their sides among the broken clay pipes, scraps of paper, dog hairs and dried mud. He saw a discarded boot without its lace and a crumpled red neckerchief that had seen better days. Muttering at the dirty habits of his customers, Bert unbolted the door. A grim-faced Digby Wise pushed past him and Bert at once slid the bolt home again.

'Where's Daisy?' the young man demanded. 'She hasn't come home. I woke up this morning and she's not there. What have you done to her, Mr Fry? Speak up quick before I smash your teeth in for you!'

'I haven't done nothing!' He stared at Digger astonished. 'Cut me throat and hope to die! I haven't touched her.'

Digger was pale, his eyes wide and scared. 'She was here last night late with one of your "special friends", so why didn't she come home?'

'Don't look at me! I'm not her ruddy keeper.'

Digger turned to examine the room as though he expected her to be hiding somewhere. 'You know who she was with,' he said. 'If they're not still upstairs I'll have to get round to his house. So what's his name?'

Bert was beginning to recover from the shock and he now took exception to the young man's attitude. Nice enough when he wanted a job, he thought resentfully, but soon turned nasty when things looked black. Young people had no respect for their elders and betters. 'Don't you come in here making trouble,' he growled. 'I'm not telling you anything. She's probably asleep upstairs. Go up and look. Third door on the right – and go quietly. If they're both there I don't want you upsetting my friend. He's one of my best customers and pays on the nail.'

Digger deliberately thundered up the stairs two at a time and Bert heard his footsteps clattering along the landing. There was a silence and then a yell and Bert set off after him, stumbling up the stairs and along the landing. Together they regarded the empty, rumpled bed.

'She's not here,' Bert cried, 'and you can't prove she ever was!'

158

Digger pointed to the bed. 'Look at that!' he muttered hoarsely. 'That's Daisy's blood!'

Bert moved to stand beside him. To his horror he saw a splatter of large bloodstains, which turned his stomach over. 'That could be anybody's blood!' he muttered, trying to hide his terror.

'If it's not Daisy's then why didn't she come home?' Digger slumped on to a large wicker basket. 'And where the 'ell is she?'

'Someone must have done her over as she was walking back.' Bert began to tug at the sheets, determined to hide the evidence. 'Someone jumped her and bashed her head in.'

'So why is the blood on your sheets and not on the pavements? Don't talk so stupid. She's dead, you fat fool, and he's dumped her body! And your friend did it in one of your bedrooms *in one of your beds.* You're going to have a lot of explaining to do, Mr Fry. I wouldn't be in your shoes for all the tea in China!'

Bert closed his eyes but a moment later snapped them open. 'They could have gone back to his place. She could be still alive.' His voice rose hopefully.

'*Whose* blood is it then?'

Bert longed to punch him. 'Christ Almighty, Digger, you're like a ruddy terrier. Won't let go! And don't ask me his name 'cos I won't tell you. I daren't tell you 'cos he'd knock me into a squashed hat.'

'In a pig's eye you won't!' Digger breathed rapidly, his face ashen. 'The bastard's done her in! You know he has! And hidden her body.'

'Don't keep saying that! For God's sake let me think.' He rubbed a fat hand over his face, closing his eyes to blot out the ghastly scene. This would be the end of him if he wasn't careful. Uncovering his eyes, he decided that urgent action was required. Any action was better than staring at the blood-stained bed. 'Get off your backside and help me!' he instructed, rolling up the sheets. 'Get that pillowcase off an' all . . . Oh God! It's gone through to the mattress. We'll 'ave to turn it over. No one'll ever know. *Come on!* Help me, you useless sod!'

Jumping to his feet, Digger backed away. 'I'm not helping you. It's your mess, not mine. You put her up to it. You provided the room and you took 'alf the money! And . . .' he wagged a threatening finger under Bert's nose, 'he was your *special friend*, remember. I'm off! I'm telling the police. Your friend's done Daisy in and he's not getting away with it!'

Bert moved quickly for a large man. He dropped the sheets and grabbed his tormentor's collar. 'And I'll tell 'em you encouraged her to do it for the money. You could have warned her off but you didn't!' He rubbed thumb and forefinger together. 'Greedy. That's what you are!'

The young man jerked his shoulders and Bert released him. They stared at each other fearfully, then, without another word, Bert took hold of one side of the mattress, Digger walked round to the other side of the bed and together they turned the mattress. Several large yellow marks stained the threadbare fabric but neither of the men commented. Urine marks were infinitely preferable to blood stains.

'We'll remake the bed. Clean sheets, if I can find any . . .' Bert looked round helplessly. 'My cousin Ada sees to the rooms.' He drew a long shuddering breath. 'Then perhaps you'd better go and look for Daisy. Pretend you haven't been here and know nothing about what she was up to. Make it look good for when the police come knocking! What d'you think? We're both going to need a good story. We'll need alibis.'

Digger shook his head. '*I'm* not looking for her. I might *find* her!'

Bert had a dreadful vision of Daisy's crumpled body lying in a ditch and his heart began to race. Had Ollie really killed one of his barmaids? He was a bit of an animal but could he have gone that far? Sweat broke out on his face. This couldn't be happening!

Suddenly Digger grabbed him by the front of his nightshirt. 'Who was it, Mr Fry? Who done for her? If you don't tell the police who it was they might think it was *you*.'

'Me? God strewth! *I* never done it!'

'I believe you, but will they?' He released him and Bert sat down on the bed while the silence grew.

Bert said thickly, 'It was Jerrod. Ollie Jerrod, the fight promoter. Boxing. Rolling in it, he is!'

'My Daisy and a rich fight promoter?' Digger stared thoughtfully at Bert. 'Where does he live, this Ollie Jerrod, when he's not whoring at the Grey Nag? And don't lie to me or I swear you'll live to regret it!'

Shaking with fright, Bert gave him the address and a moment later Digby Wise was gone and Bert Fry was left to contemplate the empty room and brood on the promise of certain trouble to come.

Oliver Jerrod lived in a large house in the middle of the town and Digger eyed it with satisfaction as he leaned against a plane tree on the other side of the street. The door knocker had been recently polished, the windows shone and the curtains looked like velvet. To Digger's practised eyes the house reeked of money and he marched straight across the road and banged with the knocker on the door before his courage deserted him. A maid opened the door, dressed in a sprigged dress with a white apron and cap. Pretty in a pert way, but Digger had no time for women at the moment. She regarded him with obvious disapproval.

'Your master in?' he demanded.

'Yes, sir,' she said in a prim voice. 'Who shall I say, sir?' Eyeing his dishevelled appearance, she laid a slight emphasis on the last 'sir'.

'A friend. It's urgent. Tell him that. Very urgent business.' While he waited Digger straightened his collar and tugged his sleeves down to hide his none-too-clean wrists. He rubbed his dirty boots against his trouser legs and ran fingers through his hair, unsure why he was bothering since this was hardly a social call. A face appeared at the lower left-hand window and a large red-faced man peered out at him. So that was Ollie Jerrod.

161

The maid reappeared. 'He says to tell you he's too busy to – Oi! Who are you pushing!' Her voice rose as Digger forced her aside and made for the first door on the left. As he burst into the room Ollie Jerrod turned from the window, his face reddening with anger.

'How dare you come in here! Get out before I throw you out . . .'

Standing his ground, Digger stabbed an angry forefinger in his direction and said, 'I know what happened last night! You and that little whore.'

The maid followed Digger to the door. 'I'm sorry, sir. I couldn't stop him.'

'Get out!'

She went, closing the door quietly behind her.

Jerrod began to bluster, eyeing Digger as though he were a wild dog about to pounce.

Digger said, 'Aren't you going to ask me to sit down?' His confidence was growing. He had expected a fight promoter to be a large and burly ex-boxer but this man, though overweight, looked weak and fleshy. His pale-blue eyes were slightly bulbous and his small mouth was over-shadowed by a large nose. It was the sort of face that made Digger feel handsome. He threw himself insolently into one of the expensive leather armchairs.

Jerrod lowered himself into a chair. 'Don't know anything about anything,' he told Digger unconvincingly. 'I was at home all last evening.'

'You were at the Grey Nag with a young woman called Daisy Pritty.'

'Never heard of her.'

'There's a witness. You were seen together.'

'Impossible!'

'He'll tell the police he saw you go upstairs with her.'

'Who is this person?'

He had lost some of his colour, Digger noticed. He said, 'Ever heard of Bert Fry!'

There was a long silence while Digger took in the details

162

of Ollie Jerrod's lifestyle. Pictures on the wall, an elaborate gold clock and a thick rug underfoot. Oh yes. There was money here.

Jerrod said, 'What if I did?'

Digger gave a short but triumphant laugh. 'The girl's dead and you did for her. The police'll come sniffing round your door like bloodhounds!'

'Dead! Jesus Christ!' Now his face had lost all its colour, Digger noted with satisfaction.

'So you see, Mr Jerrod, you're in a—'

'I never touched the girl!' he cried, his voice reedy with shock. 'If you want to know the truth I never took to her . . . *Dead?*' He shook his head vigorously. 'I never did anything to the girl and Fry will second that if he knows what's good for him. I took one look at her and changed my mind. Came straight home, if you must know.'

Digger sat back, beginning to enjoy himself. He wanted to say that the police would search Jerrod's house but that was risky because whatever he'd done with Daisy's body it was most unlikely that he'd bring it back to his own home. Better to leave that part vague.

'I don't 'ear the ring of truth there, Mr Jerrod,' he told him with a grin. 'See, that's the trouble. Because the bed you was in is covered in blood. *Her* blood. So I think you *did* touch her.' He wagged a finger insolently. 'I think you like to be a bit rough with your girls and you went too far. Police aren't going to believe you, Mr Jerrod. You know what they're like. They've got nasty suspicious minds!' Casually he crossed one leg over the other and smiled thinly. 'I could say I came by the Grey Nag to look out for Daisy and saw you and her through the keyhole! Bert Fry might remember something along the same lines. Two against one!' He drew an invisible knife across his neck and laughed.

Jerrod's eyes darted round the room as though in search of escape but then gave up. 'I gave her a bit of a tap, that's all,' he conceded. 'She was being cheeky. Wouldn't do this!

163

Wouldn't do that! Young women get like that if you're too easy with them.'

Digger said nothing. He was enjoying himself. Let the wretch stew, he thought, but just then the church clock struck twelve and he remembered he had things to sort out. He had left Molly asleep in the room. Maybe he'd take her back to Maybourne. She could go back to the workhouse, where she belonged.

Jerrod's resistance suddenly collapsed. 'Look! I might have gone a bit too far. Maybe she had a weak heart or something. She didn't look very sturdy. But I swear she wasn't dead when I left her. She was definitely still breathing, so she must have died after I'd gone home . . . Where is she now?'

Digger, a glib liar, had perfected his story on the way round. 'Waiting for the police to cart her away. So, Mr Jerrod, if you want me to help you save your bacon it's going to cost you five guineas.'

He produced a mirthless grin and Jerrod groaned. 'And what do I get for my money – apart from your so-called silence?'

Digger thought quickly. 'I leave the country for good – I fancy Australia.' A stroke of genius, he told himself. Australia had that sort of ring to it. In fact it surprised him that he hadn't thought of it before. Yes, he *did* rather fancy Australia. They had kangaroos and . . . and other weird animals – not to mention sticks that come back to you when you threw them. 'They've got gold out there, too,' he told Jerrod 'You just have to find it, dig it out and it's yours! I daresay Fatty Fry will want a silencer, but that's between him and you.' He held out his hand. 'Pay up, Mr Jerrod. I haven't got all day to waste with you.'

For the next five minutes Oliver Jerrod did his best to talk his way out of the problem but without success. When Digger got up, pretending to leave, he capitulated and lumbered upstairs to the safe. While he was out of the room Digger picked up a small porcelain statuette and a silver snuff box and stuffed them into his pocket. Jerrod came dowstairs, counted five guineas into Digger's grimy palm and then thrust a flabby fist under Digger's nose. 'If I ever see you again

I'll get one of my fighters to mash you to a pulp. Rearrange your face so your own mother won't recognize you! Understand?'

Digger gave him a mock salute and said, 'Aye aye, Captain!' then dodged past him and hurried out of the house. He made his way back to the Grey Nag, where there was still no sign of the police, and ran back to his lodgings to collect Molly. He was sorry about Daisy, she wasn't a bad sort, but she was gone and there were plenty more fish in the sea. Australian fish! He laughed, then breathed a deep sigh of relief. At last something had gone right for the first time in his miserable life.

At Havely House, the following day, the postman handed over the mail with a cheerful smile. 'Another stamp from Italy!' he told Harriet.

Thanking him, she watched him go with a feeling of dread. She did not want to be reminded of Godfrey and Amelia, and had done her best to force them out of her mind but with only partial success. Now she returned to the kitchen and opened the envelope with fingers that seemed clumsier than usual. She recognized the handwriting as Amelia's and her lips tightened.

> *Dear Harriet,*
>
> *I think you need know our plans so that you will make some of your own. I ask Godfrey to write to you but he refuse. We are now arrive from train in Italy where we will live as a married couple until Godfrey is free. He now studies the Roman Catholic faith. The children we plan to have also will be brought up in that same faith. At the moment Godfrey's mother is set against me but the grandchildren will bring about a change. I tell you all the above so that you no longer hope for Godfrey to return to you. You must accept. I am his woman now.*
> *Amelia Bianchi*

Harriet crumpled the letter and sat holding the balled paper as she mouthed a word that her mother must never hear from her lips. This was the last straw, she thought wearily. She was already feeling listless and miserable. Something she had eaten the previous evening had disagreed with her and she had been sick when she first got out of bed. Now she imagined Amelia with Godfrey, standing at the rail of the ship that would take them to Italy. Godfrey had his arm around Amelia's waist and she was leaning against him, her dark hair blown by the breeze. She imagined them next in their Italian home, padding barefoot across marbled floors and staring out over a blue lagoon fringed with palm trees and bright flowers. Lastly she imagined Godfrey returning home from work, crouching down to embrace his children who would speak to him in Italian while Amelia watched fondly from a distance.

For a while Harriet struggled to find some forgiveness for the wrong Amelia had done her but her heart was as cold as stone. She wanted to pray that something large and heavy would fall on Amelia from a great height but no doubt God would ignore that particular prayer.

'Forgive your enemies,' she muttered bitterly.

She also wanted to reply to the letter in words that would make Amelia squirm but firstly she had no address to write to and secondly she felt too lazy to do anything but wish the woman ill.

Should she show the letter to her mother? No, she decided. Why upset her needlessly? Agnes had had more than her share of grief over the years and Harriet had no desire to bring her more. Unballing the letter, she read it once more then tore it into small pieces and tossed it into the coal scuttle. Then she went slowly down to the stables to give Cummings the Italian stamp.

Cecile Wellbury slipped a bookmark into her book, laid it down and glanced up at her son. 'Something to tell me, Marcus? Then sit down, dear.' She patted the sofa. 'Something good,

I hope. I could do with some good news.' For the last two years she had suffered from a delicate digestion and was not an ideal patient. She was a woman who enjoyed her food, and the diet the doctor had given her was too bland for her liking.

Hardly good news, thought Marcus as he obeyed her invitation to sit next to her. Good news to his mother would be the announcement that he had fallen in love with an eminently sensible and suitable woman whom he intended to marry. Harriet Lester did not fall into that particular category.

'I went to see Harriet recently,' he began. 'She really has had the most awful bad luck.' He saw his mother's expression change.

'People make their own luck,' she said.

'They don't choose their families,' he said mildly.

'They choose their husbands!' She fiddled with the string of amber beads she was wearing. 'She chose to wed that Lester fellow. If you think I pity her, you're wrong. She should have married you.'

He looked at her in exasperation. 'That wasn't your feeling at the time, Mother. You and Father were adamant that the Burnetts were ruined. You were very relieved when you finally forced me to withdraw from the betrothal.'

Cecile made no effort to deny this. 'I thought you liked the Rothford girl – what was her name? Alison, was it? She came to play tennis with you several times.'

'Alison Rothford is not the sort of woman I want, Mother. She's dull and self-centred and has no conversation.'

'Then why invite her over and raise her hopes?'

'I didn't, Mother. You did.'

Cecile shrugged. Vaguely she recalled searching her friends for a suitable replacement for Harriet Burnett. Presumably Alison had not been the only one. 'If I did then it was for your own good.'

'You also invited Marion Bewle to a picnic and Eloise Crayford to a party on your birthday and—'

'I was trying to help you recover from the Burnett business. You were very depressed after that disaster and you

167

needed to find another companion. You need a wife, Marcus, and the longer you delay, the harder it will be to change your ways. Married life is a big responsibility . . .' Her frown deepened. 'The older you get, the less women will be available to you. They will all be spoken for. Teresa Markham is a very nice girl . . . '

'There you go again, Mother. I wish you could see that I am old enough to make my own choice.'

Cecile gave a long theatrical sigh, then abruptly her expression changed.

'You say you went to see Harriet? Why, for heaven's sake?'

'To ask if she would give me another chance.'

Visibly shocked, his mother laid a hand across her heart. 'Marcus! Are you out of your mind?'

'Not at all. I want to marry her. I realize that no one else will do. And I was so impressed with her, Mother. She is older and wiser and bearing up bravely under the disappointment. Most women would be hysterical in her place but she is struggling to—'

'She has only herself to blame, Marcus. Godfrey Lester, the son of her great-uncle's housekeeper! What did she expect from someone like that?'

He regarded her with exasperation. 'Mother, you're not listening to me. I knew the moment I saw her that I'm still in love with her.'

'In love with her? Don't talk such nonsense, Marcus. You are simply being romantic and it doesn't suit you.' She glanced up in annoyance as Letty, their housemaid, came into the room with the following day's menu in her hand. 'Not now, Letty. Tell Cook I'll see to it later.' She waited until the maid had closed the door and then continued. 'You are being foolishly gallant, that is all.' She glared at him. 'And don't try to pretend that suddenly Harriet Lester is a suitable wife for my son, because we both know she *isn't*. Disaster-prone! That's what she is. You must forget any such ideas, Marcus. Your father and I will never condone such a union. Harriet Lester is damaged goods, if you'll pardon the expression.'

168

She gave him a challenging look but Marcus steeled himself and returned it with one of his own. 'If she is willing to have me after the shabby way I treated her when her father died I shall—'

'He didn't *die*, Marcus. Your grandfather *died* – in his sleep in his own bed. George Burnett put a pistol to his head and blew his brains out. *He took his own life!* Very different and well you know it.'

'He's still dead!'

'Don't be flippant, please.'

Marcus sighed. 'If Harriet will forgive me for my unkindness, I shall ask her to marry me.' He held up a hand to forestall her protests. 'The truth is, Mother, that if I don't marry Harriet I shall remain a bachelor. It's as simple as that. I shall talk to Father later today when he returns from his afternoon walk.' Seeing the angry flush in her cheeks, he added, 'I don't want us to quarrel over this. I'm sure you want whatever will make me happy.'

'Not if it makes me *un*happy!' She grimaced. 'Oh! This wretched indigestion! All this worry has brought on one of my attacks. You are so thoughtless, Marcus. I need my pills. Not that they do me much good. I shall speak to Doctor Fletcher when he next calls.'

Marcus rose to his feet, hesitating. 'Within a year, Mother, I hope to be married to Harriet and maybe expecting our first child. Is that such a dreadful prospect? Isn't it what you have always wanted – for me to be a settled, family man?'

She screwed up her face. 'Not if the mother of your child is Harriet Lester. Now please fetch my pills from the bedside table. You have ruined my day, Marcus. I hope you're satisfied!'

Charles Swift hurried along the corridor of the workhouse and into the office where the undertaker was waiting. The two men shook hands and seated themselves.

'Mr Hawke, I do understand your impatience,' Swift began. 'Your invoice has been with us for nearly four weeks, which

169

is inexcusable. However, as you know, the funds come from on high, as you might say, and there has been an unfortunate delay. Mrs Fenner has written to you, promising payment as soon as we receive the money.'

Albert nodded. 'But you must understand that a business cannot thrive if its accounts are not settled. Three coffins have not been paid for and—'

'Three very cheap coffins!'

Albert bridled. 'Three very cheap coffins supplied exactly as ordered,' he amended. 'I now have to pay the timber merchant before he will deliver any more wood and I am forced to close the business while I chase up my money! I am not a rich man, Mr Swift.'

'Maybourne Workhouse is not a thriving business either, Mr Hawke. It has no reserves of cash into which we can delve at will.' Swift adopted an expression of exaggerated patience. 'We have paperwork, Mr Hawke, and we are at the mercy of the authorities, who dole out the funds with great reluctance.'

Neither followed up this discouraging information but Albert made no attempt to rise and leave the premises and before either could speak again there was a commotion outside and the door was flung open. Digby Wise came into the room, dragging Molly behind him.

Swift jumped to his feet. 'What d'you think you're doing, bursting in like that?'

'What I'm doing, Mr Swift, is returning this kid to your care. Her mother's gone and disappeared and the littl'un's not mine, so you'd best take her back. I'm—'

Swift said quickly, 'She's not our responsibility any more. She'll have to go into one of the London workhouses.'

Albert cried, 'Disappeared? How do you mean? I thought you and Daisy and Molly were together.'

Molly began to cry, loud searing sobs, and when nobody took any notice she stamped her foot and screamed. Digger cuffed her round the ear but she screamed louder than ever.

The Workhouse Master came round the table and shook her and she stopped abruptly. 'Sit down, Molly!' he

170

snapped and she sat on the floor and put her thumb in her mouth. Swift turned back to Digger. 'Have you notified the police?'

'What about?'

'About Pritty's disappearance. She has no right to abandon a child who will then become a drain on the public purse!'

'Well, I don't know anything about that but—'

'I understood the mother had a job.'

'She did. At the Grey Nag. I got her a job and the ungrateful dolly has thrown it back in me face, so to speak!'

Albert stood up, his hands tightening into fists. 'Have you and Daisy had a falling out? Is that the truth of it? And she's left you?'

'No, it's not like that.' Digger thrust out his chin. 'I gave 'em both a roof over their heads and without a word she ups and leaves. Went to work and never came back and I'm not looking after some orphan brat, that's for sure.'

Molly, realizing she was the subject of the argument, crawled under the table.

Digger went on. 'Any rate, I'm off. Going to Australia to make my fortune!'

The other two men stared in disbelief.

'Going to Australia?' Swift echoed. 'That costs money, that does. How did you get that sort of money?'

'That's my business. I'm off – that's all you need to know.'

Albert glanced at Swift, then turned back to Digger. 'Perhaps you'd better give us her last address. We might need to get in touch . . . '

'Save yourself some trouble. She won't be reading any letters where she's gone!'

Something in his tone made Albert frown. 'Won't she? How do you know that?'

For a moment he looked shaken, then said hurriedly, ''Cos she couldn't read.'

'She might get someone to read it for her. Lots of folk do. *You* may do that.'

'Meaning?' He bridled. 'I can write my name!'

171

Albert took a deep breath. 'Was there another man involved? If so we can find her and—'

Digger gave a short laugh. 'Another man? Yeah, you could say that!' For a moment his face darkened. Then he said, 'For the record, I don't know why she went or where she went or who did what to her – and to tell you the truth I don't damn well care! She brought it all on herself, trailing up to London after me with her perishing kid!' He glared at them, his tone resentful.

Molly began to whimper but nobody took any notice.

'So if she turns up . . .' Albert exchanged glances with Swift.

'She won't! Oh!' He closed his eyes. 'Oh, to hell with her!' Turning quickly, he hurried from the room, almost running in his desire to be gone.

Molly began to cry. 'I want my ma!'

The Workhouse Master shouted, 'Pipe down, Molly!' Thoughtfully, he drummed his fingers on the table. 'So he had money for the fare. Hardly destitute, was he? He could have paid something towards her keep if we'd thought fast enough.'

'But she's not his. Why should he?' Alfred frowned. 'What I can't see is how he's come by all that money. And the way he talked about Daisy . . . Something's not right there. I smell something fishy.'

'Stolen, you mean?'

Albert nodded. 'Most likely. Or forged. But it's more than that.' He shook his head in despair. 'What a mess. Can't blame her for running out on a man like him but I can't see her leaving Molly. And how come he was so sure she wouldn't turn up?'

'None of our business! Let someone else worry about that.' Swift called in Mrs Fenner and handed Molly over.

Albert, the debt forgotten, made his way outside, deep in thought. Worried and suspicious, he decided to call on Eveline Boothby and tell her what had happened. She listened in alarm and suggested they should both visit Harriet.

* * *

'Come in,' cried a delighted Harriet when she opened the door to them. 'Mama is downstairs and will be delighted to have some company! She's working on a pair of cuffs and hating every moment.' She lowered her voice. 'I think she finds it strains her eyes but she won't admit it.'

'I fear she won't appreciate the purpose of our visit,' Eveline told her as she and Albert followed Harriet into the drawing room, where Agnes rested on the sofa wrestling with her crochet. Harriet was uncomfortably aware that the drawing room had not been dusted and dead coals remained in the grate, but at least the flowers in the window were fresh and a faint smell of lavender polish still lingered. It was ridiculous, she knew, not to engage a daily woman for they could certainly afford it now, but she had felt so tired for the past week that she could not summon the energy to make the extra effort to approach the agency. It was enough to get through the day with the shopping and cooking and caring for her mother.

After the greetings they all sat down and Harriet fetched tea and biscuits. As soon as Albert began his story the mood changed and the three women listened attentively. When he had finished no one spoke for a long time.

Then Agnes gave a long sigh. 'Poor Daisy!' she whispered. 'To go off like that. She must have been very unhappy.'

'And poor little Molly.' Eveline bit her lip. 'Barely four years old and an orphan.'

'Hardly an orphan,' Harriet argued.

'As good as an orphan if her mother's run away and abandoned her!'

Albert looked round. 'Or worse! I've got a bad feeling about this.'

Eveline bit her lip. 'It doesn't make any sense, does it? Daisy was so keen to have Molly with her. Why, if she has left Digger, didn't she take Molly with her? She surely wouldn't expect him to care for the child.'

Harriet nodded. 'But somewhere Molly has a father. We just don't know where he is – or who he is. The trouble is,

I suspect Daisy doesn't know, either. I wonder if there is any way we could find out.'

Eveline shrugged dismissively. 'Even if we could find this mystery man I doubt he'd confess to being the father. How would he know about Molly's existence if she didn't tell him?' She accepted another biscuit.

Harriet turned to Albert. 'What makes you think she may be dead?'

He replaced his cup on the tray. 'Digger looked guilty. Even Mr Swift thought so. And he called Molly "an orphan kid". Why would he do that if he thought Daisy was still alive? And he said she "*couldn't* read".'

'She can't,' said Harriet.

'So why didn't he say she "*can't*"? Why say she "*couldn't*" read? Talking as though she was gone. I reckon she's come to some harm. He knew more than he was saying.'

Harriet, taken aback by his words, sought for an excuse not to believe his gloomy theory. He was an undertaker, after all. Maybe he was obsessed with death.

Eveline said, 'If she was dead someone would have found her body – and presumably they haven't. Have they?'

Albert shook his head. 'It's just a *feeling* I have. Call it intuition if you will. I want to go up to London and look for her. If she's still alive someone will know. If I find her I'll offer her a job as my housekeeper and Molly can come as well. I've thought about that for some time now but there was always Digger. The fly in the ointment, so to speak.'

Eveline reached forward and patted his hand. 'What a kind man you are, Mr Hawke. What you propose could be the making of her – if she's still alive. I must say it does sound very suspicious. And all that money Digger has come by. That too sounds rather ominous. Could he have *sold* Daisy? You do hear such dreadful things these days. White slave trade or whatever they call it.'

By this time Harriet was beginning to be infected by her companions' alarm. Suppose Daisy *was* in some kind of danger and they did nothing. She would never forgive herself.

174

She glanced at Agnes, who was obviously upset by the prospect of another calamity.

Her mother said, 'You could go with Mr Hawke, Harriet. I could manage somehow on my own just for a day or two. I could sleep down here on the sofa. A woman might find things out more easily than a man alone.'

Going to London was the last thing Harriet wanted to do but before she could think of a way out Eveline said, 'You go, Harriet. I'll look after Agnes. I could sleep in your spare room if you don't manage to get home by the evening. Your mother's right. People might find it easier to talk to a young woman. They might be suspicious of a man. On the other hand a young woman alone in London might be in some danger but with Mr Hawke you would be safe from molestation.'

It seemed the matter had been decided for her and Harriet could only nod. After a little more discussion it was agreed that they would wait one more day for news of Daisy and if she didn't turn up or send a message Harriet and Albert Hawke would travel up to London on the first available train and go in search of her. There could not be too many Grey Nags. It was not a prospect which filled her with much enthusiasm but her friends were right. Daisy Pritty could not be allowed to simply disappear. Her friends would try to discover the truth. What else were friends for?

It was nearly eleven o'clock that same night when a small brown dog of no significance wandered into an alley about a hundred yards from the Grey Nag and lifted his leg against a pile of rubbish. He wandered on, sniffing half-heartedly at anything interesting. A large rat watched from a dark corner and the dog smelled it but knew better than to attack. Instead he looked for a cat and saw a large tabby on the top of the wall out of reach. Hurling himself upwards in the direction of the cat, he began to scrabble at the wall, barking dementedly. The cat stretched lazily and proceeded to walk with infuriating slowness to the end of the wall, where it leapt up

175

on to a shed roof and disappeared. The dog fell back, staring stupidly into the space from which the tabby had disappeared.

From the nearby road he heard the clatter of hooves, a door slammed, and nearer at hand a window was pushed up and something liquid splashed down into the alley. A movement just behind him caught his eye and he saw that the rat had ventured out and was nibbling at something long and narrow and vaguely familiar. It reminded the dog of his owner's legs. Pouncing, he frightened the rat and inspected the object. It was a leg. It smelled human. Now this *was* interesting. Eagerly the dog began to bark again and scratched busily at the leg with his front paws. He went on barking and eventually he heard someone calling.

'Mick! *Mick!* Stop that racket and get back here, drat you!'

Reluctantly he abandoned his find and without a backward glance, trotted back along the alley, through the hole in the fence and back to his delapidated kennel.

Minutes later Daisy finally regained a degree of consciousness and opened her good eye. She blinked slowly but saw nothing, then closed it again. Her mouth tasted of blood and her tongue was dry but as it moved hesitatingly over her lips it touched a split in her upper lip and then discovered two missing teeth and she winced. Her head ached abominably and breathing was painful. There was an unpleasant smell around her and something was scuffling across her chest. She tried to scream but no sound came from her dry throat. When she tried to raise her head, it seemed that her neck was too weak to support it and she sank back against . . . what? A pillow? Vaguely she had supposed she was in bed but now, instead of a blanket, her slowly groping fingers met something cold and wet and she shuddered instinctively. She tried once more to open her eyes and the eye that still functioned made out a dark sky full of stars.

'Where . . . ?' she murmured and this time she managed to produce her voice but it sounded strangely clumsy and hoarse. She saw a wall opposite her but there was no window. No one would see her. She tried to move her legs but her whole body was unresponsive. Her heart was pounding and the sound seemed to reverberate within her ribs and for a while she was content to listen to the reassuring beat. If her heart was beating she must be alive. Fatty Fry's brutish friend hadn't killed her after all. A small miracle. So all she needed now was for someone to rescue her. To find her and take her back to Digger and Molly.

After what seemed an eternity she became aware of footsteps approaching and suddenly a man appeared out of the gloom. An elderly man shuffling home after a late night out. Daisy tried to raise her hand to catch his attention but the attempt caused an agonizing pain in her lower arm. Once more her voice failed her and, weak with shock and exhaustion, she gave up the uneven struggle and he passed within a few feet and went on his way unaware of her plight. It dawned on her at last that she was in a back alley and injured and she began to remember more of the events that had brought her here. Her mind moved sluggishly and she slipped in and out of consciousness, hovering between life and death. Too weak to care if she lived or died, Daisy closed her eyes and allowed herself to drift back into a dark and welcome oblivion.

Two days later Harriet and Albert Hawke arrived in London and began making their enquiries and by two thirty in the afternoon they turned up at the Grey Nag and spoke to the owner, Mr Albert Fry, who was in his yard supervising two lads who were raking dirty straw from the stables.

'Daisy Pritty?' He nodded. 'I know her. Or did. Good-looker. Wanted a job. Worked here for a few days, then disappeared. Not a word since. That's the thanks you get for helping people.' He glanced over at the two lads and shouted, 'Toddy! Stop your chat and get on with the job. What d'you think I'm paying you for?'

Albert said eagerly, 'We heard she was living with a young man called Digby Wise.'

'That's right, she was. Left him in the lurch, I reckon. He

wasn't too pleased, I can tell you. Went off to Australia, so they say. Real upset he was. Came round here looking for her.' He shrugged.

Harriet was watching him carefully. Either he was entirely innocent of any wrongdoing or he was a very good liar. She said, 'We're worried about Daisy. We think some harm's come to her. She wouldn't abandon her daughter.'

Mr Fry rolled his eyes. 'I wouldn't be too sure about that. She was no angel, that's for certain. I gave her a job because Digger asked me to. Good job it was too. Barmaid. Regular work. But off she went without a word.'

Harriet began to ask if they had had lodgings nearby but Mr Fry was having trouble with his workforce again. 'Use the wheelbarrow, you useless tykes . . . What d'you mean, you don't know where it is? Find it! God Awmighty!' He turned back to Harriet. 'Lodgings? Huh! One dingy back room. Yes, I know where it was.'

He gave them the address and Harriet and Albert set off to find it.

Harriet was suspicious. 'Gone to Australia? I don't believe it. It's too sudden. And as for being upset by Daisy's disappearance . . . If he cared that much he'd have tried to find her and apparently he didn't.'

Albert nodded. 'Most likely came by that money illegally and thought he'd better get out of the country before they caught up with him.'

A woman came to the door in answer to their knock and told them her name was Annie Welsh and she was the landlady. A thin woman with a gaunt face and jaundiced complexion, she leaned against the door jamb and folded her arms.

'Daisy Pritty? You've just missed her by a few hours,' she told them. 'Turned up here this morning looking like death. Bang, bang on the door just as it was getting light. Frightened the living daylights out of me, she did. Slumped on the doorstep, white as a blooming ghostie and all beaten up. Could hardly walk. Must have dragged herself here, though how I shall never know. Teeth knocked out, One eye all puffed up, face swollen, bruises.' She shuddered at the memory. 'But not a word about who done it. Just on and on about Digger and the kid. Molly her name was. Bonny little thing.'

Albert and Harriet exchanged triumphant looks. They had found her and she was alive.

'Did she say what had happened?' Harriet asked.

'She did eventually 'cos I made her tell me. I said if she didn't I'd call a copper. Seems some fellow bashed her about down at the Grey Nag. Half killed her if you ask me. After I told her the young chap had come back for the kid and said he was going to Australia, she just collapsed. Dead faint. I thought she'd croaked. The police come and took her off to the hospital. They said they're going to look into it but they didn't seem too interested. They never do bother with her sort.'

'*Her sort?*' Albert glared at her. 'What's that supposed to mean?'

She tossed her head. 'It means that the barmaids down there have a bit of a reputation for . . . you know. Bit on the side if there's a few extra pennies. Old Fry's a devious devil. Stoop to anything he will and the police seem to look the other way. Men! They stick together.'

Harriet said quickly, 'So she knew Digger had taken off with Molly?'

She gave a sly grin. 'Mind you, he'd slipped me a bit extra to keep my mouth shut and say nothing to no one. Not that I'd want either of 'em in my house again. Not keen on that sort.'

Albert looked grim. 'So where is she now?'

'In the hospital. Where else? The police, they sent for a stretcher and carted her off.'

'We have to find her,' Harriet explained. 'We know where her daughter is and when she's recovered we'll . . . '

Annie gave a short laugh. 'When? You mean *if* she recovers. It wouldn't surprise me if she snuffs it. That'll be murder then.' She tutted disparagingly. 'It makes you wonder, things like that happen. We've never had a murder in this street. A stabbing, yes, and burglaries and the odd rape but not *murder*. This is a respectable street.'

She pushed herself upright and took them to the end of the road so that she could give directions for the hospital. 'You won't get a cab nor a bus round here,' she advised, 'but you can walk it in half an hour.'

They thanked her and set off at a quick pace until Harriet complained of feeling unwell and they slowed down. They then got lost and it took them nearly an hour to reach the hospital and find a nurse who would talk to them about the patient. An elderly man mopping the corridor pointed out a woman seated at a table at the far end. 'Ask her.'

'Daisy Pritty?' The nurse glanced up from the paper on which she was writing. 'Yes, she's here, but you can't see her unless you're family and only at visiting times.' Her rolled-up sleeves revealed huge, mottled forearms and her expression was harassed but at least her apron was clean. 'And visiting time is nearly over.'

Harriet explained that they were friends and that Daisy Pritty had no family. 'She was born in the workhouse and her mother died when she was very young. Surely she can have *some* visitors.'

'It's the rules.' She shrugged, laid down her pen and blotted the page.

'How is she?' asked Albert. 'She's been through a terrible experience.'

'Terrible's the word!' the nurse agreed. 'She says a drunken brute of a man attacked her and knocked her out. Broke her nose and a couple of ribs. She was a mass of bruises! I've seen some sights but that was frightful.' She glanced down at the paper, frowned then picking up the pen, scratched out a word and carefully wrote above it. 'The next thing she knew she was lying in a heap of rubbish in an alley! How she found her way home in that state the Lord only knows. The doctor thinks there may be some internal damage.'

180

Harriet leaned closer and whispered, 'Suppose I say I'm her sister. How would anyone know?'

Startled by the suggestion, the nurse looked at Harriet thoughtfully. 'You'll be thrown out if Matron catches you!' she warned.

'I'll risk it!' She looked at Albert and he smiled approval. 'Give her my kind regards,' he said. 'I'll wait for you outside.'

Harriet followed the nurse upstairs and on the way slipped a sixpence into the woman's outstretched hand. Left alone, Harriet pushed open wide doors and was at once engulfed by the noise of a large ward. There were about thirty beds in it ranged down either side and most of them were occupied and many of the patients had visitors. Two nurses hurried to and fro, one carrying rolled-up bedding, the other a china bedpan. A third nurse was helping an elderly woman towards a door at the far end. Light entered through the large windows placed high on the walls and Harriet was reminded of the infirmary at the workhouse. The sounds were depressing. Someone sobbed, another coughed uncontrollably and somewhere voices were raised in argument. There were even a few shrieks of lewd laughter. A large clock on the far wall said ten to four.

'Third bed on the left,' said the ward sister, 'but she might be sleeping. And don't stay more than a few minutes or you'll tire her out.'

Filled with relief, Harriet tiptoed across the floor and stood beside Daisy's bed. Immediately her relief vanished as she saw the mess the man had made of her face. The flesh was puffy and covered with purple and yellow bruises. Areas of her hair were still matted with blood and there were deep scratches down one cheek. One eye was hidden beneath a bandage. Appalled, Harriet was glad she could not see the poor, battered body. Softly she said, 'Daisy. Can you hear me? It's Harriet Lester.'

Slowly Daisy opened her eyes. 'Where's Molly?' she asked, lisping through her damaged teeth.

'Safe and sound in Maybourne.' She didn't refer to the

workhouse. 'As soon as you're better you can come back and collect her.'

'Digger . . . Australia . . .' Tears trickled down Daisy's face and Harriet wanted to cry with her. She also wanted to shake some sense into her. Surely now she could see that Digger was no good for her!

Instead she said, 'Forget him, Daisy. You don't need Digger. Mr Hawke the undertaker is outside. He travelled up with me to find you and he wants to give you and Molly a home. You can be his housekeeper. The poor man's lonely and needs some cheerful company. He needs someone to look after him.' She did not want Daisy to consider herself an object of Albert's charity.

Daisy didn't answer. She closed her eyes and Harriet thought she was falling asleep again. The minute hand reached twelve, a nurse appeared ringing a handbell and all around her the visitors got up to leave. 'Daisy, I have to go. If anyone asks, I'm your sister. Remember that.'

She waited. At last Daisy opened her eyes again. 'Kiss Molly for me.'

'I will.' Impulsively she leaned down and kissed Daisy's hand, then hurried from the ward before her own tears started.

She rejoined Albert and they made their way back to the railway station. On the way Harriet did her best to answer all his questions. Things were bad for Daisy but they could have been a lot worse and the future did hold a few promises for her. By the time they were ensconced in the train carriage and rattling their way back to Maybourne they had talked themselves into a more cheerful mood, both buoyed up by the satisfaction of a job well done.

For Harriet the next week passed in a whirl of private anxiety as her mysterious symptoms finally alerted her to the possibility that she was expecting a baby. The bleeding she expected each month did not appear and her mother had told her enough on the eve of her wedding to know that this was what she and Godfrey had been awaiting for so long. But that was then and now the prospect of a child without a father terrified her. She moved around the house in a daze of uncertainty, hopefully imagining a variety of scenarios in which Godfrey abandoned Amelia and rushed back to Havely House and his lawful wedded wife. But how was he to know? They were somewhere in Italy but where exactly? And what of Amelia? She, also, might bear Godfrey a child, and that bitter thought cut deeply into her heart.

The most sensible thing to do was confide in her mother but before she could come to a decision Agnes broached the subject. They were sitting together in the garden – Agnes working on the crocheted cuffs while Harriet, beside her on the grass, pretended to read a book about Africa. From time to time she turned a page but mostly she stared unseeingly at the rows of small print and wished she could rid herself of the lingering nausea which now haunted her.

Agnes turned to her. 'When are you going to tell me, Harriet?' she asked gently. 'I'm your mother and I notice things. I think I know what is happening.'

Harriet closed the book with a snap and said, 'It's true, Mama. I'm with child and I don't know what to do.'

Agnes reached down and laid a hand on her shoulder. 'First thing to do is consult Doctor Fletcher. He will confirm it, I'm sure, but—'

'Angus? Oh no!'

'Don't be foolish, Harriet. He will also give you something to relieve the nausea. Trust him, Harriet. He is a good doctor.'

Harriet stared down at her hands. 'I don't want the baby if Godfrey can't share it. What am I to do?'

'Nothing, Harriet. You will have the child whether or not Godfrey returns to you. Godfrey is the loser if he doesn't see his son or daughter grow up.' She set down the crochet work and steepled her fingers thoughtfully. 'Why don't you write to his mother and tell her the news? She's the baby's grandmother and you could ask her to pass on the news to Godfrey. Then it will be up to him.'

'And Amelia!' Harriet was unable to keep the bitterness from her voice. 'She will never allow him to come back to me . . . to *us!*'

'We don't know that, Harriet. There is also the consideration that you may not want him back after the way he has treated you. You might think you do now, but it would be between you for the rest of your lives. That might be harder than you think. Let him know by all means – he's entitled to know – but don't promise anything by way of forgiveness. He has brought you so much unhappiness that—'

'That was Amelia's fault!'

'No, Harriet. *Part* of it was her fault. The major part was Godfrey's fault. He was married. He didn't have to let Amelia control him the way she did. You may not want to accept that, but we're all responsible for our own actions *and* our *re*actions! I know how you feel about Amelia but you mustn't ignore Godfrey's part in the betrayal.'

Agnes was right, thought Harriet reluctantly, but the truth was she *didn't* want to blame Godfrey for any part of what had happened. Right now she was so desperate, she wanted him back at any price. She would write to Doris Lester and ask her to tell her son that he was about to become a father.

Agnes stole a glance at her daughter. 'You mustn't forget Marcus. He has asked your forgiveness and he—'

'Mama!' cried Harriet. 'He won't want to marry me when he knows I'm carrying Godfrey's child! This baby changes everything.' She hesitated. 'Angus Fletcher has also shown that he is interested in me . . . '

'I know. I realized some months ago.'

'But neither of them will want to marry me now. I shall be alone with the child, who will have no father!' Her voice cracked and she was dangerously near to tears.

'You won't be alone, Harriet. You have me.' Agnes took hold of her hand. 'Suppose you had been expecting the child and were suddenly widowed. You would then bring the child up alone. It happens to hundreds of women and they all learn to cope. You will also. And don't write off Marcus. He may well decide that the baby makes no difference to his feelings for you. He's a good man, Harriet. Don't be too quick to judge him.'

Harriet didn't answer. Her mother was trying to help, but in her present state of mind Harriet could not see a way out of the problems that now beset her. She was also dreading the examination Angus Fletcher would have to make to determine the pregnancy, especially as he was now a personal friend.

As though reading her thoughts, Agnes said, 'Perhaps it would be better for you to see another doctor. Eveline might be able to recommend one.'

Relieved, Harriet merely nodded. She felt perversely that life was most unfair. Surely she had done nothing to deserve these misfortunes.

Seeing her expression, Agnes said, 'You will love being a mother, Harriet. It will be difficult at times but never less than wonderful. Even the wild Daisy felt she could not live without her daughter! She made sacrifices to keep her.'

Harriet swallowed. Her mother was right. She had so much more than Daisy Pritty – a devoted family, a home, enough money to live comfortably – and yet she was complaining, grumbling like a spoiled child. 'I'm sorry,' she muttered, ashamed.

Agnes laughed. 'Look at it this way, Harriet. Sam will be an uncle! Imagine that!'

After a moment or two Harriet saw the humorous side of it and joined in the laughter and the tension eased. Perhaps, she thought cautiously, being a lone mother might be bearable after all.

Letty Simms sat in the waiting room and waited impatiently for her turn to see Doctor Kilkenny. Not for herself but on behalf of her mistress, who was convinced that the pills he had given her caused her headaches. The small waiting room was hot and crowded with sick people and the idea of being among them terrified Letty. She had a lifelong fear of illness and infection and would much rather have been told to sweep a chimney instead. She was trying not to breathe too deeply because the man on her left was wheezing dramatically and might be consumptive. On her right a young woman nursed a sobbing baby, rocking it in her arms and crooning soothingly to no effect. The noise set Letty's nerves jangling and she tried to remember how many people were waiting ahead of her.

When she could bear it no longer she jumped to her feet and crossed the room to the door which had been propped open to allow in some fresh air. As she did so a man came in with his hand roughly bandaged and he sat in her empty seat which left her with nowhere to go. She was still in the doorway when the doctor called her name and she went with him into the surgery. Here there was even more chance of infection and she tried to hurry things up. Brushing aside his greetings, she plunged into her prepared speech.

'Mrs Wellbury says as these pills aren't right for her 'cos they give her a headache and she'd like you to change them.'

The doctor sighed as he took them from her. 'Mrs Wellbury never approves of any of her treatments,' he remarked as he read the label. 'She is probably taking the wrong dosage. I tell her but she forgets and doesn't bother to read the label. How many does she take at a time, do you know?'

'Two, doctor, three times a day.'

He made a gesture of annoyance. 'As I thought. It clearly says "one when needed".' He sat down and scribbled a note on a sheet of paper. Folding it, he handed it back. 'Please give this to your mistress and return the pills to her.' He looked at her closely. 'You look very pale. Are you unwell?'

'No, doctor. It's . . . I just need to get into the fresh air before I catch something.'

'Then off you go.' He smiled distractedly and sent her out into the waiting room.

Letty saw a woman standing by the door and gave a gasp of recognition.

'Mrs Lester!' she cried. 'What a surprise.' The woman

186

stared at her without a flicker of recognition. 'It's me, Letty Simms. The Wellburys' maid.'

Mrs Lester gasped. 'Oh! Letty! So it is . . .' Her voice trailed off.

Mrs Lester had reddened and was obviously lost for words but Letty filled the gap.

'Didn't know Doctor Kilkenny was your doctor. He's nice, isn't he? The mistress sets great store by him, him being sympathetic and that. I'll tell her I've seen you.' She looked at Mrs Lester and remembered that she was once going to wed Marcus Wellbury but then her father had shot himself. Still, she'd married that other man, the one who had run off with an Italian woman. What a family. One disaster after another. Letty smiled at her but Mrs Lester said nothing. Cat got her tongue, poor woman. Suddenly Letty remembered that she was still in a room filled with the sick and wounded and with a final shudder she made her excuses and left.

Cecile heard Letty return and called her at once into the drawing room.

'What did Doctor Kilkenny have to say for himself?' she asked.

Letty handed back the pills. 'He said you were taking double the dose and must only take one at a time when needed and read the label.'

'One at a time? What on earth is he talking about? I distinctly recall him saying two. It says two on the bottle.'

'No, ma'am, it says one – but guess who I saw there!'

'Don't play games, Letty. Who was it?' She screwed up her eyes as she peered at the label on top of the pill box. Letty began her story and suddenly Cecile was staring at her in consternation.

'Mrs Lester? Mrs Harriet Lester? Are you sure?'

'Certain sure! I recognized her straight away because they came here to dinner.' Her smile was triumphant.

Eyes narrowed, Cecile extracted every scrap of information about the conversation, then sent her back to the kitchen.

James Wellbury lowered *The Times* and met his wife's gaze. 'Interesting,' he said. 'What do we make of that, I wonder?'

Cecile pursed her lips thoughtfully. 'For some reason she didn't want to consult Doctor Fletcher. One idea springs immediately to mind – that Harriet might be in a certain condition and doesn't want her own doctor to know.'

'But why ever not? He's her doctor.'

'Of course he is but recently the relationship seems to have changed. Remember that Harriet visited with him one Sunday for lunch.'

'She visited the doctor socially?' James stared at her. 'I heard nothing of this!'

'Of course you did. I told you when I heard the gossip. You never pay attention, James. I overheard some tittle-tattle in the kitchen. You know what servants are like. They know everything that goes on for miles around. You could call it a grapevine.' She raised her eyebrows. 'If I'm right, that would solve all our problems because Marcus would certainly not want to raise Lester's child, so there would be no more talk of marriage! Could we be that lucky, do you think?'

He narrowed his eyes. 'Hmm . . . Marrying an abandoned wife would be bad enough but an abandoned wife *with child* would be impossible.' He folded the newspaper. 'Even Marcus would see that.' He hesitated. 'Should we tell him?'

'I think not. He won't thank us for unwelcome news. It will become obvious as the weeks go on. Better that he discovers the truth for himself.'

'Unless we're wrong and there is another explanation for her visiting Kilkenny.'

Cecile shook her head. 'I'm right. I know I am.'

'You usually are, my dear!' he said diplomatically.

Ten

Harriet told nobody that she was writing to Doris Lester. She would wait until it was safely in the post and then confide in her mother. The first covering letter went to Doris and was brief and to the point.

Dear Mrs Lester,
Would you please forward the enclosed letter to Godfrey if you have an address for him? I want you to read it so that you will understand why I am offering him a last chance to save our marriage and to share in the life of our child. Whatever his answer, you will always be welcome to visit and to see your grandchild whenever you wish. As you know we have plenty of room here at Havely House.
My fond regards as ever,
Your affectionate Harriet
PS I was so sorry to hear about the death of your mother.

When she had blotted it she thought about the joy the child would bring to Doris Lester but then realized that if Godfrey did *not* return to his wife, he would no doubt have several children with Amelia and they would also be Doris's grand-children. Her own child might well be overlooked and this thought tormented her. She tried to imagine what Godfrey would do when he learned that he was the father of Harriet's child. Perhaps he would throw up his new life in Italy and come back to the security of life at Havely House. The problem was that Amelia knew exactly where to find him if she was determined to keep him. She would turn up looking splendid while Harriet was looking shapeless and undesirable.

'Damn you, Amelia!' she muttered, furious with herself for these defeatist thoughts but plagued by them nonetheless. 'Have more faith in yourself, Harriet!'

She began the second letter in a less than conciliatory state of mind.

> *Dear Godfrey,*
> *I don't imagine that you will be pleased with my news but I believe you are entitled to know that I am expecting your child. The doctor confirmed my suspicions yesterday. Although bringing up the child without the father would not be my choice I am, as you know, in a position financially to do so and I am looking forward to motherhood. I would never refuse you opportunities to visit the child if you are ever in England again and I have made the same promise to your mother . . .*

Harriet paused. Should she refer to Amelia? She felt it would be sensible and yet she did not want to give the other woman the satisfaction of believing herself important in Harriet's world. Better, perhaps, to imply that the child drew husband and wife together and that Amelia was no longer a factor in the equation. Feeling marginally better, Harriet began to write again.

> *If you feel, Godfrey, that in the circumstances you would like to return to me and become part of the family again there will be no problem. I will forgive you the hurt you have caused me and we need never refer to it again. I'm certain we could rediscover our love for one another but in the end it will be your choice. In your absence I have receieved an offer of matrimony (when*

*I am free) but have made no decision and the baby
changes everything for everyone. I would appreciate a
letter from you either way so that I can plan the rest
of my life and make a happy home for our child . . .*

She reread the letter carefully, trying to imagine how
Godfrey would react – and how Amelia would deal with the
unwelcome news. Because of Amelia, Harriet could not bring
herself to plead with her husband nor could she allow him
to think that she could not prosper without him. He would
wonder who had made her the offer of marriage and Amelia
might fly into a passionate rage . . .

'I hope you do!' Harriet murmured. 'Show yourself in
your worst colours, Amelia.'

*I'm certain we could rediscover our love for one
another . . .*

Was she certain? Harriet did not know but, despite her
mother's warning, she did want Godfrey to help her bring
up his son or daughter. For better, for worse – she reminded
herself. If he came back . . . It was a big 'If'.

*I look forward to your letter.
   Yours, Harriet*

Before she could change her mind she slipped both letters
into an envelope, addressed it to Godfrey's mother and hurried
down to the postbox. The deed was done.

Later that same evening Mrs Fenner was once again checking
in the men who had applied to spend the night in the casual
ward. She entered the room at her usual brisk trot but at once
froze, her heart racing. Daniel Stick, obviously drunk, was
making his way round the room, stumbling and cursing. He
had a bottle of gin in his hand and the other men were eyeing
him uneasily. How on earth had he got in? she wondered
with the familiar feeling of panic. She swallowed hard and
took a deep breath. Don't let him see that you fear him, she

told herself sternly, and fixed him with what she hoped was an icy glare.

'What are you doing here, Mr Stick? You've been told to stay away from this town. I could call the police and have you arrested.'

'Do it then!' He stopped and eyed her defiantly, then took a swig from the bottle. 'They won't do nothing 'cos they're all scared witless, tha's why . . . They're afraid of me – and so are you. You and that cissy Workhouse Master and the spinster lady and that inter . . . interfering Lester woman.' He grinned blearily at the other men. One sniggered but the rest looked hopefully towards Mrs Fenner. Stick continued. 'Went to the police, she did, and put in a complaint about me. I'll do for her, I told them. Gave them a right telling off, she did. Wanted them to arrest me, she did! Said I should be locked up! Why, I asked them?' He swayed and nearly fell. When he had righted himself he said plaintively, 'I . . . I haven't done nothing.'

One of the men spoke up. 'Yes, you have! You've done plenty in your time, Stick. You turned over the undertaker's place a few weeks back!'

He scowled. 'That were nothing. I needed a bit of cash, tha's all. I never hurt nobody . . . 'Cept the undertaker.'

'Serve you right if 'e refuses to bury you!' A young man winked at Mrs Fenner. 'No coffin for you, Stick, you silly bogger! They'll 'ave to chuck you down the 'ole mother-naked!'

For a moment Stick looked shaken by this prospect. 'But I never hurt him – leastways not much.'

'That's a lie!' Mrs Fenner told him. 'You punched him and you knocked him down *and* you damaged his property, which you had entered illegally.' She was playing for time, wondering what she should do next. 'That's an offence.'

'I'd had a few, tha's all.' He waved the gin bottle as though to prove his point and drank again.

'Drink will be your undoing!' Mrs Fenner told him.

An old man nodded sagely. 'No good blaming the drink

when you've killed someone, Dan. They won't hang the bottle, they'll hang *you!*'

There was some laughter and Mrs Fenner seized the opportunity. 'That's quite enough. No drinking in here, Mr Stick. You know the rules. Take your gin and get out of here.' She held up her whistle. 'I'll count to three and then I'll go outside and call a constable.' For a moment they glowered at each other. Mrs Fenner said, 'One!'

He got up slowly and drank the remains of the gin.

'Two!' she said. He didn't move. 'Three!'

He drew back his arm and hurled the empty bottle against the wall, where it smashed into smithereens while the men gasped at his audacity. Stick walked slowly from the room, swaying as he went, and Mrs Fenner followed him at a safe distance. Once he was outside in the street she locked the door and breathed a sigh of relief. Then she looked up and prayed aloud, 'Please God, if you love me at all, get that man out of my life!'

The meeting in Maybourne Workhouse on the following Thursday was uneventful. There were no absentees, the incident with Daniel Stick was reported and the rest of the business was quickly concluded. Afterwards Eveline hurried away to visit a sick friend and Harriet remained talking with the Workhouse Master and Mrs Fenner.

Charles Swift said, 'I hear that Pritty is coming out of hospital tomorrow. Do we know what is happening next? I can't keep Molly here indefinitely if her mother is fit to take responsibility for her.'

Harriet nodded. 'I'm going to be at the hospital when she leaves,' she told him. 'I can't trust her not to disappear again. The plan is that I will bring her back to Maybourne with me and take her round to Mr Hawke's place. He is offering her a home in exchange for duties as a housekeeper . . .' She laughed as Charles Swift raised his eyebrows wordlessly. 'I know! But the man is determined to give her a chance to make good and we have to hope she takes advantage of his generosity. She will have to find her feet, so to speak, and Eveline has volunteered to take Molly for a few days while Daisy learns her duties and settles in.'

Mrs Fenner reached for her shawl. 'Miss Boothby has a heart of gold!'

'She loves the child. She misses her dreadfully.'

'Molly speaks often of her.'

Swift said, 'I can't see Pritty changing her spots. If you ask me, she's a lost cause.'

Harriet bit back an angry reply. The Workhouse Master had been kind enough to keep Molly for the past week when he had no need to do so. Molly was not an orphan. She smiled. 'She will have to work hard. I shall immediately start teaching her to read and write – she must learn if she is to make a decent life for herself and the girl. Molly will go to school when she is five and that will leave Daisy with more free time to do her work. Mr Hawke hopes that by then Daisy will be able to help with some of the simpler bookkeeping connected with the business.'

'The eternal optimist!'

'Perhaps, but I imagine the beating Daisy took recently has taught her a lesson she won't forget.'

'And you're taking Molly today?'

'If you agree.'

He smiled. 'The sooner the better! The child is a real handful. Too bright for her own good!'

Mrs Fenner made her excuses and bustled away.

Swift gathered up his papers and closed the lid of the inkwell. 'Pritty is luckier than she deserves!' he muttered, and Harriet, after a moment's hesitation, allowed him the last word.

The following day, true to her word, Harriet was waiting at the hospital when Daisy was discharged but before she went up to the ward she spoke with one of the doctors.

'Have the police arrested anyone?' she asked without much hope.

'Not as far as we know. Two policemen called but Miss Pritty was unconscious and couldn't answer their questions. Then one came back the next day but she couldn't remember much except that someone punched and kicked her and then she fainted. The police asked around at the pub where it happened but nobody knew anything. Nothing at all!'

'They would say that!' Harriet sighed. 'She told us it was a friend of Mr Fry's but she didn't know his name.'

The doctor sighed. 'Fry swears he knows nothing about it. Says she must have made a private arrangement with one of the customers. She's probably afraid to press charges because she'd have to give evidence. Women like that don't trust the police. They don't trust authority full stop!'

'Someone must have carried her outside in the middle of the night and dumped her among the rubbish, thinking she was dead. *Hoping* she was, no doubt, so that she couldn't point the finger at anyone.'

He shrugged. 'Too scared to speak up, probably. Or maybe it *is* all a blur, as she says. Trying to put it all behind her. But the main thing is that Miss Pritty has survived. We've done our part. Now you must excuse me.'

Daisy looked infinitely better than when she had gone in although she was still desperately pale. She seemed to have lost some of her spirit and spoke respectfully to the nurse who came downstairs with her. Harriet hurried forward with a welcoming smile but Daisy's response lacked enthusiasm. As soon as the nurse was gone Harriet suggested they go straight to the railway station and, if there was time, find somewhere there to buy a cup of tea and a bun. Daisy seemed preoccupied and Harriet hoped something to eat would cheer her up.

While they waited for a hansom Harriet told her that Molly was well and looking forward to seeing her mother again. Daisy listened half-heartedly and said little. At last she said, 'Digger should have come looking for me. Miserable tyke!'

They climbed up into the hansom and the cabby whipped up the horse.

195

Harriet said, 'He doesn't deserve you, Daisy. You can do better for yourself. Make something of yourself . . . I went round to the undertaker's yesterday evening and Mr Hawke showed me your room. Yours and Molly's. Two beds with matching blankets. What d'you think of that, eh? A table and chairs and a big canvas chest for your clothes . . . '

The cabby was already reining in the horses and they climbed down. Harriet paid the fare and they made their way towards a stall that sold mugs of tea and mutton pies.

After ordering, Harriet said, 'Forget about Digger, Daisy. Think about the future. What fun you'll have, you and Molly, with your own bedroom and a proper kitchen where you can cook for the three of you and . . . you like Mr Hawke, don't you?'

Daisy tossed her head. 'He needn't think I'm easy,' she said with a show of bravado. 'I'll be his housekeeper. That's all. I'm sick to death with men! Nasty brutes.' She bit into the mutton pie, ignoring the gravy that ran down her chin. 'This isn't half bad!'

'I'll show you how to make pastry,' said Harriet. 'Then you can make mutton pies whenever you feel like it!' She grinned and was rewarded with a reluctant smile. 'You'll have a day off and then you can go out with Molly and have fun. You can bring Molly up to Havely House and she can ride on Sam's pony. Or you can go down to the beach and buy ice creams – Mr Hawke's going to give you some pocket money.'

'Pocket money?' She glared at Harriet. 'I want proper wages!'

'You'll have a free room and all your food and coal in the winter and a gas light, and that's worth a lot,' Harriet explained. 'If he pays you wages you will have to pay rent, buy your own coal, pay—'

'I see.' She had finished the pie. 'I could go another one of those,' she remarked wistfully.

'Didn't they feed you in the hospital?'

'I couldn't eat the food. Me face hurt and my teeth was knocked out.'

Harriet bought another one and went on. 'When you can read and write you can—'

'I *can* read and write!'

'That's not what I understood.'

Daisy was already halfway through the second pie, ignoring fragments of pastry which fell down the front of her jacket.

'I can write my name!' she mumbled. '*And* read it.'

Harriet smiled. 'There's a bit more to it than that, Daisy. Anyway, when you can read and write well enough you might be able to help in the undertaker's shop. Write down the orders.'

Daisy paused. 'What do they order? Two dead bodies, please!'

Harriet laughed. 'People come in and order headstones or ask for details of the coffins – the prices and the wood they want used. If you do that, Mr Hawke will pay you more money. He's a very fair man, Daisy, and you must realize that. You *must* behave yourself if you want to stay there. No running off or . . .' She hesitated.

'Or stealing! That's what you were going to say.'

'Exactly!' Harriet looked at her in exasperation. Everyone was trying to save Daisy from herself but she was so obviously ungrateful. Hiding her irritation, Harriet said, 'This is probably the last time anyone is going to help you. The very last time.'

'You needn't go on about it!' Daisy looked sulky. 'You sound like the old schoolmarm down the workhouse.' She adopted a squeaky voice. ' "You're a bright girl, Daisy Pritty, but you're lazy!" '

'A bright girl? That was a nice compliment.'

'She was an old bat!'

Harriet pretended not to hear this and, with a rapidly sinking heart, pointed out instead that they would have to hurry or they would miss the train back to Maybourne.

Four hours later Daisy sat alone in their room above the undertaker's. She felt tired and unhappy and she didn't like the plans that had been made for her and Molly. She was supposed to wait a whole week before the child could join them and she wanted her now. She stared round the room, trying to pretend that she did not like it, but in fact it was very pleasant. She had never lived in such a nice place – it was much prettier than the one she had shared with Digger. But that was part of the problem. She might never see Digger again. They had said he was on his way to Australia but maybe they were lying. Maybe they were trying to keep her and Digger apart. Perhaps he was in London, arrested about what happened to her . . .

There was a knock on the door.

'Come in if you must!'

Albert Hawke put his head round the door. 'Settling in, are you, Daisy?'

'I suppose so.'

'I've made us a bit of supper if you'd like to come down. Tomorrow you can make it if you like. Help you get used to the—'

'I can't cook, Albert. I told you that.'

'You'll soon learn. You're a bright girl. A bright, pretty girl. You can have a good life.'

She scowled. 'I was having a good life before everyone started interfering. Me and Digger and Molly. We were—'

'You were nearly killed. Call that a good life?'

She stood up with an elaborate display of disapproval and followed him downstairs. In the kitchen she saw the table laid for two with a loaf, butter, cheese and a jar of pickled onions, and a little of her unhappiness faded. A full stomach always improved her mood.

She seized the bread knife and cut two very thick slices, one for each plate, and said, 'Doorsteps!'

He grinned. 'This time next week we'll be laying the table for three! That'll be fun, won't it? Molly'll liven the place up.'

He held up the big teapot. 'This goes in that corner cupboard. I bought it specially. Mine was too small for the three of us. Sugar's in here . . . and the milk goes in the pantry to keep it cool. My ma used to love the pantry. Always making stuff for it. Chutneys and jams and stuff. Wish you could meet her but she died nine years ago. Poor old Ma. She'd have loved to meet you and Molly. She'd love to know you was here, keeping me company.'

Daisy studied him over the top of her bread and cheese. She was touched to learn that his mother would have liked her and Molly. Digger had never said anything like that to her. 'I can boil eggs,' she offered. 'And fry bacon . . . and peel potatoes and once I made a rabbit stew but Digger had to skin the rabbit 'cos it turned my stomach even to think about it.' She did not add that the so-called stew was a miserable failure, watery and with no flavour.

He beamed at her, apparently lost in admiration. 'I thought you said you couldn't cook! Tomorrow we'll have a bit of bacon and you can cook it and lay the table and I'll be in the workshop polishing Silas Deane's coffin and you can call me when it's ready. I'll look forward to that.'

Daisy was amazed. It didn't take much to make this man happy, she thought as she helped herself to another pickled onion and allowed herself a tentative smile.

Two weeks passed and June gave way to July and Harriet's life was altogether quieter now that Daisy was ensconced at the undertaker's and Molly had joined them there. Snapper the dog had quickly reconciled himself to having an enlarged family and formed a firm attachment to Daisy, who was always tripping over him and scolding him to no effect. He was less sure of Molly and gave her a wide berth, hiding himself under or behind stacks of wood whenever she appeared.

Every Tuesday morning Harriet went to the undertaker's and helped Daisy with her lessons. She was a bright student but very impatient and the lessons never lasted more than half an hour.

Eveline visited them whenever she could think of an

199

excuse, taking round a jar of marmalade or a piece of ribbon for Molly's hair and it was a source of satisfaction that the child and her mother finally appeared settled.

'Although I don't promise myself it will last,' Eveline told Harriet.

Harriet also had her doubts but she kept them to herself, knowing that Eveline needed to believe all would be well. She confided in her friend about the child she was carrying and after Eveline's initial dismay it was her turn to insist that all would be well.

'Godfrey will come back to you,' she insisted. 'No man – no *decent* man – would want to lose his child. Amelia will take second place. You'll see, Harriet. And as for Amelia . . . No doubt she will have found herself a new beau within days of Godfrey's departure.'

Although Harriet had hoped that she could keep her pregnancy secret for a month or so, Angus called one morning to see Agnes and then went to find Harriet in the kitchen, coming straight to the point.

'Rumours are reaching me, Harriet,' he told her. 'I know you are expecting a child. I did suspect something earlier but you did say you would confide in me.' His expression was full of reproach.

She felt her cheeks redden. 'I'm truly sorry,' she said guiltily. 'I didn't want anyone to know, especially you, until I had come to terms with what it means to me. It was such a shock. I had begun to assume that maybe I would never have a family. I needed time to think and Mama suggested we should go to Doctor Kilkenny. She knows you have feelings for me. *Had* feelings,' she amended hastily. She sat down on a nearby stool. 'Because you are more than just my doctor I felt . . .' She swallowed. This was what she had dreaded.

'Embarrassed? Poor Harriet.' He took hold of her hands and pulled her gently to her feet. 'I wanted to know because I knew the panic you would feel.'

Harriet could see that his manner was a little more distant than last time they met. Had they already drawn apart? The idea saddened her.

He went on. 'I don't know what you are planning to do about your husband. Does he know yet?'

She shook her head. Before she could explain about the letter she had sent via his mother, Angus said, 'I want you to know, Harriet, that the child doesn't change my feelings for you.' He smiled but she could see how nervous he had suddenly become. 'In fact I think you should consider this as a proposal of marriage.'

'Angus!' The words echoed in her head. A proposal of marriage?

'I would have given you time to get used to the idea,' he said, 'but this rather changes matters.'

'Oh Angus! How on earth can I thank you? That is so generous.' She stared at him in astonishment. 'Are you sure it is what you want? It's all very sudden and you surely—'

'It *is* what I want, dearest Harriet, but I do not want to rush you.'

She drew back a little. 'I have to tell you, Angus, that I have written to Godfrey to tell him about the child and have sent the letter by way of his mother. I know he's in Italy but I don't know where. I felt I should offer him a second chance if he wants it.'

'Naturally he must be given the choice but . . .' He frowned, obviously unhappy with the possibility that Godfrey *might* return.

Harriet went on. 'I now have a responsibility to the baby and it should have the real father if possible . . . but Amelia complicates matters.' She sat down again and indicated another chair; Angus sat next to her. 'I doubt that he would give up Amelia or that she would give him up! But I felt I should make the offer and if he accepts then I shall do my best to make the marriage work.'

He nodded bleakly, unable to hide his disappointment. 'That is so like you, Harriet. But let me say this. If he comes back to you I will think him the luckiest man alive and I shall wish you all the happiness in the world. But if he doesn't ... or if your relationship still doesn't work, I shall ask you again, Harriet.'

'I don't know what to say except "Thank you".'

He stood up and kissed her gently. 'I have so many calls to make. I have to rush away. Harriet, I hope you don't mind, but I told your mother what I was going to say to you. Just that. We did not discuss the matter further. She gave me her blessing. Go up to her. She needs to talk to you. She is frail but very wise, Harriet, and you shouldn't keep any secrets from her. She doesn't need to be protected from hard facts – she has survived so much already and is stronger emotionally than she is physically.'

He took his leave and Harriet was on the way upstairs when there was a ring at the front door and she retraced her steps. Cecile Wellbury waited on the doorstep. Behind her on the driveway her groom held the horse's bridle. As usual the Wellburys' governess cart was immaculate.

'I'm sorry to come unannounced,' said Cecile, 'but I really must speak with you. May I come in, Harriet?'

Sensing trouble, Harriet reluctantly resisted the temptation to say no and opened the door further. They went into the drawing room and sat down. For a moment neither spoke and Harriet saw that Marcus's mother was greatly agitated.

'I think I know why you are here,' Harriet offered, keeping her voice steady.

Cecile took out a lace-edged handkerchief and dabbed at her face and neck before answering. 'We have heard a rumour about your condition, Harriet. Is it too much to ask if you will confirm or deny this?' As Harriet hesitated she added, 'I know I have no right to ask but ... you will understand my concern.'

Harriet struggled with her resentment. 'You are fearful Marcus will still want to marry me, is that it?'

Cecile stiffened. 'You did turn him down in favour of Godfrey Lester!'

202

'No, Cecile.' Harriet hardened her heart. 'Your memory is faulty. I may have wanted to turn him down but in fact Marcus gave me no chance to do so. He withdrew from me as soon as my father died and our family was facing a terrible scandal. No doubt you encouraged him to step aside from our betrothal.'

Now Cecile's face reddened. 'That may be so but you, Harriet, were inordinately quick to find another husband! Which makes me wonder how genuine your feelings were for our son!'

They glared at one another until Harriet reminded herself that she had fallen in love with Godfrey *before* her father's suicide. Better to let that particular argument die, she thought. With an effort she remembered her manners. 'May I offer you some refreshment?' She hoped the answer would be 'No'.

'No, thank you!' Cecile fussed with her handkerchief, then tucked it away and looked enquiringly at Harriet.

Harriet could delay it no longer. 'Am I carrying Godfrey's child? Yes, I am.'

'Ah! I thought as much!' Cecile's tone was triumphant. 'Our maid saw you in Doctor Kilkenny's waiting room. I suppose congratulations are in order . . . or maybe not. I don't know what to say. You are in an unhappy position, Harriet.'

Harriet could not bring herself to agree. 'On the contrary. I've always wanted a child and now I have one. I'm delighted.'

Cecile took a deep breath. 'I wanted you to know . . . Marcus doesn't know that I'm here . . . to know that James and I hope very much that Marcus will marry Alison Rothford.' She waited for Harriet's reply but none was forthcoming and in the awkward pause she went on. 'They have been seeing each other for some time and she is a delightful young woman. Only twenty. Unencumbered by – how shall I put it? – any *difficult* history. Marcus is un- decided but he will come round to our way of thinking as soon as he realizes that there is no future for him with you.'

'And if he fails to realize that?' Harriet answered coolly. She knew that she was being hard on Cecile but she was hurt by the woman's determination to keep her out of the Wellbury family. Suppose she had decided to accept Marcus's proposal? Cecile's attitude would have been a serious affront and would have created all manner of problems for the future.

Cecile gasped. 'Why then . . . Then we shall make it clear that he no longer has our support.' Seeing the shocked expression on Harriet's face, she abruptly changed her line of attack to one of appeal. 'You must admit that from his point of view a union with the Rothford girl is infinitely more sensible. Another man's child is . . .' she shrugged, '. . . is a great responsibility and a burden not to mention a source of future problems. Are you prepared to allow him to take on all that? If I have to be perfectly plain, Harriet, I have come here today to ask you to give him up. He is too loyal to see reason and will never face up to the truth.'

'That I am undesirable as a wife and as your daughter-in-law!' Harriet searched for a way to defend herself. 'Are *you* prepared to risk his happiness by talking him into marriage with someone he doesn't love?'

'Alison will bear him children and make a good home for him. It will be a good match. Marcus will *learn* to care for her.'

'And if he doesn't?'

Cecile's expression hardened. 'Then he will make the best of it like so many others. Marriage is not about being in love, Harriet. It is about being sensible. I was not in love with James when we married but my parents were convinced it was the right thing to do and I . . . I have never regretted it.'

There was an uncomfortable silence. Harriet studied her hands, more shaken than she liked to acknowledge. If she were honest she could see Cecile's point of view but it seemed very harsh to judge people by the misfortunes heaped upon them. Her marriage to Marcus had been 'arranged' for her by both sets of parents before she had had time to discover what true love was all about. She had fallen in love with Godfrey the first time they met. Looking back, she didn't feel that she had behaved too badly.

Cecile face crumpled suddenly. '*Please*, Harriet. I'm asking you . . . No. I'm begging you to discourage him in this matter. If you care for my son at all, let him go!'

Harriet felt an unwilling admiration for the mother fighting for her son. Would she, Harriet, do the same for *her* child if and when the time arose? And if she did, would she be right to interfere?

She rose to her feet. 'I shall look forward to the news of your son's betrothal to Alison,' she said, keeping her voice steady with an effort. 'Now I'm sure we both lead busy lives . . .' She led the way to the front door.

Cecile paused at the door. 'I'd prefer it if Marcus knows nothing of my visit . . . or the reason for it.'

Harriet nodded and opened the door and, tight-lipped, Cecile allowed her groom to help her into the governess cart. Turning to Harriet, Cecile mouthed the words 'Thank you' and Harriet gave another nod. She managed to maintain a semblance of dignity until the the sound of the horses' hooves had faded. Then she closed the door, leaned against it and willed herself not to cry.

As soon as Cecile arrived home she went in search of Marcus, who was in the barn talking with the farrier, who was not looking too happy, and her son informed her irritably that the man had been waiting nearly an hour to shoe the mare.

'I've asked you, Mother, not to take the horse without checking with me first!' Marcus grumbled. 'Mr Bottomly had an appointment here and then I find you have taken out the governess cart—'

Cecile interrupted him curtly. 'I needed it.' She turned to the farrier. 'I'm sorry you've had a wait, Mr Bottomly, but there are priorities in life and I had urgent business in the town.' To her son she said, 'I need to speak with you.' As he opened his mouth to protest she said, '*Now*, Marcus! I shall be in the library.'

She walked away, her anger surfacing. The visit with Harriet had not gone exactly as she had hoped and she was not used to being opposed. She was certainly not used to being forced to beg for favours. How could she ever have considered Harriet Burnett a suitable wife for her son? Thank goodness she had found out in time to stop a disastrous marriage. Not that she entirely trusted Harriet to keep her part of the bargain . . . Not that there had *been* a bargain, she thought anxiously. There had been no *time* for a proper bargain to be struck. Harriet had shown no humility and had practically hustled her from the house. It was unforgivable. Cecile climbed the stairs at a pace that left her breathless and waited in the library for Marcus to appear.

He, too, was out of favour. How dare he reproach her for needing the horse! And in front of the farrier! True, she *had* deliberately slipped away so that she need not explain where she was going or the purpose of her visit but that did not excuse his impatience. She wanted to reprimand him but that would not help her cause.

He came in and said, 'Why the library, Mother?'

'I don't want to disturb your father. Sit down, Marcus, and listen carefully. I have some very unpleasant news . . . about Harriet Burnett.'

She outlined the rumour she had heard and watched his expression change.

'You had no idea?' she asked. 'She didn't have the decency to tell you?'

He shook his head. 'A child! What a time to find out! Poor Harriet . . . Does the father know?'

'What does that matter? None of it matters to you, Marcus, because this rules out any chance of the two of you making a fresh start. I hope you realize that. I went to see her this morning to ask her if the rumours were true. She made no attempt to deny them.'

'Why should she?'

Cecile gave him a pitying look. 'Because she might have had some ideas about a quick marriage to someone else. Women have been known to marry in haste and pass the child off as—'

'Mother! I hope you're not suggesting that Harriet would do such a thing! I know her better than you do.' He jumped to his feet and strode over to the window.

'Don't turn your back on me, Marcus!' she snapped. 'This is serious. I have to tell you that I was not well received at all. In fact Harriet was most unpleasant. I might even say rude. I'm sorry you weren't there to see it. A very different Harriet from the sweet girl we have always imagined her to be.' Cecile was not encouraged by his expression but forced herself to continue.' I told her you were going to marry Alison Rothford.'

'You did *what*?' He stared at her, appalled. 'Alison Rothford? I would rather remain a bachelor than marry Alison.'

Ignoring this outburst, Cecile went on. 'I also asked Harriet to stay out of your life. Your father and I don't want to see you bringing up another man's child, Marcus. The responsibility . . . the burden of expense . . . It's not what we want for you.'

He rubbed his eyes wearily. 'Don't you care what *I* want from my life, Mother?'

She swallowed. 'I told Harriet that if you marry her we will no longer support you in any way.'

'You threatened her, in other words. Poor Harriet.' He sat down again, covering his face with his hands.

'She was very rude to me, Marcus.'

'I don't blame her!' He looked up, his anger mounting.

Cecile hardened her heart. 'Tell me honestly – do you want to marry her and bring up Lester's child? You don't, Marcus, although you are not yet ready to admit it. She has brought this situation on herself, Marcus, and there is no need for you to step in and rescue her.'

She waited for him to argue with her but instead he picked

up a booklet from the table and riffled distractedly through the pages. Give him time, she thought, and he will thank me for this.

At last he said, 'What can I say to her? How can I face her? I'll be betraying her for a second time.'

'Do nothing, Marcus. Write nothing. Say nothing. She will eventually understand. Your father will think as I do, Marcus. He won't want you shackled to an undesirable wife.' Seeing that he was still unconviced, she said, 'It's not as though she has been left destitute. She lives very comfortably in that big house and Mrs Bly, who does our washing, says Robert Burnett has left them all his money.'

Marcus stared at her. 'And how does Mrs Bly know all this?'

'Mrs Bly lives next door to the woman who works in the solicitor's office. She saw the papers on the desk.'

Marcus rolled his eyes. 'So much for confidentiality!'

'Now do you see? No white knight is needed!'

He nodded and slowly his face cleared and Cecile closed her eyes, weak with relief. The worst was over. 'I shall ask the Sandersons to dine next week,' she told him. 'You remember them?'

'No, Mother, I don't.'

'Steven and Clarissa Sanderson. He's something in the city and his wife was one of the Grantham girls. They have a married son, Herbert, and an unmarried daughter . . . '

Eleven

Two weeks passed and Harriet's nausea lessened much to her relief but she was still waiting eagerly for the baby to move within her. On Agnes's instructions, she rested every afternoon and took a good walk round the grounds every morning and evening. She continued to give Daisy her writing and reading lessons, sometimes being driven to the undertaker's and sometimes asking Daisy to come to Havely House. According to Albert, Daisy was settling in well and Molly was a joy. Harriet began to wonder if it was all too good to be true.

On the eighteenth of July the postman brought a letter from Italy. Harriet took it upstairs and opened it in her bedroom with trembling hands.

> *My darling Harriet,*
> *You have made me so happy with your news. A baby at last!*

Tears sprang into her eyes, blurring the words, and she brushed them away impatiently.

> *I can imagine your feelings – very mixed, no doubt – when you realized the truth. And how wonderfully forgiving you are. To offer me a chance to redeem myself and to share in the life of our child. I am coming home, Harriet, and we shall be reunited. Thank you a thousand times. You are a much nicer person than I am and I don't deserve you but will try to make it up to you in the future.*

*Amelia is distraught but I have taken her back to her
parents, who were not at all pleased to see her . . .*

Harriet felt a flutter of nerves as she read this dismissal
of Amelia. Did Godfrey really believe that Amelia would
stay away from them just because they had a child? It seemed
naïve of him to make such an assumption. The truth was
that Harriet and Godfrey could never be sure that Amelia
would not intrude once more into their lives and disrupt their
happiness. She shivered. This might be the price they would
have to pay for past mistakes.

*But they must somehow work things out for themselves.
What a fool I have been to make so many people
unhappy. Dearest Harriet, I will be with you as soon
as I can. Take care of yourself and our baby.*
Your loving husband, Godfrey

Harriet reread the letter, trying to read between the lines.
Godfrey was admitting he had made a mistake but she took
little pleasure in the knowledge. Instead she tried to imagine
how he had felt when he read her letter. Had he been secretly
hoping for a way to come home? What exactly did he mean
when he said Amelia was distraught? Angry? Hysterical?
She could visualize the beautiful face distorted by anger, the
dark eyes flashing. She knew exactly how Amelia had felt
and almost pitied her.

'But not quite!' she murmured, smiling faintly at her own
honesty.

At least Godfrey hadn't simply abandoned Amelia but had
taken her back to her parents. And he was obviously delighted
about the child.

'Your papa is coming home,' she whispered.

And Doris Lester would be thrilled to hear the news that
Godfrey was returning to his life with Harriet. It occurred
to her suddenly that as Doris's mother had died, there was
nothing to prevent her from coming to live with them at

Havely House. There was plenty of room. With the baby coming (and maybe another child in the future) it would be good for the children to have both grandmothers in their lives – and an extra pair of hands would be welcome as it was clear that Agnes was never to recover her full health.

An unwelcome thought intruded. Now she could never marry Angus Fletcher. She would have to break the news to him and he would be unhappy in the extreme. Tears pricked at her eyes. Her child would have its true father but at what a price!

'I could have been happy with you, Angus,' she whispered, aware of what she was giving up. And she would have made him happy. Angus would have been a good and loving father and a wonderful husband. He would be devastated by the news of Godfrey's return, which would signal the end of his hopes. Poor Angus was yet another person to be hurt by Godfrey's behaviour, Harriet thought with a frisson of guilt. She had made it possible for Godfrey to return and to frustrate any hopes of a marriage between her and Angus. A coldness welled up inside her as she wondered if she had made a mistake that would cost them all dearly. With a flutter of panic she put her hands together, closed her eyes and prayed to God for a happy outcome.

'Why is life so complicated?' she asked aloud, then read the letter again to find out when her husband would be returning to England. There was no date, so presumably he wasn't sure of his travel plans. She would have to be patient.

She went into her mother's room but Agnes had fallen asleep. Harriet left the letter on the bedside table so that she would see it as soon as she awoke.

Harriet was allowed little time for anxious reflection for she had another appointment. Half an hour later, throwing a shawl round her shoulders, she made her way downstairs and set off to walk to the churchyard, where Albert Hawke would be supervising the installation of Robert Burnett's headstone. Agnes had chosen marble and, being a special order, it had only just arrived. She found Albert smoking his clay pipe, his arms folded as he watched a young man bedding in the headstone. She was surprised to find Daisy and Molly there also but Albert explained that he thought Daisy should learn all aspects of the business.

The headstone looked very handsome with a dark polished surface which gleamed in the sunlight and set off the gothic lettering.

Daisy waved a nonchalant hand and pretended to read the inscription. 'In Memoriam . . . um . . . Robert Ivor Burnett . . . um . . . then some dates . . .' Pausing, she frowned then continued. '. . . and then Dearly Beloving and Resting Peace!' She glanced slyly at Harriet.

Albert winked at Harriet, who immediately understood.

'Daisy!' she cried. 'You read that! You *are* making progress.'

'I know!'

For a few moments they watched as the young labourer flattened the earth at the base of the headstone, thumping it with the back of a weighty shovel. Seeing that he had a larger audience, he straightened up, took off his neckerchief and wiped the sweat from his face. He smiled at the new arrival and said, 'It's warm work, missus!'

'I'm sure it is.'

'How's that looking for you now, Mr Hawke?' he enquired hopefully.

After a careful appraisal the undertaker signalled his approval and money changed hands. The young man touched his hat respectfully, shouldered his spade and wandered off.

Daisy tugged urgently at Harriet's sleeve and they moved away a few yards.

'What d'you think of Mr Hawke?' Daisy asked. 'A normal sort of man, would you say?'

'Very normal.' Harriet was watching Molly crawling between the graves in search of daisies to add to her daisy chain. 'Why do you ask?'

Daisy lowered her voice. 'I offered him a bit of . . . you

know! More than a kiss! He looked lonely and him never having a wife or nothing, I felt sorry for him. You would have done the same.'

Caught off balance by the confidence, Harriet floundered. 'I would? That is . . . Maybe but . . . maybe not.'

Daisy paid her answer no heed. 'And he said no! I mean, he said it in a flowery sort of way and went on about there being no understanding between us and too early to think of getting hitched . . .' She gave him an anxious glance. 'Is that normal?'

Harriet breathed a sigh of relief. She felt herself to be on firmer ground. 'Entirely normal, Daisy. It shows that Mr Hawke is a decent man who doesn't want to take advantage of you.'

'Meaning what exactly? Doesn't fancy me?' She looked pained. 'I expect it's because of my missing teeth.'

'No! It means you don't know each other very well and . . .'

'But I've been there *weeks*! I was just, like, being grateful.'

'That's very kind of you, Daisy, but I'm sure Mr Hawke didn't expect anything like that. He gives you pocket money and keeps you both, which pays you for your work. He doesn't owe you anything and you don't owe him anything.' Daisy looked unconvinced and Harriet tried again. 'Mr Hawke is treating you with proper respect, Daisy. You should feel very flattered. It's a compliment. Like saying he sees you as a . . . a lady.'

'A lady? Go on!' She glanced at Albert, astonished. 'Does it mean he likes me?'

'Certainly.' Harriet hoped that the undertaker's hearing was not too sharp.

'Oh! That's good then . . . I made some jam tarts this morning like you showed me. Twelve. Six with red jam and six with yellow jam. Mr Hawke said they were the best he'd ever tasted. The *best ever*! They were good. Molly liked them, too.'

'Wonderful, Daisy.' Harriet's smile was heartfelt. She was

aware of a sense of satisfaction in a job well done. It seemed to her just then that at least some of the troubles of the past months were over and she went home in a happier frame of mind to discuss with her mother the return of her husband.

Agnes extracted a reluctant promise from Harriet not to say anything yet to Angus about her husband's return in case – perish the thought! – Amelia should somehow change Godfrey's mind for him.

'You know how unpredictable he can be,' she warned Harriet. 'And Godfrey blows hot and cold and might get cold feet! Wait a while, Harriet. There's no harm done. A few days or even a week will make very little difference.'

Consequently, when the doctor called in that evening to see Agnes, Harriet said nothing about Godfrey's letter but felt horribly uneasy about the deceit. Her head told her that she should tell Angus the truth, but her heart warned that the opportunities to spend time together would soon be over and that prospect dismayed her. To ease her guilt she rashly invited Angus to stay for supper and, when he accepted, hurried to put together some cold mutton pie, chutneys and a dressed potato salad.

Agnes chose to eat her supper in bed, so Harriet carried up a tray. The invalid diet did not include cold mutton pie, so Harriet cooked her a small omelette, which she sprinkled with chives from the garden. In the dining room Harriet and Angus enjoyed a leisurely meal and followed it with some strawberries. When the meal was over she left the candles unlit and the two of them sat together, talking of this and that and watching the daylight fade.

Harriet described her visit to the churchyard and her delight at the progress Daisy was making.

'Daisy seemed so much calmer and Molly so contented. I began to feel hopeful about their future.'

Angus smiled. 'If Daisy turns out well it will be largely thanks to you and your mother.'

'And Eveline.'

It was at that moment that they heard a thump from upstairs. Harriet jumped to her feet. 'Mama has dropped something!' she said lightly. 'Excuse me for a moment. I don't want her to get out of bed unaided.'

She was quite unprepared for what she saw when she opened her mother's bedroom door. Agnes lay on the floor, apparently unconscious. Behind her, the lower sash window had been pushed right up, so that the curtains fluttered in the light breeze. Confused, her mind tried to make sense of what she saw. Had Agnes struggled from her bed to open the window wider and if so why? The bell was to hand.

'Mama!' cried Harriet and moved towards her but as she did so a rough hand came from behind and clamped itself round her mouth, terrifying her and effectively preventing a cry for help. For a few seconds Harriet failed to understand what was happening but then her attacker clutched her arm and twisted it behind her back until she cried out in agony. A terrible suspicion swamped her senses.

A voice said, 'Not another sound or I'll cut your throat!' and she recognized the blurred tones of Daniel Stick. Fear made her shiver and he laughed. 'Not so bold now, are you? Never thought this day would come, eh? Daniel Stick – the devil himself!' Putting his mouth close to her ear, he asked, 'Is there anyone else in the house?'

Immediately she shook her head. Better to keep Angus's presence a surprise.

'Well now, that's a bit of luck!'

She was trying to look at her mother, but now he had released her arm and was holding her hair, forcing her head back so far that she could not hold back a groan. At some stage, she thought, Angus would come upstairs to see what was happening and then she would try and call out a warning to him.

He uncovered her mouth but almost at once she felt the cold edge of a blade of some kind pressed against her throat. Harriet didn't doubt for a moment that Stick would use it at the first excuse. She caught a brief glimpse of him in the

215

mirror and could see how drunk he was. But not drunk enough, she thought bitterly. Sober enough to find his way over to Havely House to carry out the threat Mrs Fenner had mentioned to her a week ago. Why on earth hadn't she taken the warning seriously? Her mother had been attacked and she blamed herself. Why had she gone to the police in the first place? If she had left well alone this would never have happened.

Risking Stick's anger, she cried, 'What have you done to Mama?' Was she still breathing? Please God, she prayed, let Mama be unconscious and not dead. The thought of her defenceless mother glancing up at the window to see Stick climbing in made her insides churn, and that in turn made her fearful for her unborn child.

'She'll live,' he said, 'but you might not. You don't deserve to live after what you done. Whining to the police and telling them I was dangerous! Big mistake, that!' He shook her head with a violence that made her dizzy. She wanted to plead with him for the baby's sake but he might make it an excuse to harm the child. He might punch her in the abdomen. She felt cold at the very thought. Godfrey was coming home, but to what? His wife and child might well be dead by the time he arrived.

Abruptly she decided that she dared not wait any longer but must alert Angus to their predicament. Before she could change her mind she kicked out at a nearby chair and it fell with a crash.

'What the . . . ?' Daniel Stick, taken by surprise, loosened his grip on her as he reached for the fallen chair. As he did so Harriet made the most of her opportunity. She snatched up a candlestick and lashed out with it, aiming at Stick's head. It caught him a glancing blow on the left temple but it was not enough to do anything but anger him. Collecting himself, he roared with anger and lunged towards her. He was still holding the knife and Harriet saw with terror that his eyes were heavy with hate. In desperation, Harriet dodged out of his way, thanking providence that the alcohol had dulled his senses and slowed his thought processes. Harriet snatched up the chair and thrust the four legs towards him in an effort to keep him at a distance. One leg drove into his stomach and another struck his right leg making him yell with pain.

'Keep away from me!' she screamed and heard Angus's voice from below.

'I'm coming, Harriet!' His footsteps sounded along the passage. Soon he would be on the stairs.

At the sound of a male voice, Daniel Stick faltered. 'You bitch!' he muttered, staggering towards the door. Harriet stepped back, still holding the chair as protection, praying that he would pass her without further reprisals. Fortunately he was more concerned with evading capture and limped past without a second glance. He went out of the door and turned to the right. From the left, Angus's footsteps now clattered on the stairs and Harriet stumbled to the door in time to see Stick pulling himself up the short flight of steps that led to the attic.

At the same moment Angus appeared at the top of the stairs and rushed after him. He grabbed one of Stick's legs and pulled him backwards and Harriet realized with horror that Angus meant to tackle him.

'Don't!' she cried. 'Let him go! He's got a knife!'

The warning came too late and Angus stepped back with a cry of pain, clutching the side of his face from which blood dropped on to his shirt. Thus released, Stick scrambled back up the steps and dived through the door into the attic.

Breathlessly Harriet caught up with Angus. 'There's a key in this side of the door,' she gasped. 'Lock him in!'

He did as she suggested and then they both sank down on to the steps until Harriet remembered her mother and struggled up again.

'Mama!' she told Angus. 'That thump we heard must have been poor Mama hitting the floor as she fell!' With Angus close behind her she ran back to the bedroom, where they both knelt beside Agnes's still form. Angus, ignoring the blood dripping from the cut to his face, felt for a pulse while Harriet waited in an agony for his verdict.

'She's still breathing but there's a swelling just above her eye. I'll lift her back on to the bed and you can stay with her,' he instructed. 'I'll find your gardener and send him for the police.'

'He's already gone home.'

'Right, then I'll go for the police myself. You'll be quite safe while that brute is locked in. When your mother regains consciousness she'll need to see you close by. I'll be back as soon as I can.'

Moments later she heard the clatter of his horse's hooves and the sound of wheels on gravel as he raced down the drive in search of help. Harriet fetched a damp flannel and bathed her mother's face, willing her to open her eyes again. It seemed a lifetime but at last Agnes's eyelids fluttered; then she opened her eyes and gazed at Harriet fearfully as the terrible memories flooded back.

'Oh Harriet! That dreadful man. Where is he? He was here in this room!'

'He obviously came in through the window.' Harriet crossed the room to look out. 'There's a drainpipe. He must have climbed it.'

Agnes made an attempt to sit up but immediately groaned and put a hand to her head. 'He hit me,' she whispered. 'He was creeping past the bed when I woke from a doze and cried out. I tried to get out of bed but he hit me and I fell.'

'What did he hit you with?'

'His fist. I saw the knife in his other hand and I thought he was going to stab me to death! Oh Harriet!' She fell back against the pillows as she recalled her terror but at that moment there was a crash from somewhere over their heads and they both looked up.

Harriet said, 'Don't worry, Mama. He's locked in the attic and Angus has gone for the police.'

Agnes paled. 'But suppose he gets out . . .'

'We've locked him in,' Harriet reminded her. 'He can't escape.'

Relieved, Agnes shook her head, took a deep breath and tried to calm herself. 'And you, Harriet. Did he harm you at all?'

Harriet explained what had happened. 'My neck is painful where he forced my head back and he twisted my arm rather badly, but he hasn't hurt the baby and that's what matters. On the whole we've been lucky, Mama – if you can see it that way! Poor Angus was cut across his cheek and it's bleeding badly, but he is a doctor! He'll no doubt put in a few stitches but I think it will leave a scar, poor man.' She finally managed a weak smile. 'It's a blessing he was here and Stick didn't know it. It took the wretch by surprise.'

'It's a good thing Sam isn't at home.' Gingerly Agnes touched her eye and winced. 'But surely Stick must have seen his vehicle on the drive.'

'No. Since he was staying for supper I suggested he drive round the back so his horse could graze in the paddock with Sam's pony for company.' She regarded her mother with deepening concern. 'I can't believe that man could attack a defenceless old woman who—'

'I'm not old, Harriet! I'm simply older than you!' Agnes corrected her sharply. 'Nor am I defenceless. I was trying to reach something I could throw at him . . . a shoe perhaps. Anything to distract him.'

Harriet leaned over and kissed her. 'I'm sorry, Mama. It was a stupid thing to say and I should have known better. You are certainly not old.'

A hammering from the attic interrupted her and they looked at each other in alarm. Agnes said, 'I hope that attic door can withstand those blows – and where on earth are the police?'

The hammering ceased abruptly and Agnes clutched Harriet's hand. 'Has he broken down the door?'

As if to answer her, they then heard footsteps running across the ceiling, then silence followed by a crash.

'He's opened the skylight!' cried Harriet, alarm flooding back. 'He must be getting out on to the roof. Perhaps he means to climb down the drainpipe and run off . . . or to come back in here after us!' She rushed again to the window and looked up but could see nothing. Withdrawing her head, she closed and fastened the latch window. Turning, she said, 'I'm going downstairs into the garden to see what he is doing up there! I don't trust him an inch. He might be planning some reprisal against the police when they arrive.'

Agnes clasped her hands nervously. 'Reprisals? What could he do from up there?'

Harriet shrugged. 'I don't know, Mama, but I don't want anyone else hurt by the stupid brute. He can't get me, Mama, if I'm on the ground and he's on the roof! Please don't worry about me. I'll be back before you know it – and I'll lock your door from the outside and take the key with me.'

Ignoring her mother's protests, Harriet opened the bedroom door, removed the key, went out and locked it. With the key in her pocket, she hurried along the passage and down the stairs. She went out of the front door and looked up cautiously towards the roof. Slithering sounds told her Stick was clambering over the roof. But why? What exactly did he hope to achieve? she wondered. And how on earth would the constables catch him unless they followed him up there, which would be dangerous in the extreme? A cornered man could do almost anything to save himself and a cornered man under the influence of drink would be lethal.

She took a few more steps away from the building and suddenly saw him. He was pulling tiles from the roof and Harriet knew at once what he intended. He would throw the tiles at anyone who approached him. She had thought the encounter almost at an end but instead it was becoming worse.

'He's going to kill someone,' she muttered fearfully. 'He won't be taken without a struggle.' She stepped further out into clear view. Daniel Stick sat with his back against a chimney, a pile of tiles beside him.

'Mr Stick!' she shouted. 'Please go back into the attic. If

you slip you'll fall to your death! It's not worth it, Mr Stick. Please give up and—'

'Go to hell!' he shouted back. 'No one's lugging me back to that stinking jail!' He laughed crazily. 'Nice view from up here! I can see the workhouse and . . .' He turned his head sharply. 'I see them. They're coming!' He stood up. 'Come on then, you rotten bastards! Come and get me!'

Sure enough Angus drove up with two constables and they leaped from the trap and, seeing Stick, went into a huddle. Angus shouted to Harriet to go inside but she made one last appeal to the man on the roof.

'Go back inside, Mr Stick, while there's still time. Save yourself!'

His answer was a string of oaths and threats which sent a shiver down her spine. He was never going to give up without a fight, she realized, her heart hammering. If she were entirely truthful, she didn't care if he killed himself but she worried about the two young constables and Angus.

The two constables had already run into the house and Harriet could imagine them rushing up the stairs towards the attic steps and a possible disaster. Stick obviously guessed what they were planning and stood up, preparing for the approaching battle. In answer to her appeal he hurled down one of the tiles and Harriet ducked as it flew harmlessly past her to smash on the gravel.

'Go inside, Harriet!' shouted Angus. 'We'll deal with him.'

From above Stick shouted, 'Tha's what you think, you bogger!' He swayed and took a few stumbling steps forward. 'If I go I take her with me!'

One of the constables was already hauling himself through the skylight on to the roof and, seeing this, Stick grabbed a couple of tiles and began to scramble down the roof towards the edge. It was a miracle he managed to stay upright but he did and for a long moment Harriet stared up at him, paralysed with fear and indecision. Nothing seemed real but at that precise moment she thought she felt the child move within her. Distracted momentarily, she hesitated and the next

221

moment she was again aware of Stick. He had stepped forward, his arms outstretched as though in flight and was threatening to jump from the roof – and he was directly above her . . .

As the full horror of her predicament dawned, Harriet froze. She had only one thought. Stick was going to kill her and the unborn child and she was powerless to stop him. Fortunately Angus was not. He moved fast, hurling himself towards her. He caught her round the waist and dragged her out of the way as Daniel Stick fell to the ground beside them with a flat, dull sound that would echo through Harriet's mind for the rest of her days.

An hour later the police formalities were concluded. Stick's broken body had been removed to the hospital mortuary. The hospital doctor had stitched the gash in Angus's face and had reassured Harriet that her child was unaffected by what had happened. Angus drove them both back to Havely House. They were both silent as they drove through the darkened streets and Harriet thought long and hard. Aware that Angus had saved her life, she was no longer prepared to act on her mother's advice regarding Godfrey's return, she reflected. There was no way she could continue to act out the lie and as soon as they were in the kitchen, waiting for a pan of milk to heat through, she blurted out the news as gently as she could. At once she saw the happiness drain from him.

'The letter came this morning but Mama wanted me to keep it private for the time being. She thought he might not . . .' She swallowed. 'She thought Amelia might still manage to keep him in Italy. I'm sorry I deceived you.'

Holding a handkerchief to his still oozing wound, he searched for the right words and Harriet's heart ached for him.

'I ought to say how pleased I am,' he said slowly, 'but that would be a lie, Harriet . . . but since that's what fate has decreed, I see I must accept it. But I do seriously wonder if Godfrey is good enough for you.'

'I hope he is and he *is* my husband – and the baby's father.

I admit that when I thought he had gone for good . . .' She hesitated, not wishing to sound disloyal. 'I knew that you and I could be happy together.'

'We still could be, Harriet.' His eagerness made her want to cry. 'You don't have to take back a man who has treated you . . . who has treated women . . . in such a cruel way.'

Harriet blinked. 'Are you saying he ill-treated me?'

'Not physically. No. I mean that first he left Amelia and then you and now he is leaving Amelia for the second time. Will he stay with *you* when he comes back? Can you be sure of that, Harriet, or are you going to spend the rest of your life see-sawing between hope and despair? All I want is to make you happy and secure. I wanted us to have a family and a good life together.'

Harriet hardly knew what to say to him. She had expected him to bow out politely and now that he was prepared to argue his case she was afraid she would be persuaded.

'I did promise to love him for better or for worse,' she told him. 'And the baby changes things. I didn't expect Godfrey to want to come back, but he does.'

'Does he, Harriet?' His tone was increasingly bitter. 'Maybe he has just grown tired of Amelia and her dramatic ways.'

'Don't say that, Angus.' Troubled, she looked at him. Hearing him put some of her own secret fears into words was unsettling. 'He loved me once. That I do know.' She looked at the blood which now soaked the handkerchief and hurried to the bathroom to fetch a clean towel. He accepted it distractedly and pressed it to his face.

'He doesn't love you enough,' he argued, 'or he would never have left you. If you were my wife you could rely on me, Harriet. I would always be at your side.'

Harriet could no longer look at him because she feared the change of tone in his voice. 'I've made you angry, Angus,' she said. 'I'm truly sorry.'

Startled by the accusation, he softened his tone. 'It's your news that's made me angry, not you.' He took out his watch and looked at it. 'I must go. Suddenly I feel I have no right to be here alone with you at this time of night. By tomorrow you might be reunited with your husband.' He stood up. 'I'll see myself out, Harriet. Take the milk up to your mother and have some yourself. Plenty of sugar. You've both been badly shocked.'

Harriet held out her hand. 'Please let us remain friends. I owe you so much. Without your help this family would be a sad affair.'

He regarded her at length, then kissed her hand. His face was anguished. 'From now on we must remember to be Doctor Fletcher and Mrs Lester,' he said.

Harriet nodded, hiding the hurt his comment had caused.

'I'll visit your mother in the morning.' As he clambered up into the pony trap he picked up the reins, then glanced down at her. 'If he ever leaves you again I shall still be waiting, Mrs Lester. You have my word on that.'

Twelve

In London, on the seventh of August, Godfrey boarded the earliest Maybourne train, tossed his bag into the luggage rack overhead and sank down into a corner seat with a sigh of relief. He looked dishevelled and had had no sleep the night before because his money had finally run out and he could not afford lodgings. There was no way he would lower himself to apply to a casual ward in the nearby workhouse. His departure from Italy had been fraught with problems and caught between guilt and anticipation he was emotionally drained. He had been unable to shave but had washed his face and hands under a street pump. His clothes were rumpled and he longed for a change of shirt but he had been travelling for five days and the few clothes he had with him already needed laundering.

'Morning!' An elderly man settled in the opposite seat and pushed a basket under the seat. A clucking noise suggested that the basket contained a chicken.

Godfrey gave a brief nod. The events of the last few months had worn him down and his mood was sombre. Every choice he had made had brought its difficulties and his mind still reeled under the strain. When he had received Harriet's letter about the baby he had examined his conscience and, after an hour praying for guidance in a nearby church, he'd finally realized where his future lay and had insisted on leaving Amelia with her parents. Bitter memories of their rows had haunted his undignified escape – slipping from the house while she slept and travelling by farm cart and on foot to the nearest train station. He had left Amelia a letter asking her forgiveness and enclosing most of his money.

The man opposite caught his eye. 'Going to be hot today!' he said.

'Yes.' Godfrey answered reluctantly, unwilling to enter into a conversation.

'Going far, are you?'

'To Maybourne.' He looked at the talkative man and saw that he appeared even more dishevelled than he did himself. They were then joined by a young woman with three small children while outside on the platform porters scurried to and fro delivering luggage to the van at the front of the train and passengers peered into the doorways of the train in search of vacant seats.

'Morning, ma'am. It's going to be hot.'

Godfrey thanked heaven that the chicken man had transferred his interest to someone else. He wanted to think about his approaching meeting with Harriet. How would she greet him? he wondered. He tried to picture them with their arms around each other, a passionate kiss and a deep and lasting happiness. Harriet had said she would forgive him and they would start afresh, but could she really put the past behind her? Perhaps she could, for the baby's sake, but it wouldn't be easy for either of them. Doors began to slam shut and the train guard strode past, his green flag at the ready.

A late flurry of footsteps, another door slammed and then the whistle sounded and with a whoosh of steam, a grinding of gears and a scream of metal wheels the train lurched forward and slowly settled into its rhythm as it gathered speed along the track.

Godfrey turned away from his fellow passengers and stared out of the window. He was trying to imagine himself and his wife when their child would be born – a son or daughter. They would be a family. That had been their dream . . .

'Oh Harriet!' He whispered the words, oblivious to those around him and then frowned as the hateful question resurfaced in his mind. Who was this person who had dared to offer Harriet matrimony? Not Marcus Wellbury, that was certain, for he had blotted his copybook when Harriet's father died. Who else did she know? Would she be making comparisons? Suppose she decided a reconciliation wasn't possible after all . . . Would she leave him? If so his desertion of Amelia would have been pointless. Closing his eyes, he longed for sleep and the chance to forget everything but even the rocking of the train could not soothe his shattered spirit.

Eveline, Harriet and Agnes were having tea in the garden later that day. Harriet had baked some scones and Eveline had brought some raspberries from her garden. They sat in the shade of an elderly chestnut tree enjoying the slight breeze. Harriet was pleased to see how much better her mother looked – her recovery from Stick's attack had surprised them all. There was a flush in her cheeks and her conversation was animated. The three women had talked over the details of the morning's meeting at the workhouse and were agreed that Charles Swift was a conscientious Master and were pleased he had agreed to stay on for another five years. Although Agnes no longer attended the meetings she still retained a strong link through Harriet and had recently suggested that the inmates should attend a summer picnic in the grounds of Havely House by way of a special treat.

Eveline had been informed of Godfrey's imminent return, so inevitably the talk turned eventually to the subject of his return.

Agnes smiled as she spread cream and jam on to her scone. 'I can forgive him anything now that I know he loves his child.'

Eveline looked at Harriet. 'Are you hoping for a boy or a girl?'

'I have no preference but I expect Godfrey wants a son. Men do, don't they? Mama has saved the family christening gown which Sam and I both wore.'

'And does Sam know about the baby and about Godfrey's return?'

'I wrote to him as soon as I received Godfrey's letter.' She brushed crumbs from her skirt. 'He'll be home for the holidays soon and Doris Lester has agreed to come and live with us so we shall be one big happy family!'

As she spoke a shadow passed over Eveline's face and Harriet regretted her words. Quickly she said, 'And I hope you, too, consider yourself part of the family, Eveline. I'd be honoured if you'd agree to be the baby's godmother.'

Eveline beamed. 'Godmother? Oh Harriet, I'd be delighted.'

Agnes nodded. 'You are an honorary member of our family, Eveline! Always welcome . . . Oh!' She glanced past Harriet towards the end of the drive. 'We have company. It's a policeman. I think it's Sergeant Tulley.'

Harriet sighed. 'Not again! It seems we shall never hear the last of Daniel Stick! I'm told I have to appear at the inquest as a witness but they have delayed it once already.' She stood up. 'There's plenty of tea in the pot if anyone would like another cup. Help yourselves while I deal with our visitor.'

Crossing the lawn, Harriet produced a smile but to her surprise the sergeant's expression was guarded.

'Mrs Lester, I have some news for you. I wonder if we—'

'Don't tell me, they have postponed the inquest again!'

'No. I wonder could we go inside. I have . . . That is, it's rather hot today.'

She looked at him in surprise and saw that he did look uncomfortable in his heavy uniform. 'We could move under the trees.'

'I'd prefer to go inside, Mrs Lester, if you don't mind. I'd . . . I'd like a glass of water.'

'Certainly.' She led the way. 'Are you feeling unwell, Sergeant?'

He hesitated. 'A little unhappy, Mrs Lester, but I'll explain when we get inside.'

Harriet directed him to the drawing room and brought him a glass of water. To her surprise he made no attempt to drink it. Instead he insisted that they both sat down and something in his eyes sent a frisson of fear down her spine.

'Oh no! Not Sam!' she cried. 'Something's happened to him! Please tell me at once!'

'Not Sam, Mrs Lester.' He seemed intrigued by his shoes and bent to retie a shoelace. 'Mrs Lester, there's been a derailment. An accident. The London train. Just a few miles from London.'

Harriet stared at him, uncomprehending. 'Not Sam?'

'Sam's fine, Mrs Lester, but there were casualties. Serious casualties. Your husband was travelling . . . '

'Godfrey! On the train from London?' For a few seconds her face lit up, then her eyes widened. 'Casualties? Dear God! Is he hurt?'

The sergeant nodded, then handed her the untouched glass of water. 'Take a few sips,' he suggested. 'Steady your nerves. The news isn't good.'

Obediently she drank a mouthful of water but her hand was trembling and she set down the glass. 'Is he in hospital?'

'Mrs Lester, I'm afraid your husband is dead. He was killed in the crash along with two other poor souls and eight injured. I'm so sorry.'

Harriet watched him, trying desperately not to believe him, searching for another way of understanding what he had told her. 'He was *killed*?'

'Yes. I'm sorry to bring such terrible news.'

She told herself it was a mistake. 'But how did you identify him? How do you know . . . ? You can't be sure!'

'We found a letter in his pocket. It's from you at this address. Mrs Lester, I'm afraid there's no doubt at all. It is your husband.' He rose to his feet. 'With your permission I'll call Miss Boothby in. You need somebody with you and I know your mother is too frail. I'll break the news gently to your mother.'

Without waiting for her permission, he left the room and Harriet was left to her thoughts. Godfrey was dead! He was on his way back to her but had been killed in a train crash.

229

He had come all the way from Italy and had died only a few miles from Maybourne. Instinctively she put a hand on her abdomen where the child was growing and closed her eyes. 'Your papa . . . !' she whispered. 'Poor baby! Oh God! You will never see your papa!' And Godfrey would never see his child. Tears filled her eyes and ran unheeded down her face. And I will never see Godfrey again, she thought. We will *never* be a family.

Moments later Eveline rushed into the room, sat beside her and took hold of her hands. 'My dear! What can I say? Such terrible, *terrible* news!'

They stared at each other and then Eveline put her arms around Harriet and they cried together until Sergeant Tulley returned. He said, 'Mrs Lester, your mother needs someone but first I must ask you a few questions.'

'I'll go to her.' Eveline hurried from the room.

Harriet, trembling with shock, found a handkerchief and wiped her eyes.

The sergeant said, 'It's about his other relatives who should be—'

'Oh! His mother!' Harriet cried and covered her face with her hands. 'She is living in Dorset but I have her address. Poor woman. She adored her son. She'll be devastated by the news. Who will tell her?'

'The police can deal with it. Don't fret yourself. You have enough to think about with that little one on the way.' He produced notebook and pencil and Harriet gave Doris's address. The sergeant advised her gently that she would be needed to identify Godfrey's body and it was agreed she would delay that task until the next day.

Thinking about Doris's loss added immeasurably to Harriet's grief and by the time Eveline and the sergeant eventually left them, both Harriet and Agnes were close to breaking point. Fortunately, just before eight o'clock, Angus Fletcher, alerted by Sergeant Tulley, turned up to offer much-needed support.

* * *

The next day the doctor was tied up by his surgeries and house calls and Eveline volunteered to accompany Harriet to the hospital where the bodies of the crash victims were being kept until the police and railway authorities had finished their enquiries into the disaster.

'I'd love to accept your offer,' Harriet told her friend, 'but then there will be no one to stay with Mama. I really am able to deal with this on my own, Eveline. I'll go up by train and be back again within an hour or two.'

'By *train*?' Eveline stared at her. 'Can you bear it?'

'I have to. Life has to go on, doesn't it? And I feel the need to *do* something. Something positive. If I don't keep busy I fear I shall sink into a deep depression.'

Eveline regarded her doubtfully. 'If you insist, Harriet. I'll willingly stay with your mother but you have had a terrible shock and you mustn't overdo things.'

Before she could change her mind, Harriet set off for the station and had only a twenty-minute wait for the next London train. When she reached her destination she took a taxi to the hospital and was shown into a small room where a police constable was taking down names and addresses of those who came to enquire. He was young, probably no more than twenty-two or twenty-three and the strain of his work was apparent. He was pale and fidgeted frequently with the collar of his tunic.

'Name?' He gave her a quick glance, then concentrated on the form he was filling in.

'Mrs Godfrey Lester.'

His pen scratched its way across the form. 'Address?'

She gave it and he wrote again. She said, 'My husband had been abroad . . . to Italy. He was on his way home.' These few facts were intended to head off any awkward questions.

'We have a piece of your husband's luggage. A bag in which we found the letter. Would you like to take it away with you?'

She nodded and he crossed to a table at the far end of the

room and came back with Godfrey's bag. Inside she found a few clothes, toothbrush and comb and two presents wrapped in tissue paper. One was labelled *To my darling Harriet* and the other *To baby*. Harriet broke down at the sight of these mute proofs of Godfrey's love for her and minutes passed before she could see clearly enough to sign the receipt.

The constable said, 'I'm sorry, Mrs Lester, for your loss. The railway authorities also offer their condolences.'

Harriet nodded distractedly and when the form was completed she was asked to wait a moment. After a further wait a man carrying a blue folder appeared and introduced himself as Mr Hollander. She followed him downstairs and into the white-tiled mortuary where four bodies lay on trestles, each covered with a white cloth. Without hesitation he guided her to the first trestle and gently drew back the white cloth. Harriet gasped. Her husband looked calm and his face was untouched. No sign of blood or broken bones. It was a relief to see him looking normal – in fact she would have been unsurprised to learn that he was only sleeping and not dead at all. 'How exactly did he die?' she asked.

He opened the folder and consulted the first page to refresh his memory.

'Your husband was thrown from his seat and crushed . . .' he placed his hand over his chest, 'here when the wall of the carriage collapsed on to him. The other two victims were found in the same area and had similar injuries. I can assure you it would have been very quick. And almost no pain. It would have been a merciful death, Mrs Lester.'

'Would he have had time to know he was dying?'

Mr Hollander hesitated, then nodded. 'I believe he would but it would have been a very brief realization before the end came.'

So Godfrey would have known that he would never see them again. Harriet drew in a long shuddering breath. Had she, by writing that letter, somehow drawn him towards this unhappy end? For a moment her senses reeled but, frantic with the prospect of possible guilt, she quickly thrust the idea into the darker recesses of her mind. This was not her fault. How *could* she blame herself for the accident? It was the responsibility of the railway.

Harriet glanced around. 'There are four bodies here,' she said. 'Not three.'

'The third person, a woman, died of her injuries a few moments ago.'

He spoke so dispassionately that Harriet had to remind herself that doctors and nurses must be able to distance themselves from their work to avoid the constant trauma of unavoidable deaths. She turned back to Godfrey. So peaceful, she reflected sadly. Why had the last few months of his life been so full of anguish and despair? If only Amelia had stayed away from them. Harriet wondered who would tell Amelia of Godfrey's death. Presumably she should be notified in time for the funeral – she did love him – but it was not Harriet's job to try to get in touch. Doris Lester might do so but in her heart Harriet hoped that Amelia would *not* appear at the funeral.

She sighed. If only she could turn back the clock. Perhaps with hindsight she could have dealt more sensibly with the threat of Amelia.

'Mrs Lester?'

Startled, she realized that Mr Hollander was speaking to her. He was hinting that it was time to go. He said, 'The police will tell you when you can arrange for collection of the body so that you can make plans for the funeral and notify an undertaker.'

Harriet leaned over and kissed Godfrey's cold face and smoothed his hair. She would remember only the good times they had shared. She whispered, 'Goodbye my dearest. I'll talk often of you to your child so that you will never be forgotten.'

The church clock struck twelve noon as the last of the mourners entered the church for the funeral of Godfrey Lester. Harriet sat in the front row with Sam on one side and Doris

Lester on the other. The date was the twenty-ninth of August
– after an agonizing three-week delay caused by the contin-
uation of the police investigations into the accident. Doris
had moved into Havely House and Harriet was grateful for
her comforting presence. Sam was on holiday from school.
In the pew behind Harriet, Angus Fletcher sat alongside
Eveline Boothby and, further back, Daisy sat with Molly.
The doctor had advised Agnes to stay at home and not risk
her health further, for which Harriet had been secretly
thankful. Albert Hawke was supervising the funeral.

The coffin supported a large wreath of lilies – a farewell
from the family – and the church was full of flowers from
well-wishers. The choir was in place and the bell-ringer
waited. The service had begun and the first prayers offered
up. Then, at a signal from the organist, the congregation rose
to sing 'Jesu, Joy of Man's Desiring'. At the same moment
the church door creaked open and footsteps sounded sharply
on the flagged floor as a latecomer entered.

Heads turned to see this late arrival and only Harriet stared
grimly ahead. Intuition told her that this was the person she
most dreaded. This was Amelia Bianchi. Doris, however,
had turned and now her plump face paled. 'It's *her!*' she
whispered. 'Oh my Lord!'

Amelia, aware of the impact of her entrance, walked the
length of the aisle, her head held high. Dramatic in deepest
black with a black lace shawl covering her head, she carried
a long-stemmed red rose. As she walked towards the coffin
the vicar blinked in confusion and the organist faltered and
missed a few notes. Behind Harriet the singing petered out
and whispers began. Sam, astonished, cried, 'It's Amelia!'
and the name was repeated and wondered over.

Amelia gave the vicar a brief nod of acknowledgement as
she passed, then halted before the coffin. Fascinated in spite
of herself, Harriet watched transfixed, vaguely aware that
Angus had reached forward to lay a reassuring hand on her
shoulder. A few people tried to continue singing but most
had stopped to enjoy the intriguing spectacle of a beautiful

stranger interrupting the funeral. Harriet's heart was heavy. This was the image people would take away with them. Not the grieving widow but the audacious mistress. Trust Amelia to have the last word.

Now Amelia rested her free hand on the coffin and her head was bent as she muttered a prayer in Italian. The vicar cast an anxious look in Harriet's direction, but she shrugged helplessly. Amelia then laid the rose on the coffin and turned to face the congregation. She crossed herself and retraced her steps along the aisle. The creaking door indicated her exit. But where would she go next? Harriet uttered her own prayer. 'Please God, don't let her come back to Havely House. I couldn't bear it.'

She need not have worried. Amelia Bianchi was not waiting at the graveside and had apparently disappeared into thin air. Presumably, *hopefully*, she had returned to Italy. The service recovered and continued normally. Godfrey's body was lowered into the grave and the gravedigger picked up his spade and began his work as the mourners drifted away.

Back at Havely House, Harriet told Agnes what had happened and her mother was furious. 'That dreadful woman!' she cried.

Harriet sighed. 'She must have cared for him to come all this way to be at his funeral.'

'Or was determined to spoil his funeral with her dramatics!' Agnes fumed. 'She was determined to have the last word! To upstage you.'

Secretly Harriet felt exactly the same about her rival but said, 'Let's hope we have seen the last of her.'

Angus appeared at her side and suggested they should have something to eat.

'Good for shock!' he whispered and Harriet smiled. She felt exhausted by the emotional strain and had no appetite but forced herself to eat a little ham and salad. Two hours later, when most of the guests had gone home, Angus sought her out and led her to a shady corner of the garden.

'The worst is over, Harriet,' he told her. 'Forget Amelia's

235

performance. Look on it as the last fling of a desperate woman. Your husband is decently laid to rest and you have your child to look forward to.'

Harriet nodded. 'I still have my mother and Sam, and Doris is a kindly soul. I'm very lucky.'

'I hope one day, before too long, you will have a new husband, Harriet. I hope you will become Mrs Angus Fletcher.'

'Oh Angus!'

'I know this is not the time to ask,' he told her earnestly, 'and I promise I will be patient, but I adore you, Harriet, and am determined to care for you and your child – and for all your family. I will love you, Harriet, as you deserve to be loved.'

'I love you, too, Angus.' Harriet took his hands in hers. 'I will marry you, Angus, but not yet. I need time to have my baby – which will give me time to grieve for Godfrey. I have to come to terms with the past. Will you wait for me?'

'Most certainly!' His smile was radiant. 'You've made me the happiest man in Maybourne, Harriet. Probably in the world!'

Harriet was longing to kiss him. She said, 'We've waited so long, Angus. Do you think this might be the moment for a first kiss?'

He frowned, pretending to think about it. Then he said, 'I think it might!'

And it was.